East Wind Coming

By
Hirayama Yuichi
&
John Hall

Paperback ISBN 978-1-78092-380-2
ePub ISBN 978-1-78092-381-9
PDF   ISBN 978-1-78092-382-6

Published in the UK by MX Publishing
335 Princess Park Manor, Royal Drive, London, N11 3GX
www.mxpublishing.co.uk

Cover design by www.staunch.com

CONTENTS

Forward by the author

By Hirayama Yuichi

One hundred years has passed since the publication of "Studies in the Literature of Sherlock Holmes" by Ronald Knox in 1912. That's four generations of Sherlockians in United States and Britain. On the other hand, there have been only three generations of Sherlockians in Japan, as its history didn't begin until after World War II.

It is said the first Sherlockian meeting in Japan was in 1948, with Richard Hughes, Edogawa Rampo, Yoshida Ken-ichi and others attending. But this scion society had only one meeting, and then Hughes moved to Hong Kong. The real history of Japanese Sherlockiana began with Dr. Naganuma Kohki and his first book, *Sherlock Holmes no Chie* (Wisdom of Sherlock Holmes), published in 1961. He was an earnest Sherlockian and the first Japanese to become a member of The Baker Street Irregulars. Naganuma's generation was an introductory age. He wrote nine books on Sherlockiana, most of which were overviews of western studies and investigations. Before Naganuma, we had only a few articles on Sherlockiana, and it was unusual for us to give such consideration to detective stories.

The second generation was that of Dr. Kobayashi Tsukasa and his wife, Ms. Higashiyama Akane. They began the Japan Sherlock Holmes Club in 1978, the first nation-wide Sherlockian society in

5

Japan. The couple was tireless Sherlockian evangelists, publishing many books to spread Sherlockiana all over the nation. I also became a member of JSHC when I was just a high school student. JSHC once had more than one thousand members, and remains one of the largest Sherlockian societies in the world.

As the third generation of Sherlockians, I have seen Sherlockiana imported and developed. Now it is time to export the results. In 1991 I began publishing an international Sherlockian magazine, *Shoso-in Bulletin*. At that time, there was *The Baker Street Journal*, *Sherlock Holmes Journal* and many other Sherlockian magazines but most of them were American or at least printed in English. I planned to introduce Sherlockiana to Japanese and other non-English speaking countries. In 2004, the bulletin's final volume, vol.14, was published. I believe the journal succeeded in its mission. This series of published articles are not only from the United States, Canada and the United Kingdom, but also from France, the Czech Republic, Italy, Spain, Liechtenstein, Switzerland, Germany, Denmark, Sweden, Russia, Belgium, Australia, New Zealand, India, Malaysia, Brazil, Hong Kong, and Japan.

This volume contains all of my own articles published in *The Shoso-in Bulletin*, and several that appeared in *The Baker Street Journal*, *The Ritual*, *Canadian Holmes*, and other Sherlockian magazines printed in English. (One of them was translated into Italian, and published in an Italian magazine.) After twenty years of writing, I believe it is a good time to sum up my overseas works.

In these writing and publishing endeavors, there are two people who supported me the most; without their help, it would not have been possible to write even one Sherlockian article in English. The first one to thank is Mr. John Hall of England. I met John when I attended the general meeting of the Northern Musgraves. He is a famous Sherlockian scholar, and I always admire his vast knowledge and kind gentlemanship. We wrote some articles together and exchanged Sherlockian questions and answers. It was a fun game and good training as a Sherlockian. All of these articles are included in this book.

The other friend is Ms. Mel Hughes of the United States. She was the co-editor of *The Shoso-in Bulletin*. She was previously a professional editor, and without her help, *The Shoso-in Bulletin* would not have continued as long as it did. I thank her so much for her great support and help.

I also thank to Ms. Peggy Perdue of Canada. She assisted us in the completion of this book. She checked my poor English with great patience.

In this book, names of Japanese people are written in our traditional style, family name first, for instance HIRAYAMA is my family name, and YUICHI is my personal name.

Forward by the author

By John Hall

Yuichi and I first met about twenty years ago (doesn't bear thinking about!) and began co-authoring articles on Sherlockian Topics soon after. It was Yuichi who thought of the format which is here used, namely that each of us should ask the other three questions on each of the cases in the Sherlockian canon; the other would then supply – as best as might be – answers, the questioner would then, if need be, respond. The intention being that there should be eventually be either a consensus of opinion on, or two markedly different readings of, the particular topic.

It worked reasonably well, apart from the fact that other things came along and prevented our completing studies of all sixty of the cases. We hope, however, that such as we did complete might be of some interest to other students of this most fascinating of subjects, Sherlock Holmes and his works.

Sherlock Holmes in Japan

Japan is a Maple-White Land of Sherlockiana. Nobody knows even of its existence. But there are more than one thousand Sherlockians and many papers and books, which include many that have been out-of-print in the West for many years.

There is a cliff between your countries and mine. That is a language cliff, which is very high and dangerous. If you want to get over it alone, you need to make even more of an effort than that of Professor Challenger. This is a rope for you. I hope it helps your climbing.

First of all, I must tell you a history of Sherlockiana in Japan.

The first translation of the Canon was in 1894. It was "The Man with the Twisted Lip" in the magazine *Nihonjin*. You may be surprised at this fact. At that time, our ancestors tried at western ways so hard in order to keep our independence. Most Asian countries were under the reign of western Empires except Thailand, China and Japan. Our ancestors decided to make Japan as "rich and strong". They followed Germany in establishing an army and educating children. They also followed the British style of economy, navy and culture. It had been believed for a long time that British products were always first class.

In 1916, *Adventures* was translated. In 1929, the entire Canon except *His Last Bow* was translated into Japanese. From 1931 to 1932, most of works of Doyle were translated in eight volumes. Nobuhara Ken translated the Canon by himself in 1951. This translation is the most well read now.

You can find several Japanese names in the member list of The Sherlock Holmes Society of London. The first Japanese Sherlockian was the late Dr. Naganuma Kohki. He was the first Japanese member of The Baker Street Irregulars and published nine Sherlockiana books.

The first Japanese Sherlockian society "The Baritsu Chapter" was established in 1948. The members were Mr Richard Hughes, Count Makino, Dr Naganuma and some other Japanese and Western

9

people. The society donated a plate to The Criterion Bar of London which was stolen a long time ago. This society had only one meeting. After that, it moved to Hong Kong. The society and Mr. Hughes's name are found in De Waal's *The World Bibliography of Sherlock Holmes and Dr. Watson* as a Hong Kong society.

In 1977, Dr. Kobayashi Tsukasa and his wife Mrs. Higashiyama Akane established The Japan Sherlock Holmes Club. Now its members are more than one thousand. It must be one of the largest Sherlockian societies in the world.

This society publishes the news letter "The Baker Street News" ten times a year, and the magazine *The World of Holmes*. Regrettably, all articles are written in Japanese.

Japanese Sherlockians inclinations are interesting. As we had no Victorian times in our history, it is important to know how people lived in this time. There are papers with titles like "English Cooking", "Victorian Gentlemen's Hats", "Victorian Maps" etc. For British Sherlockians, these are easy matters. It is sufficient to only ask their grandparents. At one meeting which I attended, there was an argument on Holmes' washroom. No one knows where and how it was.

Another interest of Japanese Sherlockians is writing parodies. So many parodies are published in private Sherlockian magazines. Most of writers are young beginners. It is sad that there are only a few stories which are attractive enough to translate and show you.

Sherlockian collections are fun for us, too. It is not popular to collect books in English, because of their lack of knowledge of English. The most famous collector's items are nine Dr. Naganuma books. They are not easy to find, and are expensive. If you want one, you need twenty pounds per Dr Naganuma book. Though you can buy two good Sherlockiana books in English with this, as there are not many Sherlockians who can understand English, they cannot have the Agra treasure.

It is believed in Japan, that Sherlockian papers like "Dr Watson was a woman" or "Who was the king of Bohemia?" are relics of the past. It was Dr Kobayashi who advocated it first. He was a psychiatrist and translated Sam Rosenberg's *Naked is the Best Disguise* in 1982. I think his tastes lay in such psychiatric or psychological works, literary studies and studies of Victorian era.

But I think this is not true. There are such books as *You Know my Method* by Sebeok, and *The Sign of Three* by Eco & Sebeok. On the other hand, there are also much more "classic" studies published. It is clear Eco and Sebeok's works are not Sherlockiana. They used Holmes as material for their study. Japanese Sherlockians need Victorian era studies because of our lack of knowledge. These two are not Sherlockiana at all.

As we have only ten or fifteen years history of Sherlockiana excepting the late Dr. Naganuma, several interesting books which are out of print in the West are now sold in Japan.

It was *Sherlock Holmes; a Biography of the World's First Consulting Detective* by W. S. Baring-Gould which Dr. and Mrs. Kobayashi translated and used to call together Japanese Sherlockians. This book is available as a paperback edition now.

After that, many good books were translated into Japanese.

1962 THE *LIFE OF SIR ARTHUR CONAN DOYLE* by John Dickson Carr
1973 PROFILE *BY GASLIGHT* by Edgar W. Smith
1975 THE *SEVEN-PER-CENT SOLUTION* by Nicholas Meyer
1978 THE *ENCYCLOPEDIA OF SHERLOCKIANA* by Jack Tracy
1980 *SEVENTEEN STEPS TO 221B* by James Edward Holroyd (paperback now available)
1982 THE *SHERLOCK HOLMES COOKBOOK* by Fanny Cradock
1982-83 *THE ANNOTATED SHERLOCK HOLMES* (available in 21 volumes)
1983 CONAN *DOYLE* by Ronald Pearsall (paperback now available)
1984 CONAN *DOYLE* by Julian Symons
1987 THE *PRIVATE LIFE OF SHERLOCK HOLMES* by Vincent Starrett
1989 *THE NEW ADVENTURES OF SHERLOCK HOLMES* by M. H. Greenberg (paperback now available)

These are only a sample.

The most incredible translation is *THE MISADVENTURES OF SHERLICK HOLMES* edited by Ellery Queen. It is not a joke. It was published in 1983-84 in two volume paperbacks by Hayakawa Shobo Co. I do not know why Hayakawa could publish it. But Japan is the only country where this book is available now.

In addition, original books are also published. Most of them are written by Dr. and Mrs. Kobayashi. Another member of The Baker Street Irregulars, Mr. Tanaka Kiyoshi published a book for beginners. Two other books are anthologies by members of JSHC.

You might wonder why there are so many Sherlockians in these tiny islands in the Far East. Some British Sherlockians asked me this question when I visited their home country. Always, I told them two answers.

One is, as I wrote in this article, in Sherlock's time our country changed very much to be a modern nation. Our teacher was Germany and Britain. We learned their languages, industries and their ways of life. The Canon reminds us our old school days.

The other is that there are many points which resemble modern Japan. Now Japan, like Victorian Britain, is one of the most developed countries which many people visit. The Emperor of the time's reign was over sixty years. We can find ourselves in the Canon.

Fifty years ago, when the Baker Street Irregulars gathered, America resembled Victorian London. And now Japan does. Fifty years later, there might be millions of Sherlockians in China!

If you are interested in Sherlockiana in Japan, I am pleased. If you want to know a new world of Sherlockiana, that is not German, nor French, you need to study Japanese. Holmes says, "What one man can invent another can discover".

(The Nezire Zanmai vol.1, 1991)

"The More Deeply Sunk Impression"

"No, no, my dear Watson. The more deeply sunk impression is, of course, the hind wheel, upon which the weight rests. You perceive several places where it has passed across and obliterated the more shallow mark of the front one. It was undoubtedly heading away from the school. It may or may not be connected with our inquiry, but we will follow it backwards before we go any farther."

These are the words of Sherlock Holmes in "The Priory School" which have led to many arguments. Every Sherlockian and even the literary agent agree that it is impossible to know the direction of a bicycle from impressions which have " passed across and obliterated the more shallow mark of the front one".

According to *The Adventures of Conan Doyle* by Charles Higham,

Conan Doyle waited for a wet day and then took his bicycle out to the Devil's Punchbowl, a valley near Hindhead, rode it, and examined the track. He was alarmed to discover that his correspondents were right. He had imagined that the track of the hind wheel overlaying the track of the front wheel when the machine was weaving in mud would indicate the direction.

But it is the fact the Master found the right direction. Perhaps he knew some other facts Watson did not write?

The eminent Sherlockian T. S. Blakeney says in *Sherlock Holmes: Fact or Fiction?*, p106-107,

In any case, Holmes probably had a dozen other small indications to guide him ; though he might mention only one factor, he usually had others in reserve, as evidenced in the twenty-three additional points of difference in the joint letter of the Cunninghams.

If so, there is another question. What did Holmes know?
Blakeney also says,

It is there pointed out that the depth of the mark of the rear wheel, when the bicycle was going uphill, would indicate the direction of travel, for on the down slope it is very markedly less.

Other students consider several things which may be what Holmes knew. But my impression is they are too feeble and non-systematic to be a deduction of the Master.

Some years ago, I happened to find a book concerning techniques of detection. Its name is *Hanzai Sousa Gijutsuron* (The Techniques of Crime Detection) and it was written by Hourai Masayoshi and published by Souzou-sha in 1940. The author is a Japanese man who lived in Manchuria. He might be a member of The Police of Manchuria. In this book, I found an interesting part concerning the problem that we are discussing now. I wonder if Mr. Hourai studied with "a textbook which shall focus the whole art of detection into one volume."(ABBE)

Hourai says in his book (p355-358),

How to know the direction from wheel impressions

It often occurs that we must know the direction from wheel impressions in detecting crime.

It is very difficult to judge direction from wheel impressions only, because they are only prints of two or one continuous lines on the ground. If it is a horse or cattle carriage, or a cart pulled by a man, we can deduce it from foot prints. But we must not forget this might be false evidence. Wheel impressions of motorcars and bicycles are much more difficult because of the absence of foot prints.

But it is easy to judge direction from deductions based on observations upon these principles and on general circumstantial evidence.

1. As a wheel advances, the edges of both impressions make layers and incline towards the direction of progress.

2. At the bottom and edges, there are surface fissures towards the direction of progress.

3. Stones and other solids in the impressions are pushed toward the direction of progress, and we can find the marks of where they were.

4. If there is a flat big stone in the way of a cart, even though there is an impression on that side, we can find no prints about 10cm from the edge of the other side of the stone.

5. When a cart turns around a corner at more than 15km/hour, a wheel kicks out soil from an impression towards the inside, namely the right hand side if it turns right, left hand side if it turns left. And the soil kicked out is scattered like the spokes of a wheel in the opposite direction of the direction of progress, namely backwards. In addition, the impression on the side of the turn is deeper, and appears to lean into the ground.

6. A car or a bicycle that runs over a pool on its way will scatter muddy water in the direction of progress, and each splash lengthens toward the direction of progress.

7. If there are specific types of soil or lime on the way, the direction of their impression is the direction of progress.

In "The Priory School", Holmes says "Look here, Watson! There is a watercourse across the moor. You see it marked here in the map. In some parts it widens into a morass. This is particularly so in the region between Holdernesse Hall and the school." And "Right across the lower part of the bog lay a miry path. Holmes gave a cry of delight as he approached it. An impression like a fine bundle of telegraph wires ran down the centre of it. It was the Palmer type."

As it was so miry, Lord Saltire might leave his footprints when he could not manage his bicycle well. But Herr Heidegger fell down. Watson writes, "There was a broad, irregular smudge covering some yards of the track. Then there were a few footmarks, and the tyre reappeared once more." But at this time, he must have been upset and so left no footmarks which showed the right direction.

Though it was a morass, Hourai suggests that "this dry weather" might make it dry enough to produce layers, fissures and inclines.

Watson says "Holmes sat down on a boulder and rested his chin in his hands." It is not impossible that there were small stones which were moved by bicycle wheels or which interrupted the impressions.

It is also provable that "If there are specific soils or limes on the way, the direction of their impressions is the same as the direction of progress." It is evident that the bicycle of Lord Saltire passed "the peaty, russet moor", "the broad green-belt" and "a small black ribbon of pathway".

I think these clues are enough to find the direction Lord Saltire took, but there was more evidence which aided the deductions of the Master. After he uttered, "Following the path backwards, we picked out another spot, where a spring trickled across it," Holmes must have found "muddy water scattered in the direction of progress, each splash lengthening toward the direction of progress."

Herr Heidegger was "undoubtedly forcing the pace" to more than 15km/hour. Watson noted that "there was a broad, irregular smudge covering some yards of the track" and "the tracks of the tyre began to curve fantastically upon the wet and shining path." These are the prints noted by Hourai. Holmes must have found soil kicked out by a wheel toward the impression..

Sherlock Holmes must have observed the seven points and marks noted above, although he did not tell them to Watson.

I do not know why Hourai knew the Master's method. It is impossible to read this in a textbook written by Holmes since no such text has been published even in Britain. He might have met Holmes somewhere. There are some books concerning Holmes's visit to Japan during the Great Hiatus, but they were written fifty years after the publication of Hourai's book.

I am considering the possibility of a Japanese son of Holmes. His name is Akechi Kogoro, who is as famous a detective as Holmes in Japan. He resembles the Master much more than Nero Wolf. From my study, he was born in 1894. If this theory is right, Hourai Masayosi learned the technique from the son of Holmes, Akechi Kogoro.

References
1 Charles Higham *The Adventures of Conan Doyle* Pocket Books, 1976
2 T. S. Blakeney *Sherlock Holmes: Fact or Fiction?* John Murray, 1932
3 Hourai Masayoshi *Hanzai Sousa Gijutsuron* Souzou-sya, Tokyo,

1940, pp355-58

4 Kano Ichiro *Hokku-shi no Ikyou no Bouken,* Kadokawa, Tokyo, 1984.

5 Hirayama Yuichi *The Akechi Kogoro Chronology* privately printed, Tokyo, 1989, pp52-55.

(*The Nezire Zanmai* vol.1, 1991)

Appendix; In the first appearance, I wrote Hourai's name incorrectly as Sanekita. I apologize for my mistake.

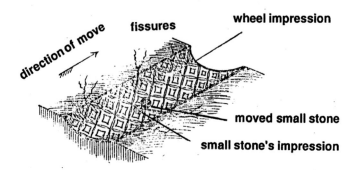

fissures

wheel impression

direction of move

moved small stone

small stone's impression

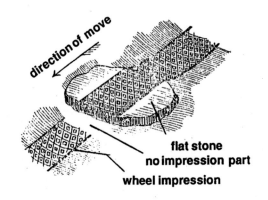

direction of move

flat stone
no impression part

wheel impression

Modified from *Hanzai Sousa Gijutsuron*

The Japanese Rivals of Sherlock Holmes

There was a boom in "The Rivals of Sherlock Holmes" ten years ago. Many Victorian and Edwardian detectives were brought back to life. In Great Britain, Dr. Thorndyke, The Old Man in the Corner, Sexton Blake, Max Carrados, Martin Hewitt, Lady Molly... In the U.S.A., the Thinking Machine, Craig Kennedy, the Infallible Godahl, Uncle Abner, Philo Gubb. You can find Arsène Lupin and Joseph Rouletabille in France, and even in Austria, you can meet Detective Dagoberts.

But none of the editors of omnibuses mentioned "The Japanese Rivals of Sherlock Holmes". There are more than a hundred rivals and uncountable episodes in which they solved mysteries. Their books are called "Torimonocho (Crime Files)". Their field of investigation is Edo, the former name of Tokyo under the Shogunate. Some of them are officers but most of them are half-official-half-private detectives called "Okappiki" or "Goyoukiki". They were heroes in movies and have also been on television programs. "Torimonocho" is called a "Horse Opera" in Japan. Even now, seven programs a week are broadcast in my city.

Before telling you about the Japanese rivals of Sherlock Holmes, I must explain of the system of police departments in the Edo period. It is very different from that of modern times, but worked pretty well.

*   *   *

The office was called "Machi-Bugyosho". It was not only a police department. Its responsibilities were the administration of justice and police services for citizens except samurais and those associated with temples and shrines. There was the Ometsuke and Metsuke system for samurais and Jisha-Bugyo for those in religious orders.

The Machi-Bugyosho was started in 1631 by Tokugawa Iemitsu, the third Shogun of the Edo period. When we think of London, whose police force was founded by Sir Robert Peel in 1829, this system of the Shogun might be ahead of its time. If we seek for the origins of the Machi-Bugyosho, however, we can even go back to "Kebiishi", in the Heian period, more than a thousand years ago.

It is distinctive that there were two Machi-Bugyoshos, "Kita (North) Machi-Bugyosho" and "Minami (South) Machi-Bugyosho". It does not mean that Edo (Old Tokyo) was divided into two parts. It was just that one division accepted cases for one month and then the responsibility to take up new cases would switch to the other division in the following month. A Machi-bugyosho which closed its case window managed cases from the former month. Police officers and others were not off duty but continued their work during the "off" months.

The chief of the Machi-Bugyosho was called the Machi-bugyo. He was one of the Hatamotos, the Shogun's knights.

There were two ranks of officers, Yoriki (upper officers) and Doshin (regular officers). They were divided into many types of occupation, but I will mention police officers only now. There were no Yoriki among police officers. Only twenty-four Doshins were patrol officers. They were called "Jomawari-Doshin" and "Rinjimawari-Doshin". In addition, two Doshins called "Onmitsumiwari-Doshin" investigated in disguise. These three groups were called "Sanmawari (the three patrols)", and were in a position to be promoted.

As you can imagine, twenty-six officers were not sufficient for maintaining public safety in Edo, a city with a population of more than one million. Each Doshin had some non-samurai followers called "Komono", and some unofficial men called "Goyoukiki". Goyoukikis were the Doshin's private subordinates. Most of them held other jobs for a living. Goyoukikis had men called "Teshita" or "Shitappiki". Some of them were embryo hooligans, others were ordinary citizens.

Some of the Japanese rivals of Sherlock Holmes are Doshins. They appear in The *Crime files of Agojuro*, *The Crime files of Mutturi Umon* (Umon the Silent), *The Crime files of Ikeda Daisuke* and others.

Most of them are Goyoukikis. And the origin of Torimonochos was a Goyoukiki. His name is Hanshichi of Mikawa town, written by Okamoto Kido.

*　　　*　　　*

Okamoto Kido was born in 1872 as a son of a former samurai who worked at the British Legation in Tokyo. He was a newspaperman, a Kabuki playwright, and a translator. He was good at English and translated Conan Doyle's work "The Captain of the Polestar".

Okamoto Kido wrote "A Memory of *the Crime Files of Hanshichi*" in 1927.

It was April 1916 when I decided to start writing "The Crime Files of Hanshichi". In those days, I had read some of the adventures of Sherlock Holmes, but had not read through all the series yet. As I had an opportunity to go to The Maruzen Bookstore, I bought The Adventures, The Memoirs and The Return of Sherlock Holmes and did with them. I found a great interest in detective stories, and I wanted to write some detective stories by myself. Of cause I had read some works of Hume and other writers, but these were the works of Doyle which stimulated me.

He also wrote about other non-Holmes stories he read.

There were no detective stories of the Edo period. If I wrote a modern detective story, it must be a copy of the western style. If it was in the Edo style it would be something quite different altogether.

His first Hanshichi story "The Soul of Obun" appeared in the January issue of *Bungei Club* in 1917. His last and sixty-eighth story was "The Two Wives" in 1936.

He described Hanshichi as "a hidden Sherlock Holmes in the Edo period" in "The Soul of Obun". He kept Holmes in his mind when he wrote this series.

He used a technique of Holmes, too. He said in "The Mikawa Comic Dialogists", "Hanshichi watched his right hand palm and judged that he must be a comic dialogist playing a drum." He also used a trick of "The Norwood Builder" in this episode to lure a criminal to come toward him from a shrine.

It is not said that *The Crime files of Hanshichi* is a complete rival of Sherlock Holmes. Some of its episodes are ghost stories, and several are not Hanshichi stories. Though Hanshichi had some "Shitappikis", it would be beyond their power to be a Watson.

*   *   *

The most famous Goyokiki is "Zenigata Heiji" by Nomura Kodo (1882-1970). All three-hundred and eighty-four stories and novels of Heiji are written by one writer. It was 1931 when the first story "A Virgin in Gold" appeared.

The author Nomura Kodo was an admirer of the Canon. He said in his essay "The Birth of Heiji", "...Japanese readers cannot think of the existence of Conan Doyle without Sherlock Holmes. It is common sense that we would not care about Doyle if he didn't write the Sherlock Holmes stories."

In his high school days, he asked his English teacher to use the Canon as a textbook. He continued his interest in Holmes and Arsène Lupin after he became a newspaperman. In his essay "Before Zenigata Heiji", "My interest in Leblanc went off. The works of Conan Doyle are sound enough to withstand re-reading, but not those of Leblanc which are only showy. The difference between Doyle and Leblanc is clear."

He also respected Okamoto Kido's Hanshichi. He said, "These stories and the Sherlock Holmes stories of Conan Doyle are the two biggest detective stories of western and eastern world in quality and quantity."

The start of *Crime files of Heiji* was a request from an editor of a new magazine called *Oru Yomimono*. This editor asked Nomura for a crime file series like that of Kido's Hanshichi. Heiji is a rival of Holmes and Hanshichi. Nomura Kodo gave Heiji a remarkable ability. Like The Old Man in the Corner and Max Carrados, this is a tradition for rivals of Sherlock Holmes. Heiji catches criminals by pitching a heavy coin at them as a weapon. Nomura took this idea from *Suikoden* which is a classic of Chinese literature.

One of the biggest differences between Heiji and Hanshichi is the existence of a Watson in Hachigoro. He is a tall easy-going Shitappiki whose resemblance to Watson is described with the words "my dear Watson rushed into the mysterious case first and foremost" in "Jigoku no Mon (The Gate of Hell)". He tells Heiji all the trivial news occurring in Edo, and Heiji solves a mystery with some of this information. Hachigoro is not only a Watson but also a newspaper of Edo.

Heiji bears some resemblance to Holmes. Though he was always poor, he never received any money from the people concerned in the cases. He was sometimes called "Shikujiri Heiji (Heiji the Miscarriage)". He connived with many criminals because he felt sympathy for them. He hated crimes but not criminals. It reminds me of how Holmes took the responsibility for judging criminals on himself in BLUE, DEVI, ABBE, 3GAB and BOSC. He says in BOSC, "I have done more real harm by my discovery of the criminal than ever he had done by his crime." He drank little but is a heavy smoker. Heiji wanted no fame. He never felt uneasy even when his rivals stole credit for his work. Though Heiji worked for Machi-bugyosho, he disliked samurais who were men of power. He was a defender of the common people. The biggest difference between Heiji and Holmes is the existence of his wife, Oshizu. She was a good Mrs. Hudson for Heiji and Hachigoro.

There are many Heiji stories that were influenced by the Canon. The most famous one is "Neko no Kubiwa (A Cat Collar)". A retired merchant was treated cruelly by his adopted son and his wife. One morning, the old man was found dead in his room. His throat was cut and the murder weapon which the victim owned was found in the garden far from the dead body. His favorite cat was smeared with blood. The heartless son was arrested. Heiji saw that it was really a suicide. The old merchant despaired of his and his small daughter's future. After cutting his throat by himself, he inserted the knife into the cat's collar. The cat was astonished and jumped out of the room. This is the plot of THOR. There is another case which used this plot. This is "Arasoi no Odori (The Dance Match)". The criminal must have known the case of "A Cat Collar". She killed her employer, and disguised it to look as if the victim committed suicide as in the plot of THOR. In this episode, the murder weapon was linked to a cart.

There are two episodes which used the plot of MUSG. In "Fujimi no Tou (The Mt. Fuji Viewing Tower)", the treasure was found under the shadow of a tower which was burnt down as told in a spell. In "Yaso no Shi (The Death of Yaso)", Yaso was found dead between a stone case and its lid. He planned to steal the treasure in it just as Brunton opened the heavy flagstone.

In "Aya no Tsuzumi (A Drum with Figured Cloth)", the criminal shot the victim's shadow like in EMPT. In "Ofune Otan", the trick of the finger print of John Hector McFarlane in NORW was used but modified into a foot print. Heiji asked a doshin to wash down a female begger like that of TWIS in "Bijo o Araidasu (Washing out a Beauty)". She made herself dirty to avoid an admirer and being killed by her brother in law.

In "Hanami no Adauchi (The Revenge at the Flower-viewing)", we can see an example of "when you have excluded the impossible, whatever remains, however improbable, must be the truth," Holmes' famous quote from BERY. We also see this quote in "Hanami no Hate (After the Flower-viewing)": "Moreover, what is winding around the neck is a speckled band, an apron lace that looks like a snake."

But such similarities do not diminish *The Crime files of Zenigata Heiji*. Nomura Kodo's intention is to create "A Utopia of Law". Heiji's humanity touched the hearts of many readers. A one hour television series of Heiji stories broadcasted eight-hundred and eighty-eight programs. This may show how much Japanese people feel sympathy toward Heiji and Hachigoro. Former Prime Minister Yoshida Shigeru, the only Japanese person whose wax doll is displayed at Madame Tussaud's of Baker Street, said his favorite book was *The Crime Files of Zenigata Heiji*. This made him rise in popularity a lot. Heiji is the ideal defender of law for us.

Twenty-six years after the first Heiji story "A Virgin in Gold", Kodo wrote the last Heiji story "The Sound of a Rifle" when he was seventy-five years old and suffering from an eye illness.

*   *   *

I was astonished at an advertisement in the *Mainichi Shinbun* newspaper on July 14 1985. It told of a videocassette devoted to the famous actor Hasegawa Kazuo who was a star of samurai movies. This videocassette included excellent scenes from his movies. The names of the movies which had scenes included were listed in the advertisement. I found *The Crime Files of Zenigata Heiji and The Speckled Snake* among these names. Hasegawa Kazuo played Heiji in movies many times. Heiji was his most successful part. But Nomura Kodo never wrote a case of Heiji's called *The Speckled Snake*. I wonder if it was "The Adventure of The Speckled Band". If so, Hasegawa Kazuo was the first person who performed in this story of Holmes.

I visited a library to investigate what it was with great

expectations. This movie was made in 1956 by Daiei Kyoto Movie. The director was Kato Bin, Zenigata Heiji was played by Hasegawa Kazuo and Hachigoro was played by Sakai Shunji.

In conclusion, it is not "The Speckled Band". It is an original story about false gold coins made up for the movie. The villains kidnapped gold workers, shut them in a secret underground factory to make false gold coins, and tattooed pictures of a speckled snake on the craftsmen to find them when they escaped from the factory.

But it told me how Heiji is close to Sherlock Holmes.

*　　*　　*

It was 1917 when the "Torimonocho" was created by Okamoto Kido. He is an Edgar Alan Poe of the "Torimonocho" which based their style on the Canon of Sherlock Holmes. Nomura Kodo who wrote Heiji in 1931 is like Conan Doyle because he established "Torimonocho" and many "Rivals of Heiji".

There was another reason why so many rivals appeared in the late 1930's. The power of the army grew and detective stories which the military considered insincere were oppressed. Many jobless detective story writers began to write "Torimonocho" to live. One of them was Yokomizo Seishi, one of the most famous Japanese detective story writers. He started his career as a writer in 1921, but he began to write *The Crime Files of Ningyo Sashichi* in 1938 and had to give up writing detective stories soon after. "Torimonocho" was his only way to live during war time.

Takahashi Hidehiro says in "The Appeal of Ningyo Sashichi", "In contrast with *The Crime Files of Zenigata Heiji*, we find an interesting fact when we compare Heiji and his wife Oshizu and Sashichi and his wife Okume. Heiji is a serious strong character and Oshizu is obedient. On the contrary, Sashichi is a handsome flighty man and Okume is a jealous person. The flightiness of Sashichi who is handsome like an actor was developed in contract to challenge the serious, strong Heiji. This was what Yokomizo Seishi wanted to say. The jealous character of Okume describes her vivid character, and also stands out in contract to Sashichi."

The next boom of "Torimonocho" came after the war, when restrictions on publications were relaxed. In 1949, the year when Nomura Kodo wrote the 200th episode of Heiji, The Torimonocho

Writers Club was founded. The first president was Nomura Kodo. It was also the year when "Heiji Happyakuyacho", the first Heiji movie with Hasegawa Kazuo appeared. In 1950, Kodo wrote 31 Heiji episodes. This is the best record of "The Crime Files of Zenigata Heiji".

After the appearance of realistic mystery stories as represented by Matsumoto Seicho, Torimonocho and detective stories became old-fashioned. The Torimonocho Writers Club was absorbed in The Japan Mystery Writers Association. The time of the Torimonocho has gone, though some writers still provide Torimonocho stories.

There are excellent Torimonocho writers even now. Ikenami Shotaro writes *Onihei Hankacho*, and Tsuzuki Michio's *Namekuji Nagaya Torimono Sawagi* is considered the best modern Torimonocho. The descendants of Hanshichi, Heiji and Holmes are still alive today.

(*The Nezire Zanmai* vol.1, 1991)

Some Problems
in *Lestrade and the Hallowed House*

For anyone, it is difficult to understand the cultures of other countries. We may misunderstand foreigners as being strange or undeveloped. There is no absolute truth in the world. Five hundred years ago, when we first met western people who ate beef and pork, our ancestors thought they were "Nan ban-Jin", savages from the south because they sailed from the Philippines. Now, western people think the Japanese and Icelanders are savage because of their whale catching.

Understanding life styles of other countries is very hard, too. Even now, there are many misunderstandings about Japan in movies made in U.S.A. and Britain. I could not find any sign of Japan in *Karate Kid 2*, and in *The Blade Runner*, there are many funny neon signs in Japanese. We Japanese enjoy 007's *You Only Live Twice* as a comedy. Tiger Tanaka's secret weapon is a subway of Tokyo! I could not stop laughing when I saw 007's disguise to become Japanese. In *The Man with the Golden Gun*, Sumo wrestlers attack 007. I wonder what they were doing in Hong-Kong.

If one wishes to create movies or books concerning a foreign country, one must investigate its culture and life style. It is very unfortunate that some Western people's understanding of Japan and the Japanese is still at the level of *Mikado* by Gilbert and Sullivan. Three years ago, a Sherlockian pastiche was translated into Japanese. I was so surprised by it. There are too many mistakes about Japan for a detective story. It cannot be a detective story, if readers cannot believe the author. The name of this pastiche is *Lestrade and the Hallowed House*, by M.J. Throw. I bought the original edition and found that some of worst mistakes were corrected by the translator.

As you know, Japan is one of the largest Sherlockian countries, so it is sad that you get wrong information about it from Sherlockiana. I would like Sherlockians of the West to know the real history and life styles of Japan.

In this book, the murderer used a Japanese sword as a murder weapon. Constable Dickens, who was called "our walking encyclopedia" said "(a) tachi, sir, is the shorter of the two swords carried by the Samurai or warrior class of Japan."(page 159)   His encyclopedia had a misprint. "Tachi" is not the shorter sword, but the longer one.   ("Elementary, my dear Watson, elementary.")

Inspector Lestrade and Sergeant Dew visited the Strand Palace Hotel to see the Japanese embassy. The year of this case must be 1901. Mycroft Holmes mentioned that the embassy had come to London to discuss the Anglo-Japan alliance, which was formed in 1902. It is natural for a special embassy to have visited London, but the Japanese legation already existed at 4 Grosvenor Gardens, London. I cannot understand why they did not visit that instead.

"It opened to reveal a wizened little man in saffron colored robes who bowed almost double to Lestrade."(page 159) I wonder who he was. Visiting Europe at that time cost so much that only selected people could go. I cannot understand this man's mission. Also, in Japan, bowing "almost double" is only for the Emperor, not for an inspector.

"From nowhere two men in armor had rushed the length of the room to the little old man's rescue."(page 160) Our modern army never used armor like they did in the good old days. The Meiji revolution in the middle of nineteenth century was the last war samurai participated in, but most of them did not put on armor, because of the development of rifles. The modern army followed after the German army in all aspects. You may remember that Japan won the war over Russia in 1904-1905.

"Ishiro Yamomoto, Charterhouse and Sandhurst," (page 160) is not a name of a Japanese man. The translator changed his name into the acceptable name, "Ichiro Yamamoto". It is unnatural for a Japanese army officer to have studied in Britain. As I mentioned, the Japanese army followed that of Germany, so promising officers were allowed to study in Germany in those days. One of the most famous novelists in Japan, Mori Ougai, who was also an army doctor, studied in Berlin and Dresden. On the other hand, navy officers studied in Britain. Admiral Togo, who won the Battle of Tsushima, studied at Cambridge and Plymouth. Many Japanese battle ships used in the Japan-Russia War were made in Newcastle.

"'Ordinarily my man would have urinated on his back, but...'"

(page 160) Never is this ordinary in Japan. That is not the behavior of samurai.

"'Actually, it's Mr. Ishiro,' the officer explained. 'In Japan we reverse the order of names. Another archaic practice.'" This practice is true, but "Ishiro" doesn't sound like a family name. "Yamomoto" is strange as a personal name, too, but the latter is better as a family name than the other. Mr. Trow reversed the name twice. The translator corrected this point too.

"The only furniture here was a series of wooden blocks on the floor and the carpets were missing. He sat cross legged on the polished board and invited Lestrade and Dew to do the same.

'I'm sorry about this, gentlemen. Personally, I should have thought "when in London..." but the wheels of progress grind slow.'" (page 161)

The Japanese army's style was completely westernized but only for food, underwear and words. All the soldiers studied with desks and chairs, and slept in beds.

"Saki or Darjeeling?"(page 161) is a spelling mistake. Not "saki" but "sake," Japanese rice wine.

"...When our business is concluded, Inspector Lestrade, would you like to have this girl?'

'Have...?' Lestrade nearly dropped his cup. He glanced at Dew, whose smile vanished at once.

'She is a geisha, Inspector. A lady of pleasure. It is her sole purpose in life to please honoured guests.'"(page 161)

"...the geisha, naked now and sitting demurely beside a bath of hot fragrance."(page 164)

I had the same feeling as Inspector Lestrade. A geisha is not a prostitute. Some of them might act disrespectfully, but first of all, they must be treated as women in show business. Prostitutes were called "yujo". "Yujo" lived in restricted places and belonged to houses of prostitution. It is impossible that a yujo came to London with the Japanese embassy.

"In the days of the Shogunate you'd probably have lost your testicles or at least had your tongue split."(page 161) Such punishments were never done in Japan. They are those of China. I believe that the embassy was a fake.

"It will mean that your subordinate will accept favours.'"(page 162) This is the first time one hears of a prostitute being forced on guests. In Japan, high ranking prostitutes could deny a customer. It was the gentlemen's pleasure to win her heart. They played a love game.

'"...we don't let them wear their swords in public. Well, they're such a nuisance getting on and off the bus.'

'But you let them wear them in London, Colonel Ishiro,' Lestrade commented.

'Oh, the natives love it. No offense, Lestrade.'"(page 162)

It was 1876 when wearing swords was prohibited. A quarter of a century had passed, and neither Ninjas nor samurais wearing swords existed in 1901.

'"This one,' he pointed to the longer of the two swords thrust through each man's waist sash, 'is the katana. The other, I fancy, is the one you're interested in, the tachi."(page 162)

Again, "tachi" is not the shorter sword, but the longer one. "Katana" means sword, including both the shorter one and the longer one. The longer one was called "tachi" or "daitou."

'"One word from me now and they would kill each other or themselves."'(page 163)

Never.

'"What you have there is a pillow,' Ishiro explained. 'You probably lose yours in the Chinese laundry. We slice some of ours for sword practice."(page 163)

We never use wood blocks for sword practice. It damages the sword. Usually, bound straw is used for this purpose. But a master of sword can cut apart even a steel helmet.

"'Is the point of the sword ever used?' he asked.

"'By a samurai, never. You see, we Japanese don't have the problem you English have; this extraordinary inability among your cavalry officers to decide whether the edge or the point of a sword is more effective. I suppose,' he scanned the middle distance while draining his second cup, 'I suppose it could be used that way, but if that was how your murderer struck, Inspector, he is not from Japan.'"(page 163-164)

Kendo, the Japanese fencing as a sport, has several winning tricks, such as cutting the face, hand, or body with a sword's edge, and stabbing. One of the most famous injury cases under the Shogunate is the Matsu-no-rouka case in Edo castle. A feudal lord named Asano Takuminokami struck at Kira Kouzukenosuke, who was a master of court ceremonies. Asano injured Kira's forehead and his back, but could not kill him. After that, Asano was blamed for his lack of knowledge of fencing. It was said that if Asano wanted to kill Kira, he should have stabbed him with the point of the sword, instead of cutting with its edge. I suppose if stabbing was the way Inspector Lestrade's murderer struck, he is from Japan.

I conclude this article with a quotation from this book.

"'Nonsense,' Lestrade slapping his shoulder." (page 164)

Bibliography

1 Trow M.J., *Lestrade and the Hallowed House*, London: Macmillan, 1987
2 Trow M.J, *Resutoredokeibu to sannin no houmuzu*, Tokyo: Shinchosha, 1989 (Japanese edition)
3 *Henna Nippon*, Tokyo: JICC, 1990
4 Kiyoyuki Higuchi, *Edo seifuzoku yowa*, Tokyo: Kawaideshoboshinsya, 1988
5 Brinkley Capt. F., A *History of the Japanese People*, New York: The Encyclopedia Britannica, 1915

(*The Nezire Zanmai* vol.2, 1992)

Another Solution of "The Lion's Mane"

By Hirayama Yuichi and Mizuochi Masako

At one of the meetings of "The Red Circle of Niigata", on July 9th 1989, we discussed many aspects of "The Lion's Mane", one of the stories that causes so many arguments. At this meeting we had been reexamining all the adventures of *The Casebook of Sherlock Holmes*, and we had an animated discussion about this story on that day.

It is believed that this is one of the records which the Master himself wrote. There are some arguments about the author, but Dr. Narita will explain this in detail. There are also so many other questionable issues in "The Lion's Mane."

Of all the questions, the most knotty problem was why Holmes did not recognize the fact that the body of Fitzroy McPherson was wet from sea water. According to Holmes's statement, "I was slow at the outset -- culpably slow. Had the body been found in the water I could hardly have missed it. It was the towel which misled me. The poor fellow had never thought to dry himself, and so I in turn was led to believe that he had never been in the water. Why, then, should the attack of any water creature suggest itself to me? That was where I went astray. Well, well, Inspector, I often ventured to chaff you gentlemen of the police force, but Cyanea capillata very nearly avenged Scotland Yard."

If "the poor fellow had never thought to dry himself," he must have been wet. The eminent Sherlockian Nathan Bengis wrote in his article "Sherlock Stays After School," "You should have known from the very first that McPherson had been in the water, and could not have been out of it by more than a very few minutes. How? By the very simplest of deductions. McPherson's body must still have been wet when you examined it. The lining of this Burberry overcoat must have been moist, as would also his hair. His canvas shoes, unlaced because he had not had time in his mortal agony. That you should have failed to notice all this water, merely from the dryness of his towel should have passed belief."

If McPherson was attacked by Cyanea capillata, he must have been in a "considerable lagoon." At least, his back should have been in water to be attacked with the feelers of Cyanea capillata.

However his towel was "folded and dry." If he got into water and did not use his towel, his body must have been wet with sea water.

Bengis considered that the Master overlooked this point. It is, however, too elementary to miss for Sherlock Holmes. We cannot accept such behavior in the Master's investigations. Even if he did make a mistake, there must have been some trick we do not understand.

If McPherson's body was wet, it is unlikely that Holmes did not recognize this fact. There is only one solution. Holmes was right when he told us, "The poor fellow had never thought to dry himself, and so I in turn was led to believe that he had never been in the water."

When Ian Murdoch was attacked by Cyanea capillata, "his clothes (were) in wild disorder." Stackhurst "threw some clothes about him" when he found Murdoch in an "infernal agony." Murdoch could not put on his clothes by himself nor walk to the school. He said, when he was attacked, that "it had taken all his fortitude to reach the bank." His heart was not as weak as that of McPherson, but McPherson could put on "his Burberry overcoat, his trousers, and an unlaced pair of canvas shoes." It is doubtful that a man who is "obviously dying" could dress himself even if he was a Victorian gentleman. Holmes thought that "he had suddenly huddled on his clothes again - they were all disheveled and unfastened." It must have been difficult for a man with great pain to put on trousers.

According to Holmes' statement, it is clear that McPherson was taking off his clothes when he was attacked by Cyanea capillata. He took off his Burberry overcoat and shirts, and sat down on his heels to unlace his canvas shoes. Cyanea capillata made an attack on his bare back,. He was taken aback, and threw it away into the lagoon. He stood up with his overcoat to protect his back from the next attack. He ran away from his enemy at seaside to his school.

There is one problem with this theory. Cyanea capillata cannot fly.

We found a unique opinion in *The Annotated Sherlock Holmes* which solves that contradiction. Hedgpeth wrote in an annotation, "The possibility never seemed to have occurred to Holmes that this disarming young man . . . had secured a Cyanea in some manner and placed it in the tide pool with diabolical malice aforethought . . .beyond all doubt this dark, brooding, 'ferocious tempered' young man, disappointed in love and capable of throwing innocent dogs through windows, had conceived a most ingenious crime and to allay suspicion had caressed his own monstrous pet."

We agree with Hedgpeth that Ian Murdoch was the criminal. We also believe that he developed the murder plan, and another man committed it. Hedgpeth thought Murdoch placed Cyanea capillata in the tide pool with diabolical malice aforethought. There is a problem with this crime. If Cyanea capillata did not attack McPherson, what would Murdoch have done? Would he continue "some algebraic demonstration before breakfast" every day until it attacked McPherson? If McPherson found and killed Cyanea capillata before he swam, did Murdoch intend to put another one in the pool? This is a crime of possibility. Murdoch might be safe from the hands of law, but he needed so much luck.

McPherson and Maud Bellamy were engaged. They kept it secret because "Fitzroy's uncle, who is very old and said to be dying, might have disinherited him if he had married against his wish." Murdoch must have known that because "for a year or more Murdoch has been as near to McPherson as he ever could be to anyone." He had no time to waste.

We think another man threw Cyanea capillata on McPherson's back when he sat down on his heels to unlace his canvas shoes. The flying jellyfish hurt him, but not as serious as it would have in the sea. He shook himself free, and it dropped into the tide pool. McPherson took his overcoat, and ran away.

Who was the other man/men? We believe they were Tom Bellamy and his son William. They did not want Maud Bellamy married to McPherson. Tom Bellamy said "I object to my girl picking up with men outside her own station." Clearly it means McPherson. He "who owns all the boats and bathing-cots at Fulworth", did not want a poor teacher as his son in law. He was a fisherman. It was easy for him to find a poisonous jellyfish. But as a teacher of Mathematics, Murdoch must have had no knowledge of fish. Tom Bellamy angrily told his daughter "I tell you, Maud, not to mix

34

yourself up in the matter". His attitude showed he knew about the case.

On the other hand, it seemed Tom Bellamy liked Ian Murdoch. Murdoch visited the Bellamys soon after the case to tell about it. Tom Bellamy said, "This other gentleman of yours let us know the news." He treated Murdoch as a gentleman, but according to his daughter, he had "prejudice against" McPherson. Maud wanted to marry McPherson, but her father and brother wanted Murdoch as their son/brother in law.

Maud Bellamy might have known their scheme. She said, "Bring them to justice, Mr. Holmes. You have my sympathy and my help, whoever they may be." And as for her attitude, "[it] seemed to me that she glanced defiantly at her father and brother as she spoke."

On that morning, Murdoch insisted upon some algebraic demonstration before breakfast, to inhibit anyone going to the tide pool to watch the crime. It also establishes his alibi.

Tom and William brought Cyanea capillata in a bucket near the tide pool, and hid themselves there.

McPherson came there alone. He took off his shirt, and sat down on his heels to unlace his canvas shoes. They threw the jellyfish at McPherson. It hit his back, and fell down into the tide pool. McPherson put on his overcoat and ran away. Tom and William also left quickly.

Holmes and Stackhurst found McPherson and came to the tide pool. Cyanea capillata was already in the pool, and the Bellamys were gone, too. They could find nothing. Murdoch appeared, and Holmes asked him notify the police. Murdoch left for the village to call a policeman. After that, he visited Bellamy's house to tell of their success. He was promised the marriage to Maud, and a job at the company of her father. It was the reason he answered, "I had intended to do so" when he was told by Stackhurst, "You will kindly make fresh arrangements for your future as speedily as you can,"

However, as Holmes said, "On the morning of the crime he can surely prove an alibi. He had been with his scholars till the last moment, and within a few minutes of McPherson's appearance he came upon us from behind. Then bear in mind the absolute impossibility that he could single-handed have inflicted this outrage upon a man quite as strong as himself," Murdoch heard that the police intended to arrest him. He was a prudent criminal. If not for Holmes, he would have been arrested by Inspector Bardle of the

Sussex Constabulary. He hurt himself with Cyanea capillata when Stackhurst came to the tide pool. He cried out in order to to be discovered by Stackhurst. He left Cyanea capillata in the pool as evidence of the accidents. It made him look completely innocent.

Although our plot proves Sherlock Holmes' misdetection, all the evidence but the death of McPherson's dog supports it. We could not find out why this dog was killed. It might be an accident, but as Hedgpeth wrote, it is unlikely that an Airedale terrier with so much hair could not protect itself from an attack by a jellyfish. It might have been poisoned by the murderer, as he said. But we could not find any reason why Murdoch or the Bellamys did it. We hope further study will answer this question.

Bibliography

1 Bengis, Nathan, Sherlock Stays after School; Illustrious *Client's Second Case-Book* New York: Magico Magazine, 1984
2 Baring-Gould, William S., the *Annotated Sherlock Holmes* New York: Clarkson N. Potter, reprinted in 1978
3 *The Red Circle Gazette* No.25 Niigata: The Red Circle of Niigata, 1989
4 Doyle, Sir Arthur Conan, The *Complete Sherlock Holmes Short Stories* London: John Murray, reprinted in 1971

(*The Nezire Zanmai* vol.2, 1992)

The Master and "Baritsu"

The largest problem concerning Japanese Sherlockiana is the meaning of "Baritsu." This Japanese style of wrestling saved the Master's life from Professor Moriarty in "The Empty House."

Baritsu is widely accepted as a sort of Judo among Eastern and Western Sherlockians, but it was not called by its right name "Judo" or "Jujutsu." Therefore, it has caused some arguments.

Count Makino, who was a member of The Baritsu Chapter, wrote a paper on this problem which was read by his grandson, Yoshida Ken-ichi at the first meeting of the society on October 11, 1948. In his opinion, Baritsu is "Bujutsu," the martial art of the Samurai. Bujutsu includes Jujutsu, Kenjutsu (Japanese fencing), horseback riding, castle designing and all other skills for war. It is difficult for Western people to pronounce "Bujutsu" correctly.

Ralph Judson believed that it was Mr. Barton-Wright's "Baritsu." Both Count Makino and Judson thought that, when Watson (or Doyle) wrote EMPT, although Holmes told him "Judo" or "Jujutsu" he used the wrong word. "Bujutsu" is a vague concept, and "Baritsu" did not appear until 1899.

On the other hand, there is a unique paper on this problem. Iijima Akira thought Baritsu is not Judo, but Sumo. Sumo is traditional Japanese wrestling. In 1991, Sumo wrestlers visited London and wrestled at the Royal Albert Hall. There is a TV program on Sumo in the UK, so Sumo is becoming popular in Holmes' homeland. Iijima believes that according to the description given by Holmes, the skill he used was not that of Judo, but that of Sumo, which is all about pushing out.

His theory is attractive, but unlikely. There are not that many people who do Sumo even in Japan. Judo is much more popular than Sumo among amateur sportsmen.

I agree with other scholars who think Baritsu was Judo. Kano Jigoro, Father of Judo, founded Kodokan in 1882. Jujutsu had been one of the martial arts, but Kano improved it to the point of being a modern sport for not only Samurais, but also children and elders, and named it "Judo." Judson says, "It takes roughly seven years to become proficient in this art and reach instinctive actions and reactions to every kind of attack, it is likely that he started his training around 1883-1884." If Judson is right, and Holmes was trained in Judo, he must have been one of the earliest students of Kodokan. Saigo Shiro, who was the model for the movie "Sugata Sanshiro" directed by Kurosawa Akira, received the black belt in 1883. As he studied Jujutsu before he entered Kodokan in 1882, he needed only one year to receive the black belt. In 1990, a man of seventy-nine joined Kodokan, and attended practice every morning. One year later, he passed the examination for the black belt. It is not impossible for a talented person to get a black belt in a short period of time.

I think, however, Sherlock Holmes did not need a black belt to fight with Professor Moriarty. Professor was an old scholar whose friends were books. He made evil schemes but did not conduct them by himself. He was a man of brains, not of hands and feet.

If Sherlock Holmes had a black belt, he would not have made such a scene in "The Reigate Squires."

His words were cut short by a sudden scream of 'Help! Help! Murder!' With a thrill I recognized the voice as that of my friend. I rushed madly from the room on to the landing. The cries, which had sunk down into a hoarse, inarticulate shouting, came from the room which we had first visited. I dashed in, and on into the dressing-room beyond. The two Cunninghams were bending over the prostrate figure of Sherlock Holmes, the younger clutching his throat with both hands, while the elder seemed to be twisting one of his wrists. In an instant the three of us had torn them away from him, and Holmes staggered to his feet, very pale and evidently greatly exhausted.

This is recorded in "The Reigate Squires" which took place in 1887, according to a chronology of Baring-Gould. It is easy for a trained Judo wrestler to throw two men in a second. It can be concluded from this passage that Holmes did not know Judo in 1887, or if he did, he was only a beginner.

It was 1889-1891 when Kano Jigoro visited Europe to study education. Most of the time he stayed in Germany, but he also visited Britain. I think Holmes met Kano at that time in Europe or in Britain, and learned the elementary skills of Judo. Watson had already left Baker Street because of his marriage in 1889. The good doctor might have not known about his friend's new sport.

The first foreign student of Kodokan was Captain H. M. Hughes of Britain, who started his training on August 14, 1893. I believe Captain Hughes was the Master in the Great Hiatus. Holmes found himself in need of more training in Judo at Reichenbach, and visited Tokyo to get his black belt. After that, he visited Tibet by an eastern route.

Kano Jigoro wrestled with a Russian officer on a ship on the way to Japan. The officer was much taller than Kano, so he tried to restrain him with his arms. Kano rolled his back and moved left and right so as not to be caught. The officer got irritated and stepped forward. At that moment, Kano grasped him and threw him down. It was a combination of "Koshinage" and "Seoinage." I think the fatal match of Holmes and Moriarty had a resemblance to this match. Holmes could not bring down Moriarty (he could not take "Ippon"), but Moriarty "with a horrible scream kicked madly for a few seconds and clawed the air with both his hand. But for all his efforts he could not get his balance, and over he went."

My conclusion is: The Master was not always a master. He might have been a beginner.

Bibliography

1 *The Mystery Writer's Club of Japan Monthly Bulletin.* No.1-50. Tokyo: Kashiwa Shobo, 1990.
2 Judson, Ralph. "The Mystery of Baritsu: A Sidelight upon Sherlock Holmes's Accomplishments." *BSJ Christmas Annual*, No.3 (1958) 10-16.
3 Iijima, Akira. "The Study of Baritsu." *Sherlock Holmes Kiyo*, Tokyo: Vol.1, No.2, 1990.
4 "Minami Shigeo." *SERAI*, No.21 (1991) 11.
5 Baring-Gould, William S. *The Annotated Sherlock Holmes*. New York: Clarkson N. Potter, 1967.
6 Oimastu, Shin-ichi. *Judo Hyakunen*. Tokyo: Jijitsushin-sha, 1976.
7 Togawa, Yukio. *Shosetsu Kano Jigoro*. Tokyo: Yomiuri-shinbunsha, 1991.

(*The Shoso-in Bulletin* vol.3, 1993)

The Hound Commentary in Japan

The Hound of the Baskervilles, one of the most important adventures of Sherlock Holmes, is also popular in Japan. According to Nakanishi, HOUN took first place in the best canonical stories contest of The Japan Sherlock Holmes Club. One hundred and fifty-seven members voted, and HOUN scored 384 points; REDH, 278; and SPEC, 208. The REDH's score was more than hundred points lower than that of HOUN. When asked to state why they considered HOUN the best, members mentioned its fine descriptions of the supernatural and nature.

It is safe to say that HOUN is one of the most loved stories in Japan. I would like to introduce summaries of monographs regarding HOUN written in Japan, and add some of my opinions to them. It will probably help your understanding of current studies on HOUN in Japan.

A HOUN bibliography in Japan

According to Arai's study, HOUN was translated for the first time in 1916, by Kato Choucho, and was published by Tengendo. It was named *Meiken Monogatari* (A tale of a good dog). I have no idea why the translator used such mismatched name, because I myself have never even seen this book.

In 1923, Nobuhara Ken translated HOUN under the title *Ma no Inu* (The Monster Hound), and it was published by Hakubunkan. Nobuhara is the first one to translate all the adventures of Sherlock Holmes in Japan. Even now, his works are the most popular version of the Canon for Japanese Sherlockians.

Nobuhara continued to retranslate the Canon all his life. He published *Baskerville no Inu* in 1929, and participated as one of the translators of *All Works of Conan Doyle* published in 1931-33. He translated the entire Canon and several of Doyle's other works. His Canon was again published in 1952 by Getsuyo-shobo, but there were too many misprints. He published it again through Shincho-sha in

1953. This edition is being published even today with slight alternations, and most Japanese Sherlockians have these books on their book shelves.

Children's HOUN in Japan

Most Japanese meet Sherlock Holmes while they are in elementary school. All school libraries have children's adaptations of Sherlock Holmes and Arsène Lupin stories. There, we meet for the first time, detective and suspense stories.

There are many translators for such adaptations. Most of them translate the Canon as correctly as they can, but such a translation is often too difficult for children in the Far East. They have never seen hansom cabs or gaslight. One of the most memorable adaptations is that of Yamanaka Minetaro (1885-1966). He adapted all the Canon and they were welcomed by children. His works are not faithful to the original Canon, but he knew how to let children enjoy the stories. Recently, some Sherlockians claim that such adaptations do not help to know the real image of Sherlock Holmes, but it is true that Yamanaka's works presented the joys of detection and Sherlockiana to many people. Most Japanese read faithful translations in their junior high school years, so I think there is not much to fear. It is the way I first experienced Holmes, too.

Fifty years ago, Yamanaka was one of the most famous juvenile story writers in Japan. He finished the military academy of Japan first in his class, and entered the military college. He met Chinese students at the academy, dropped out of college to go to China, and participated in the Third Revolution. In the end, he became the chief of staff of Sun Wen (1866-1925), the founder of the China national party. Later, he returned to Japan because of confrontations with other staff members, and started his career as a novelist.4 One of the most famous of his works is *Crossing the Enemy Camp* (1930). It is a documentary novel about Japanese soldiers who investigated Russia. He also wrote the Hongo Yoshiaki series, which are spy adventure novels. He was a Sapper or a Japanese Ian Fleming.

When World War II ended, he could not write military novels any more, and started to translate the Canon for children.

His adaptation of *The Hound of the Baskervilles* for children was published in 1955, as *Yako Kaiju*. It means "a monster glimmering in night." It is of course, the hound owned by Stapleton. He also changed several points which were difficult for children.

For example, Sir Henry Baskerville lived in Scotland, instead of Canada, and the follower at Oxford Street used a blue automobile taxi. In his other adaptations, most of the characters used cars, instead of horse carriages. But we cannot blame Yamanaka. The Sherlock Holmes of Basil Rathbone took cars and airplanes and even fought Nazi spies.

Sir Henry Baskerville telephoned Holmes to say that the post office master of Grimpen handed Sir Henry's telegram to Barrymore.

Dr. Mortimer told Watson that his spaniel was stolen by a hound. He explained that his kennel was broken into by the hound, and his spaniel disappeared. Large footprints of the hound were left there. In the original, his puppy went to the moor and disappeared, but in this adaptation, the hound attacked Dr. Mortimer's kennel. The spaniel was named "Moon." I wonder how Yamanaka found such a name.

Beryl Stapleton lost her handkerchief at a fish market at an intersection in the village, and Cartwright took it to Holmes. Holmes found that this handkerchief had the same perfume as that of the letter of warning.

In the end, the hound attacked Sir Henry on the way home from Stapleton's house. Holmes, Watson and Cartwright (Inspector Lestrade does not appear in this adaptation.) fired upon the hound. Although four bullets hit it, the hound did not die. It ran away and they followed it into the moor. The hound attacked Stapleton. Holmes shot it but was too late. Both Stapleton and the hound died. Stapleton had a black shoe in his hand. It was the stolen shoe of Sir Henry.

As the above shows, Yamanaka's adaptation is much clearer than the original story. In the original, Stapleton disappears and his death in the moor is suggested. For children, it is vague and leaves them frustrated. Yamanaka says in his preface, the original story is too complex for Japanese children today. His works are precious for small readers reading the Canon for the first time. There are many boys and girls who have never read Christie's or Hammett's works because there are no children's adaptations of Christie or Hammett, but all of them know about Sherlock Holmes. I consider Yamanaka's contribution to Japanese Sherlockiana to be very large.

The Legend

It would be a poor expert who could not give the date of a document within a decade or so. You may possibly have read my little monograph upon the subject. I put that at 1730."

"The exact date is 1742." Dr. Mortimer drew it from his breast-pocket.

Sherlock Holmes might have felt some uneasiness when Dr. Mortimer told him the exact date of the document. His words "poor expert" shows that he had confidence in giving the exact date of the document. He referred to his monograph with complete self-confidence, but actually he was on the borderline of being a poor expert himself.

It is known that the original legend which Conan Doyle heard from Robinson is that of Sir Richard Cabell. "He was a gentleman of evil repute and on the night of his death, black hounds breathing fire and smoke raced over Dartmoor and howled around his manor house."

In British legends, there are many such evil animals connected with the death of aristocrats. Foxes, white owls and white birds are seen before deaths in these families. It is interesting that in all other legends, animals prophesy death, but are never the cause of death itself. While on the contrary, the hound of the Baskervilles causes the death of Sir Hugo.

Legends of black hounds are common in Britain. They can be found in Norfolk, Ireland, Somerset, Scotland and Devon. These black hounds are a kind of devil, and cause death to those who gaze upon them.

Our legend has these two elements. This hound was a messenger from hell. Sir Charles believed that it prophesied the death of Baskervilles. The hound also killed those who watched it like in other black hound legends. For example, the friends of Sir Hugo. With only a glance, they lost their life.

But the hound also punished an evil man, Sir Hugo. I cannot understand why it appeared and revenged the girl's death. Was it a coincidence that the hound attacked Sir Hugo? Was it a miracle? I cannot tell whether it came from hell or heaven.

His findings about the man with bushy black beard

Sherlock Holmes and Dr. Watson watched as "a bushy black beard and a pair of piercing eyes turned upon us through the side window of the cab."

He was Stapleton in disguise, and Holmes mentioned that "--in all probability it was a false one. A clever man upon so delicate an errand has no use for a beard save to conceal his features."

An experienced detective could reach such a conclusion, but only some hours later, Holmes asked Dr. Mortimer the following question.

"Have you among your neighbors or acquaintances on Dartmoor any man with a black full beard?"

Holmes asked Sir Henry to send a wire to ascertain whether Barrymore was really at Baskerville Hall or not. When he received a telegram "have just heard that Barrymore is at the Hall" from Sir Henry, he said "there go two of my threads, Watson." He believed that Barrymore was one of the most suspicious men in this case. Holmes also told Watson that "if they are innocent it would be a cruel injustice, and if they are guilty we should be giving up all chance of bringing it home to them. No, no, we will preserve them upon our list of suspects." He still thought they might be criminals, even after Sir Henry's wire. It showed his strong suspicion against Mr. and Mrs. Barrymore. This attitude of Sherlock Holmes does not coincide with his previous utterance. If he thought the beard was false, he needed to ask Dr. Mortimer "have you among your neighbors or acquaintances on Dartmoor any man without a beard?"

If he did, this case would have ended there. According to the cabman, the follower was a man, not a woman. Barrymore had a black full beard. Frankland was a "grey-whiskered and red faced" man. Barrymore was not fool enough to show his bearded face to Sherlock Holmes. Frankland could not put a false beard over his real whiskers. Dr. Mortimer was with Sir Henry. It is an old maxim of Holmes that when he has excluded the impossible, whatever remains, however improbable, must be the truth. Only Stapleton remained.

The Northumberland Hotel

It is widely accepted that the Northumberland Hotel was the Northumberland Arms, at whose site, there is now the Sherlock Holmes Pub. Kobayashi et al. think that this hotel is too small for Sir Henry Baskerville who inherited seven hundred and forty thousand pounds. They consider that the Hotel Victoria of Northumberland Avenue which opened in 1887 was the one originally planned as the Northumberland Hotel. According to *Baedeker's London and its Environs* of 1905, this hotel had five hundred rooms and an orchestra during meals. Its room charge was from five shillings to six shillings. Breakfast was 3s. 6d, lunch was 3s. 6d, and dinner was 5-6s.

I think this hotel was too large if you consider the descriptions by Dr. Watson. Sir Henry Baskerville arrived at Waterloo Station before noon on the first day of this case. He met Dr. Mortimer and decided to stay at the Northumberland Hotel. This must have been around noon or a little later. At two o'clock on the second day, Sherlock Holmes and Dr. Watson were invited to lunch at the hotel. Holmes asked at the hotel, "have you any objection to my looking at your register?" and noted that "There were only "two names had been added after that of Baskerville." It is an extraordinary thing that there were only two people who checked in at a large hotel of five hundred rooms within twenty-four hours or more. This description is suitable for a smaller hotel, like the Northumberland Arms.

The Plan

Saneyoshi wondered why the hound obeyed Stapleton's orders. According to the descriptions, the hound was "bought in London from Ross and Mangles, the dealers in Fulham Road. It was the strongest and most savage in their possession. He brought it down by the North Devon line and walked a great distance over the moor so as to get it home without exciting any remarks." The hound must have been mature enough to attack Sir Charles when Stapleton bought it in London. Saneyoshi is amazed that Stapleton crossed the moor alone with the savage hound. He believes that Stapleton might have been a genius at dog training.

Saneyoshi also writes that it was impossible for the hound to attack Sir Charles or Sir Henry in the dark. Dogs cannot find even their own master from scores of meters away at night. If dogs cannot see, they must follow the scent of their game. Which means they would never have "sprang over the wicket-gate and pursued the unfortunate baronet," but only have followed Sir Charles instead.

If Stapleton wanted to make the hound attack the Baskervilles, he should have pointed them out and ordered it to do so. If he did so, someone might have seen him, but the hound would not stop attacking its victims.

Saneyoshi concluded that Stapleton's crime plan with the hound had not much chance of success.

The Hound

Saneyoshi also commented on the breed of the hound. According to Paget's illustrations, he considered that it was mostly bloodhound. Saneyoshi wondered why Ross and Mangles dealt in mutts. Endo wrote that first generation cross breeds were produced and sold intentionally, a practice that continues domestically until the 1930's.

In another paper, Endo stated that Dr. Mortimer's spaniel was an Irish water spaniel.

Stapleton

There are some arguments about Stapleton even in Japan. Kanto proved that models for Stapleton were Alfred Wallace (1823-1913) and Henry Bates (1825-1892) who were mentioned in *The Lost World*. Kanto also mentioned some evidence within the work.

In another paper Kanto wrote that Stapleton was not Roger Baskerville Jr. He reconstructed the Baskerville's family tree and found that Roger Sr. was born in 1842 and Stapleton was born in 1854. If Stapleton was Roger Jr., his father was only twelve years old when he was born. Kanto concluded that Stapleton was Jack Baskerville, an illegitimate child of the father of Charles, Roger and Henry's father. Jack and Roger Jr. from South America cooperated in the scheme. Jack committed crime, and after that, Roger was going to claim the property.

Kanto's findings on the ages of the Baskervilles is very attractive and will probably cause many arguments.

Other problems

Yagame et al. estimated the magnification of Frankland's telescope. It was 270 magnification, and its diameter was 135mm.

Kawasaki discussed the knowledge of archaeology of Stapleton and Dr. Mortimer.15 He found that Stapleton had deep knowledge of this matter, but Watson did not.

Bibliography

1 Nakanishi, H. "Holmes Monogatari Best 10" *I Love Sherlock Holmes*, Kobayashi T. and Higashiyama A. ed. Tokyo: DBS Britannica, 1987

2 Arai, S. "Holmes Monogatari Inyushi" S*herlock Holmes Zatsugaku Hyakka*, Kobayashi T. and Higashiyama A. ed. Tokyo: Tokyo tosho, 1983 pp.248-9

3 Arai, S. "Nihon ni Okeru Conan Doyle, Sherlock Holmes Bunken Mokuroku" *Sherlock Holmes Zenshu* Vol.21 Tokyo: Tokyo Tosho, 1983 (translation of *The Annotated Sherlock Holmes*)

4 Yokota J. *Nihon SF Koten Koten 3* Tokyo: Shueisha, 1985 pp.112-23

5 Doyle, A.C., *Yako Kaiju* trans. by Yamanaka M. Tokyo: Popura-sha, 1955 (translation of HOUN)

6 *The Annotated Sherlock Holmes* Vol. II Baring-Gould W.S. ed. New York: Clarkson N. Potter, 1967 p.10

7 Hirayama Y. "Baskerville-ke no Inu" *Shosetsu Sherlock Holmes*, Kobayashi T. and Higashiyama A. ed. Tokyo: Tokyo Tosho, 1987

8 Kobayashi T. and Higashiyama A. *Sherlock Holmes eno Tabi* Tokyo: Tokyo Shoseki, 1987 p.10

9 *Baedeker's London and its Environs* Leipzig: Karl Baedeker, 1905

10 Saneyoshi T. *Sherlock Holmes no Kimete* Tokyo: Seinen Shokan, 1980

11 Endo T. "Holmes to Inu 3" The *World of Holmes* Vol.9 Tokyo:

Japan Sherlock Holmes Club, 1987

12 Endo T. "Holmes to Inu 2" *The World of Holmes* Vol.8 Tokyo: Japan Sherlock Holmes Club, 1986

13 Kanto S. "Stapleton" *Kaidoku Sherlock Holmes*, Kobayashi T. and Higashiyama A. ed. Tokyo: Tokyo Tosho, 1987

14 Kanto S. "Stapleton no Shoutai" *The World of Holmes* Vol.8 Tokyo: Japan Sherlock Holmes Club, 1986

15 Kanto S. "The True Identity of Stapleton" *The Grand Game; A Celebration of Sherlockian Scholarship volume two 1960 - 2010* The Baker Street Irregulars, 2012.

16 Yagame Hiromi ed. "Frankland ou no Bouenkyou nitsuiteno Kousatu" *The World of Holmes* Vol.5 Tokyo: Japan Sherlock Holmes Club, 1983

17 Kawasaki T. "The Hound of the Baskervilles and Archaeology" *Sherlock Holmes Kiyo* Vol.2 No.1 Nara: The Sherlock Holmes Research Committee, 1991

(*The Hound* vol.1, 1992 & *The Shoso-in Bulletin* vol.3, 1993)

Some Problems on the Translation of the Title of *A Study in Scarlet*

The purpose of this article is to examine meanings and translations of the word "study" as it appears in the title "A Study in Scarlet", and the relationship between them and the title.

The title "A Study in Scarlet" has been translated into Japanese as "Hiiro no Kenkyu" since Nobuhara Ken's translation of 1931. "Hiiro" means "Scarlet," "no" is "in," and "Kenkyu" is "Study." This is the most popular translation of this title now. However, "Study" has several choices of translation. "Kenkyu" means "Devotion of time and thought to acquiring information, esp. from books, in the pursuit of some branch of knowledge."[1]

Tsuchiya Tomoyuki suggested another translation in his article.

Holmes says "I might not have gone but for you, and so have missed the finest study I ever came across: *a study in scarlet, eh?* Why shouldn't we use *a little art jargon*? There's the scarlet thread of murder running through the colorless skin of life, and our duty is to unravel it, and isolate it, and expose every inch of it." (Italics by author)

Tsuchiya paid attention to this phrase, and wrote that the translation must mean a "sketch made for practice in technique or as a preliminary experiment for a picture or a part of one."[2] His conclusion is that the same phrase used as the title of this episode must have the same meaning.[3] Eminent Sherlockians including Tanaka Kiyoshi and Kobayashi Tsukasa support his opinion. They use his title translation "Hiiro no Shusaku" in their Sherlockian articles and books. In Japanese, "Shusaku" means "sketch."

Tanaka has written an article on this problem.[4] In Nobuhara's STUD, he translated the word "study" from "the finest study I ever came across" as "Jiken", i.e., "Case." Tanaka said this translation was a free translation, and "Shusaku" was better for this word. He also asked his foreign Sherlockian friends about this problem, and most of them supported "Shusaku."

I was interested in foreign opinions, so I looked in *The Oxford Sherlock Holmes*.[4] Its editor Owen Dudley Edwards points out another time the word "study" was used.

> "'Oh! a mystery is it?' I cried, rubbing my hands. 'This is very piquant. I am much obliged to you for bringing us together. "The proper *study* of mankind is man,' you know."
> "You must study him, then," Stamford said, as he bade me good-bye. "You'll find him a knotty problem, though. I'll wager he learns more about you than you about him. Good-bye." (Italics by the author.)

Edwards wrote as follows in the footnote to this "study."

"Although Holmes will later use the term 'a study in scarlet', and although Holmes and ACD mean different things by it, we are to understand that Watson's study of Holmes will prove to be in scarlet, both from the vividness of the impression and from the nature of its preoccupation."

Edwards considered that the meaning of the title has no relation to that of Tsuchiya's suggested meaning. In Edwards' opinion, the title in STUD should be translated as "Hiiro no Kenkyu" "devotion of time and thought to acquiring information, esp. from books, in pursuit of some branch of knowledge."

I further examined this important problem.

Can "study" from "the finest study I ever came across" be translated as "Jiken", i.e., "Case"? I looked in my dictionary again, and found the meaning to be a "thing that is or deserves to be investigated." Remembering that this phrase was spoken by Sherlock Holmes, the eminent criminal investigator, it is natural to translate the word "study" into "case."

Concerning the second "study," from the phrase, "a study in scarlet, eh?", I agree with the three Sherlockians mentioned above that it means "sketch." Holmes made a joke here. The Master was cheerful, because of the interesting affair and he said this case was "the finest study I ever came across," and hit upon the joke, "study in scarlet, eh?" The latter "study" includes the meaning "case", but most of the meaning was "sketch."

There is one more "study" in this text. The third "study," is found at the end of STUD, as spoken by Holmes to Watson. "That's the result of all our *Study in Scarlet*; to get them a testimonial!" (Italics by the author)

Tsuchiya and Tanaka did not argue about this third "Study".

Can this phrase be translated as "sketch" or "case"? Unfortunately, it cannot, I believe. I cannot imagine the "result" of a "sketch." What is it? Tsuchiya referred to Whistler's artwork, "Study in Brown" or "Study in Gray and Pink" in his article; he thought that "sketch" was not a "practice", but a "completed artwork." If we accept his point of view, we still cannot understand the "result" of "completed artwork." It is difficult to conclude that the meaning is "sketch." or "case." It is more natural to translate the third "study" as "Devotion of time and thought to acquiring information, esp. from books, in pursuit of some branch of knowledge."

Another question remains. There are three meanings of the word "study," and we must decide which one is best as the title of the story "A Study in Scarlet." Tsuchiya and Tanaka did not discuss this matter, because they considered "study" to have only one meaning, "sketch."

I paid attention to the third "study" in "That's the result of all our *Study in Scarlet*; to get them a testimonial!" (Italics by the author). This time "Study in Scarlet" was written with capital letters, but the other time, "a study in scarlet, eh?" it was not. I find "Study in Scarlet" with capital letters on the title page and in the third example only. It is not difficult to say that these two phrases have a close relationship. Therefore, most of the title's meaning must be "Devotion of time and thought to acquiring information, esp. from books, in pursuit of some branch of knowledge." Of course part of the meaning is still "sketch" or "case"; however, we must choose only one of them when translating the into another language, especially non-western languages.

My conclusion is that the title of STUD should be translated as "Hiiro no Kenkyu," or "The-pursuit-of-some-branch-of-knowledge in Scarlet."

Bibliography;

1 *The Concise Oxford Dictionary*, Fifth Edition, Oxford University Press, 1964.

2 *ibid.*

3 Tsuchuya, T. "'Hiiro no Kenkyu' wa Goyaku Datta" *Shosetu Sherlock Holmes* Kobayashi, T. and Higashiyama, A. ed. Tokyo: Tosho, 1987, pp174-175.

4 Tanaka, K. "'Kenkyu' ka 'Shusaku' ka" *The World of Holmes*, Vol.14, Tokyo: JSHC, 1992, pp.7-16.
Tanaka does not show his method in this article. As a result of a questionnaire depends on its method so much, I cannot judge his result now.

4 Doyle, Arthur Conan: *A Study in Scarlet*, edited with an Introduction by Owen Dudley Edwards, Oxford University Press, 1993.

(*The Shoso-in Bulletin* vol.3, 1993)

A Second Look at the
Sherlock Holmes Museum

Illustrations by Hirayama Hiroko

It was a cloudy day in early June 1993, when my wife Hiroko and I got off the tube at the Baker Street station. I could not remember how many times I have been to the "Mecca" of Sherlockiana. It was the second time Hiroko visited Baker Street.

I planned to show her all of the Sherlockian points of interest at Baker Street, and one of our most important aims was to visit the "notorious" Sherlock Holmes Museum.

It was in the northern part of Baker Street, which was not called Baker Street in Holmes times, but "Upper Baker Street." Most of the original Baker Street buildings were destroyed during World War II by von Borgs, and there remained little Victorian feeling. However, most of its northern part escaped such violence. These buildings resembled those of old photographs taken in late nineteenth century.

It was the second time for both of us to visit the museum. We planned to visit the Granada Studio Tour in Manchester, and then the Sherlock Holmes Pub near Charing Cross station to compare the recreations of the sitting room of the great detective.

The museum's entrance was a small, ordinary entrance to a town house. Its ground floor was a restaurant. One might have missed it if there was not a "policeman" in costume. We were not the only visitors. There were two American gentlemen before us, and we waited for a while for "Mrs. Hudson." She needed some minutes to open the door after the bell was rung by the "policeman." She was too young to be "Mrs. Hudson," we thought. The entrance was narrow, and there was no space for Holmes' clients to wait. We paid £10 for two. There was a register book, and we found many American and Japanese names.

There was a stair in front of the entrance. I counted its steps, and there were really seventeen steps to the first floor. It was the main reason the owner insists that this house is the real 221B. I checked the floor, but could not find any evidence of change, so I might be able to say that these seventeen steps were original.

There were two rooms on the first floor. The larger one was the sitting room of Holmes and Watson, and the smaller one was the bedroom of Holmes.

First we entered the sitting room. Along the south side wall, there was a couch upon which Holmes lounged in a purple dressing-gown in "The Blue Carbuncle." Over the sofa, we found a dinner table near the east side windows for Holmes and Watson. I was reminded of a scene from the Granada Sherlock Holmes series. Brett-Holmes and Burke-Hardwicke-Watson had breakfast and dinner at a table on this side. This room was a little small for their sitting room, because there was no place to sit down between the sofa and the dinner table!

At the center of the room, there was a small octagonal table and the basket chair mentioned in BLUE and IDEN. Such a table was often seen in British films and TV programs, but I could not understand its name and purpose. Many British Sherlockians said in their articles that the furniture of this room was not in Victorian style. However, most visitors, including me, could not distinguish the difference. I hope British Sherlockians will give some detailed advice on this.

Just on the left side of the entrance, there was a large decorative writing table belonging to Dr. Watson. There was also the good doctor's hat and twin elephant dolls, a souvenir from India,. In front of the fire, we found a round table and two chairs for Holmes and Watson. They sat down there and argued their cases. On the table, there was a copy of *The Times* and Holmes' pipe. Next to the fire, near the window, Holmes' chemical experiment table was full of bottles of medicines. I wondered how Holmes experimented there with an oil lamp. It was dangerous and might lead to an explosion if the materials were handled carelessly.

On the other side, there was a small table for Holmes. I was surprised to see that it was too small for him. A book was open on the table, and I found a drawing of "Cyanea Capillata" there. Last time I saw it, it was open to another page. It might be a small improvement.

The fireplace was a simple one. I could not find a curved poker, however, Holmes' unanswered correspondence was transfixed by a jack-knife into his wooden mantelpiece. There was also a photo of Irene (?), a Persian slipper without tobacco, pipes, a magnifying glass, a bull's-eye lantern and a tobacco jug. Holmes' violin was left between the mantelpiece and chemical experiment desk. This must be the worst place for a violin, one of the most delicate musical instruments.

There was a door to Holmes' bedroom on the west side, between Watson's desk and Holmes' desk. This situation resembled that of the Granada's series, too. But the sitting room in Granada's series was an "L" shaped one, and its shorter arm was used for a chemical experiment area. This museum's sitting room was square and much smaller.

Holmes' bedroom was small. There was a window and two doors. His simple bed was near the south side wall, and the fireplace was in the corner. Two chests, a mirror and a jar for face washing were at the opposite side of his bed. Many photographs of criminals were hung on walls. However, there were no descriptions of this room in the Canon, so we were not reminded of any cases Watson had written about.

The large room on the second floor was an exhibition of small items related to the Canon. However, most of them were toys and dolls that you could purchase easily anywhere. The only one which drew my attention was a life size bust of Holmes, in his dressing gown and holding a pipe. There was no description of it. If any reader knows about it, I would like your help.

The small room on the second floor was a souvenir shop last time, but now there were some books and pictures related to the Canon. However, none of them drew my attention.

The third floor was closed last time, but this year we could go upstairs. The small room was closed, and the large room was a new souvenir shop. Most of items could be found at other shops, and most of them were a little expensive. I purchased a neck tie with silhouettes of Holmes.

We were surprised to find more stairs going up. There was a toilet! I have never seen the 221B toilet. I am not convinced that it was in a garret. There must have been difficulty to produce a toilet there. We also found some trunks there.

Most Sherlockian magazines said that this "notorious" museum was too "commercial." We felt that its admission price, five pounds each was expensive for that exhibition. That of Madame Tassaud's was 5.95 pounds, that of Museum of London was three pounds.

However, this place is convenient for foreign visitors. This time, we were lucky to have plenty of time to visit Manchester, to see another 221B Granada Studio Tour. Its Holmes museum was produced by the Northern Musgraves, and was full of interesting Sherlockian items, but Granada's 221B was different from its television scenes, and admission was nearly ten pounds. (We needed train tickets, too.) Other exhibitions, for example, *Coronation Street*, were not familiar to us. If I were just a Sherlockian, I might have hesitated to visit Manchester just for the studio.

The Sherlock Holmes Pub of Charing Cross had another Holmes' sitting room. This room was in a corner of its restaurant, and was separated by glass walls. We could not enter this room, and it was too small. Its original exhibition, forty years ago, might have been larger, but now it was just a lumber room. We could see it through a window of a passageway, but if we have supper at this restaurant, we would need more than ten pounds each.

If we blame this museum for being too "commercial," we must blame the Granada Studio and Sherlock Holmes Pub, too. I know its owner's naughty attitude when it was opened might have caused unpleasant experiences for British Sherlockians. However, we overseas visitors have limited time and money to visit England. We want to visit as many as Sherlockian places as we can. We are not satisfied with this museum, but we cannot omit it when we visit London from the Far East.

(*The Shoso-in Bulletin* vol.4, 1994)

The Entrance of the Sherlock Holmes Museum

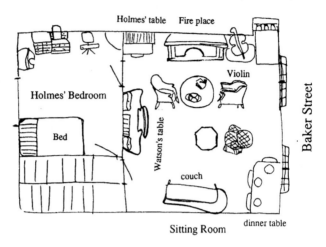

The First Floor

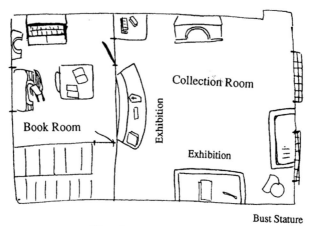

Collection Room

Exhibition

Book Room

Exhibition

Bust Stature

The Second Floor

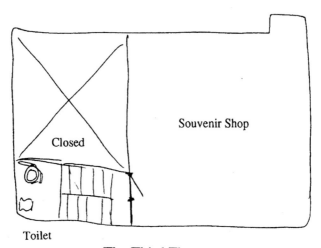

Closed

Souvenir Shop

Toilet

The Third Floor

59

Prophecies of Nostradamus and the Canon

Michael Nostradamus (1503-1566) was born in Provence, France. He studied medicine at the University of Montpelier, where Holmes also studied chemistry during the Great Hiatus.

He lived in Salon, and published his first almanac, consisting of enigmatic poems of prediction. He continued publishing this series, which is called *Centuries*. According to Henry C. Roberts, "They were written in "quatrains," or verses of four lines, with their meaning purposely obscured to prevent his being labeled a magician." The *Centuries* referred not to calendar years but to the fact that there was a series of 100 quatrains to each section; thus, a century of quatrains means 100 verses."

Nostradamus was welcome in the royal court of France, and Catherine de Medici consulted him with great interest. It is widely known that he predicted the death of Henry II by accident, the life of Napoleon, the fame of Pasteur, and Hitler and World War II.

I do not know if he was a real prophet or not, but if he was, didn't he predict one of the most important and famous persons in the world? Yes, his name is Sherlock Holmes, the Master. He is the most well known British man who ever lived, and the Canon is translated into many languages around the world.

It is not in vain, to search for verses related to the Master. I have found several interesting results. It might be proof that Holmes really existed. (However, this goes without saying for serious Sherlockians.) All the verses in this article are from Henry C. Roberts' *The Complete Prophecies of Nostradamus* (1982).

(1) Scandal in Bohemia

The first Nostradamus verse about Holmes is about SCAN.

A king shall be troubled by the answer of a lady,
Ambassadors shall despise their lives,

The great one being undecided, shall counterfeit his brothers,
They shall die by two, anger, hatred, and envy.

(Centuries 1, 85)

Roberts states, "Note the mid-twentieth-century abdication of Edward VIII caused by his love affair with Wallis Simpson. Nostradamus also makes his first reference to the assassinations of the Kennedy brothers."

His theory might explain the meaning of this verse, however, it is curious that two cases (Edward VIII and Kennedy) are included in one verse. There are some contradictions in his interpretation. It was Edward VIII, who made great trouble, not with Mrs. Simpson, but with the British people. Edward and Mrs. Simpson lived peacefully in France. No one made an attempt on their lives. Did JFK betray his brothers, Robert and Edward? No, they cooperated well. Two of them, John and Robert were killed, but what this verse says is that the other two (brothers) were dead because of "the Great one." John did not kill Robert and Edward. Edward is still alive.

Sherlockians would be reminded of SCAN when they read this verse. The first line reads, "A king shall be troubled by the answer of a lady." It is easy to understand this king is the King of Bohemia, and this lady is Irene Adler who "Threatens to send them the photograph."

The second line means these words of the king: "Twice burglars in my pay ransacked her house. Once we diverted her luggage when she travelled. Twice she has been waylaid. There has been no result." They are clearly criminal attempts on Irene Adler, by the king's agents, who were described by Nostradamus as "Ambassadors." Such illegal behavior might cause her serious injury.

"The great one" is none other than the Master, Sherlock Holmes. This should be clear to anybody. Holmes, disguised as a Non-conformist clergyman, found out where the photograph was. However, he did not take it back that night. He left it there, and returned to 221B. He wanted to show the king his skill, and postponed his final work. "I shall call with the King tomorrow, and with you, if you care to come with us. We will be shown into the sitting-room to wait for the lady, but it is probable that when she comes she may find neither us nor the photograph. It might be a satisfaction to His Majesty to regain it with his own hands." It was his fault that he was "undecided." It caused Sherlock Holmes to "stagger back, white with chagrin and surprise."

His manner caused "counterfeit" victory to the king.

The largest problem is the last line. Watson said at the beginning of this story, "the late Irene Adler." It is clear Irene Adler died before July 1891, when SCAN was published in the *Strand*. One of the two that died is Irene, I believe. The other is her husband, Mr. Godfrey Norton. Is there any connection between her death and her husband's? It is interesting that Watson called her "the late Irene Adler," not "the late Irene Norton." Watson knew the truth of her death, but did not describe it in detail. His expression suggests there were some problems between Mr. and Mrs. Norton, and it is not impossible they led to this tragedy. I believe Godfrey killed Irene, and she killed him, too. The reason would be a problem of the fair sex, and its result was "They shall die by two, anger, hatred, and envy."

There are also interesting results from the view point of mystic mathematics. In SCAN, one figure appears frequently. It is "seven."

This episode was published in the *Strand* in July, the 7th month of 1891. Watson put on seven pounds since last meeting Holmes. There were seventeen steps in 221B Baker Street. (In mystic mathematics, seventeen and seven have the same meaning.) The King of Bohemia was "hardly less than six feet six inches in height," that is, about seven feet high. His name was Wilhelm Gottsreich Sigismond von Ormstein, Grand Duke of Cassel-Felstein, and hereditary King of Bohemia. He had seven names. The crest of the King of Bohemia was a lion with a tail torn into two ends. Total of the ends, head, two hands, two legs and two tails, is seven. The King gave Holmes 700 pounds. Irene returned home at just seven o'clock. Edgar W. Smith thought the King of Bohemia was Edward VII. This verse was chapter 1, number 85. 1+8+5=14. 14 is 7 plus 7.

In ancient Egypt, they used a kind of divination with three dice. In this type of fortune-telling, "seven" means "embroiled in a scandal." This meaning coincides with the story and the title of SCAN. There are two scandals in this episode. The first scandal is that the marriage of the King of Bohemia was threatened by Irene Adler. The second scandal is Irene Adler running away with Godfrey Norton. These two explain why the total of Nostradamus's verse numbers was 14.

Tarot card fortune-telling says the reverse meaning of "seven" is: "defeat, miss at the last moment, plan breakdowns suddenly, overwhelmed by other, cannot achieve something with responsibility."

Readers will be reminded of the last scene of SCAN. "Sherlock Holmes staggered back, white with chagrin and surprise." Watson says "how the best plans of Mr. Sherlock Holmes were beaten by a woman's wit." Just as this card says.

This is not all the information included in this verse. According to Nakamura Kei-ichi of Hitotsubashi University and Daniel Lege, another calculation reveals definite proof. This verse is chapter 1, number 85, as we saw above. 1=1, 8=8, 1+8=9, root of 1+8 is 3, (5x8)/2=20. This means March 20, 1889, the date of SCAN as proposed by Baring-Gould (1955), Christ and Blakney. It is not a mere coincidence such a date was produced from these numbers.

If Sherlock Holmes really existed, Nostradamus' verse must have spoken the truth. Any serious Sherlockian will accept the former, however, I do not know if his other verses on world history are true, especially his claim that the world will collapse in 1999!

(2) The Speckled Band

This episode is one of the most important ones in the Canon, and it was not difficult to find a verse on SPEC. Like others, it is not hard to understand.

By a wild name one shall be called,
So that three sisters shall have the name of Fate
Afterword a great people by tongue and deeds shall say,
He shall have fame and renown more than any other.
(1-76)

One of the famous scholars of Nostradamus, Henry C. Roberts claims "Nostradamus very definitely feels that a Messiah will come." Uchida Hideo, a Japanese scholar of Nostradamus, wrote "Man's nickname might have its origins in his activities before his birth." No readers would not find what they want to say, and would not agree with them.

However, from the Sherlockian point of view, it is clear the man who "by a wild name one shall be called," is none other than Doctor Grimesby Roylott. He is described thusly: "he shut himself up in his house and seldom came out save to indulge in ferocious quarrels

63

with whoever might cross his path. Violence of temper approaching to mania has been hereditary in the men of the family, and in my stepfather's case it had, I believe, been intensified by his long residence in the tropics." And when Dr. Roylott visited Baker Street, the manner he leaves is, "hurling the twisted poker into the fireplace he strode out of the room." Also, the name "Roylott" resembles "riot".

In the second line, "three sisters" means Mrs. Stoner and her twin daughters, Julia and Helen. Dr. Roylott began his evil career tied into their destiny. These three were "the name of Fate." Watson said that Mrs. Stoner "was killed eight years ago in a railway accident near Crewe." However, I think Mrs. Stoner was killed by the doctor, making it looked like an accident. "Three sisters" ruled the destiny of the man of "a wild name." Of course, Julia was killed and Helen was attacked by a poison snake.

The third and fourth lines should be considered as one. They do not deal with the case itself, but the great reputation mentioned in the fourth line is, of course, that of Sherlock Holmes himself.

In Conan Doyle's "The Best of Sherlock Holmes" selection of 1927, SPEC took the first place. He always mentioned it as "the grim snake story." The eminent mystery writer Edogawa Ranpo also chose it for inclusion in his best ten stories of the Canon. Edogawa examined many mystery anthologies, and found that SPEC ranked sixth in frequency of use. In 1959, the *Baker Street Journal* published a list of favorites, and the first place story was SPEC. Even in Japan, the third place story of The Japan Sherlock Holmes Club's "The Best of Sherlock Holmes," was SPEC. It is true that "Afterword a great people by tongue and deeds shall say, He shall have fame and renown more than any other."

In this verse, the figure "three" was mentioned, and this is important. It is interesting that there are many "threes" in SPEC.

First, this episode occurred "early in April in the year '83." Helen Stoner was "a woman of thirty." Roylott family's estate was in three counties, Surrey, Berkshire and Hampshire. Dr. Roylott married Mrs. Stoner, and had three new family members. Three people lived in his house, Roylott, Julia and Helen. Their three bedrooms were in one wing. Julia told Helen "About three in the morning, I heard a low, clear whistle." Of Roylott's household income, Holmes said "through the fall in agricultural prices, not more than £750. Each daughter can claim an income of £250, in case of marriage." When two daughters married, Roylott could receive only one third of his income. Julia died when she was thirty. Three people, Holmes, Watson and Helen examined Stoke-Moran. In this story, three criminal doctor's names, Roylott, Palmer and Pritchard were mentioned. Roylott committed his crime after three o'clock. Three members of the Roylott's family died in this story. And three people, Helen, Armitage and Westphail lived. This story was written on thirty-three pieces of paper.

"Three" means "Empress" in Tarot card fortune-telling. There were exactly three females in this story. The meaning of this card is "marriage." Roylott got his fortune through his marriage, and committed murder to prevent the loss of the fortune throught the marriages of two daughters.

Like SCAN, we can get the date of this adventure from the number of the verse. It is chapter 1, number 76. $1=1$, $1+7=8$, $7+6+70=83$, $(7+1)/2=4$, $6=6$. This means April 6, 1883, the date of SPEC as proposed by Baring-Gould. In addition,
$$\log 761 = 2.8813847\ldots$$
Almost 2.9. Sherlock Holmes was born in 1854, and he was twenty-nine years old in 1883.

Roberts believed that this verse was one of the vaguest ones, but now it is very clear for us.

(3) The Five Orange Pips

Thirty of London shall secretly conspire,
Against the King, upon the bridge the plot shall be made,
These satellites shall taste of death,
A King shall be elected, fair, and born in the Low Countries.

(4-89)

Roberts said "The Guy Fawkes gunpowder plot against the British Throne is clearly outlined here." Guy Fawkes intended to assassinate King James I and members of Parliament with bombs in the Houses of Parliament, on November 5, 1605. This case is now widely known as the "Guy Fawkes Day" festival. However, there are several problems with Roberts' interpretation.

In the second line, "upon the bridge the plot shall be made," but Fawkes and his fellows set up their bomb in the basement of the

Houses of Parliament. Roberts may insist that Nostradamus mixed up Westminster Bridge and Westminster Palace. It is true both of them have the same name, and the Palace is at the foot of the Bridge. But "on the bridge" is far different from "in the basement." I would prefer to read this line as it is, and I think another case occurred on or near a bridge. It is nothing other than the murder case of John Openshaw, in FIVE. "The plot shall be made" means assassins thrust Openshaw over the embankment into the Thames river. "Against the King" is that K.K.K. members committed lynching, which is against the law of Britain. In British court, prosecution is done in the name of the King or Queen. Breaking the law is in opposition to the Crown. In addition, Waterloo Bridge was famous for suicides, like Sakata-yama Mountain, Mihara-yama Mountain or the Takashimadaira housing development in Japan. The K.K.K. members wanted the death of young Openshaw to look like suicide, but at the last moment Openshaw cried out, and the scheme failed. However, the police misunderstood it as an accident.

Returning to the first line, the "Thirty of London" are clearly K.K.K. members, and as in Kabbalah, we must consider this figure as "3+0=3". It coincides with the number of Americans on the "Lone Star." The German and Finish people had no relationship with Black people. One of the three was Captain James Calhoun. The three conspired to kill Openshaw.

Jumping to the third line, "These satellites" must be Sherlock Holmes and Dr. Watson. Lonely Openshaw asked them to help him, but he was killed before Holmes and Watson took any action. They lost the fight without taking any action. It was the biggest humiliation for them. Holmes said "That hurts my pride, Watson," and "It is a petty feeling, no doubt, but it hurts my pride. It becomes a personal matter with me now." "He sprang from his chair and paced about the room in uncontrollable agitation, with a flush upon his sallow cheeks and a nervous clasping and unclasping of his long thin hands." In this way , these satellites tasted of death.

However, the Lone Star was punished by Heaven, and sunk in a storm. God himself, who gave power to the King, punished the villains instead of the King. "A King shall be elected" may refer to this.

The last question is about "born in the low countries." I cannot find any explanation for this phrase, though if we pay attention to "low," this word has a curious relevancy to deaths in this case. All of them died in a low place.

First, Colonel Elias Openshaw was found dead. "We found him, when we went to search for him, face downward in a little green-scummed pool." Its depth was two feet. Openshaw's "father had fallen over one of the deep chalk-pits which abound in the neighbourhood, and was lying senseless, with a shattered skull." John Openshaw died in Thames, near the Waterloo Bridge. Finally, the K.K.K. criminals sunk with their ship, in Atlantic Ocean.

Moreover, most of people in this case went to the land of dead. The "low countries" may mean "the land of dead." However, Henry Roberts' "Guy Fawkes" theory cannot explain the phrase either. I would like to hear your ideas about it.

Finally, I will try to calculate the date of this case from the number of the verse, Chapter four, number 89. We can use 4. 8 and 9.

$8*9/4=18$, $8=8$, $9=9$, $9=9$, $4*9*(\sqrt{4})/(\sqrt{9})=24$.

September 24, 1889 is the date given by Professor Christ.

Bibliography

1 Roberts, Henry C., *The Complete Prophecies of Nostradamus* (new revised edition), Nostradamus Co., New York, 1982.

(*The Shoso-in Bulletin* vol.5, 1995, and vol.6, 1996)

The True Identity of King of Bohemia

It is an undisputed fact that the last true king of Bohemia was Ferdinand I (reigned 1526-1564), and that after his death, the Kingdom of Bohemia was absorbed by the Holy Roman Empire. "A Scandal in Bohemia" is estimated from1887 to 1889 by various chronologists, and it is clear there was not a king of Bohemia in the late 19th century.

Scholars have proposed the names of several noblemen as the real identity of the King of Bohemia in SCAN. However, some were already married by 1887-89; most others were too old or too young.

L. W. Baily[1] and Julian Wolff[2] proposed the Crown Prince Rudolf as the King of Bohemia. Rudolf was a son of Franz Josef, Emperor of Austria, and Elizabeth of Bavaria, Empress of Austria. Rudolf was born in 1858, and he died in 1889. He married to Saxe-Coburg, Stephanie of Belgium in 1881. It would have been impossible for him to say "I am about to be married."

Julian Blackburn[3], E. V. Girand[4] and Michael Harrison[5] suggested Prince Alexander ("Sandro") of Battenberg, Prince of Bulgaria (1857-1893). He was a nephew of Tsar Alexander II of Russia, and "Alexander was expected to be a faithful servant of St. Petersburg, but . . . he began to take a more independent line. This eventually disturbed Russia so much that her agents organized a conspiracy against Alexander among discontented army officers. One night in August 1886, they burst in on the Prince, forced him to abdicate on pain of death, and removed him to Russia."[6] Alexander married Johanna Loisinger (1865-1951), an opera singer in 1889. If Loisinger was the real Irene Adler, there would be no reason for SCAN to occur, because they married successfully. In addition, Alexander had already resigned as Prince of Bulgaria in 1886. He was not a monarch in SCAN time.

John D. Cleark[7] and Goran Sundholm[8] considered Albert Wilhelm Heinrich von Hohenzollern, who became Kaiser Wilhelm II in 1888, as the King of Bohemia. Wilhelm II was born in 1859, and his father was Frederick III, Emperor of Germany. His mother was

Victoria Adelaide Mary, Princess Royal, eldest daughter of Queen Victoria of Britain. He married Augusta Victoria von Schleswig-Holstein in 1881. The king was going to marry to "Clotilde Lothman von Saxe-Meningen, second daughter of the King of Scandinavia." John B. Wolf pointed out that Wilhelm II "was married to Princess Auguste-Victoria zu Schleswig-Holstein; Schleswig-Holstein being the Danish duchies of the second German Reich."[9] Schleswig-Holstein is very near to Denmark, but it is not a part of Scandinavia.

T. S. Blakeny[10] thought it was Archduke Franz Ferdinand of Austria (1863 -1914). He married to Sophie Josefine Albina Choteck in 1900. However, D. Martin Dakin says "nothing is known of any arrangement with the Scandinavian royal house, but he fits better than anyone else." Charles A. Meyer[11] and Edgar W. Smith[12] indicated the Prince of Wales, later Edward VII, King of Britain, as the King of Bohemia. Actually, he had many mistresses, and his bride was Princess Alexandra of Denmark, "daughter of the King of Scandinavia." The other monarchs mentioned in this article did not have brides who were from Scandinavia. It is the largest positive factor for Edward. However, he married in 1863, and was already a father of six children and too old in the late 1800s to be the 30-year-old king in the story. The King of Bohemia must have married in late 1880s, and his bride must have been from Scandinavia.

At that time, there were two kingdoms in Scandinavia. One was Sweden and the other was Denmark. Sweden's king was Oscar II (1829-1907), but he had four princes and no princesses. And his grandchildren were too young to have married by 1887-89.

The other king was Christian IX of Denmark. He was born in 1818, acceded in 1863 and died in 1906. He married to Princess Louise Wilhelmina of Hesse-Cassel in 1842, and had six children. His eldest son, Frederick VIII, King of Denmark, was born in 1843. His eldest daughter, Princess Alexandra was born in 1844 and married to Edward VII of Britain. His second son, Prince William George, born in 1845, became the King of Greece, George I. Christian's second princess, Dagmar "Marie" of Denmark, was born in 1847. She was married to Alexander III and became the Empress Marie of Russia. Their third princess, Thyra Amelia Caroline, was born in 1853, and married to Ernest Augustus, Crown Prince of Hanover and third Duke of Cumberland in 1878. The third prince, Valdemar, was born in 1858 and married Princess Marie d'Orleans.

Frederick VIII's eldest daughter, Louise Caroline Josephine, was born in 1875, and was only thirteen years old in 1888 -- too young to be a bride for the "King of Bohemia." She married Prince Frederick von Schaumburg-Lippe in 1896. The daughters of Alix, Marie and Thyra are not members of Glücksburg family. Prince Valdemar's only daughter was born in 1895.

Prince William George, King George I of Greece and his wife, Olga Constantinovna, Princess of Russia, had four princes and three princesses. Their eldest daughter, Princess Alexandra of Greece was born on 18 August 1870. She married Grand Duke Paul Alexandrovich Romanov on 5 June 1889. As far as my research has found, this is the only marriage of a Glücksburg princess between 1887 and 1889.

Though Princess Alexandra was a Princess of Greece, she was also a member of Glücksburg, the Danish Royal family. It is not exact to say she is a "daughter of the King of Scandinavia," but she was a granddaughter of the King of Scandinavia, and a daughter of the King of a member of the Scandinavian Royal Family.

Grand Duke Paul Alexandrovich Romanov was the King of Bohemia? He was born in 1860, and was 29 years old when he married. The King of Bohemia said "I am but thirty now." His father was Alexander II of Russia and his mother was Princess Marie of Hesse-Darmstadt. It is a well known fact that the Romanov family had married extensively into the German aristocracy: Alexander II's mother was Princess Alexandra (Charlotte) of Prussia. But the most famous example is Catherine II (the Great), Empress of Russia (1729-1796). She was a daughter of Christian Augustus, Prince of Anholt-Zerbst and married to Peter III, Tsar of Russia. It is natural that Grand Duke Paul disguised himself as a German noble, and that Watson used a German pseudonym for him.

The King of Bohemia said "I am about to be married." Though the Canon says "it was on the twentieth of March, 1888," Blakeney, Brend, Christ, Dakin, Folsom, Hall and Zeisler consider that it was March, 1889. This coincides with that fact Grand Duke Paul's marriage was 5 June 1889, only three months after Holmes' involvement in the affair. The King of Bohemia also said "You may know the strict principles of her family." King George I and Queen Olga "led a happy, but simple life with their large family." [6]

The King of Bohemia "could hardly have been less than six

feet six inches in height, with the chest and limbs of a Hercules . . . with a thick, hanging lip, and a long, straight chin suggestive of resolution pushed to the length of obstinacy." The king had a moustache and no beard in Sidney Paget's illustrations. The Grand Duke Paul "was a very tall, thin, broad shouldered man with a rounded forehead, a long thin nose, a moustache and no beard."

The King and Irene Adler met in Warsaw, which was a part of the Russian Empire at that time. Adler was "Prima donna *Imperial Opera of Warsaw*" [emphasis added]. It is natural that a member of Russian Imperial family visited the Imperial Opera of Warsaw. If he was a German noble, the opera houses of Berlin or Vienna were probable destinations. The Grand Duke Paul "was charming, elegant, humorous, a good dancer and a great favorite among the ladies." It is not hard to imagine Irene and Grand Duke Paul falling in love.

A Grand Duke is not a king, but then, Prince Alexander ("Sandro") of Battenberg, Crown Prince Rudolf, Kaiser Wilhelm II, Archduke Franz Ferdinand, Edward VII were not kings at the time of SCAN, either. It is not an important problem. The most important points in favor of Grand Duke Paul are, one: he married a member of the Glücksburg family; two: his marriage was just after the SCAN; and three: he was about thirty in late 1880s. I consider Grand Duke Paul as the most believable candidate for the King of Bohemia.

Grand Duke Paul had two children, Maria Pavlovna, was born on 6 April 1890, and Grand Duke Dmitri Pavlovich (the man who killed Rasputin), born 6 September 1891. Princess Alexandra died on 12 September 1891. In 1902, he married Olga Valerienovna Karnovich, Princess Paleij, as a morganatic marriage, and had three children. This second marriage caused a scandal in Russian society, forcing Grand Duke Paul to leave Russia to reside in Paris until 1912. This scandalous love affair of Grand Duke Paul supports my theory that he was the actual "King of Bohemia." He returned to Russia and lived "not far from the Alexander Palace, where Nicholas II and his family lived . . . when his health permitted, he commanded the First Imperial Guards Corps at the front, ranking as a full general of cavalry."

He was arrested and killed by the Soviets on 29 January 1919, at Fortress Peter & Paul, Petrograd, Russia.

Bibliography

1. Bailey, L. W. "The Scandal Behind the 'Scandal,'" *SHJ*, 9, No. 3 (Winter 1969), pp.82-85.
2. Wolff, Julian. "The King of Bohemia," *Practical Handbook of Sherlockian Heraldry*. Compiled by Julian Wolff. New York: [Privately Printed], 1955. pp.22-23.
"The Arms of the King of Bohemia," *BSJ*, 15, No. 3 (September 1965), 147- 149.
3. Blackburn, Julian. "The Identity of the King of Bohemia," *BSJ*, 21, No. 2 (June 1971), pp.114-116.
4. Girand, E. V. "On the Antiquity of Scandal in Bohemia," *BSJ*, 23, No. 3
(September 1973), 162-169.
5. Harrison, Michael. "Sherlock Holmes and the King of Bohemia: The Solution of a Royal Mystery," *Beyond Baker Street: A Sherlockian Anthology*. Edited and annotated by Michael Harrison. Indianapolis/New York: The Bobbs-Merrill Co., [1976], pp. 137-172. illus.
6. Kroll, Maria, Lindsey, Jason; *Europe's Royal Families*, Country Life Books, London, 1979
7. Clark, John D. "The King of Bohemia?" *BSJ*, 15, No. 3 (September 1965), pp.142-146.
8. Sundholm, Goran "Vem var Kungen av Bohmen?" *Baker Street Cab Lantern*, No. 7 (1969), pp.17-20.
"Who Was the King of Bohemia?" Tr. by the author; revised and edited by Herbert A. Eaton. *VH*, 4, No. 3 (September 1970), pp.2-4.

9. Baring-Gould; The Annotated Sherlock Holmes volume I, Clarkson N. Potter Inc., New York, 1967, pp.354

10. Blakeney, T.S.; *Sherlock Holmes Journal*, vol.3, No.2, pp15-16.

11. Meyer, Charles A. "Some Thoughts on A Scandal in Bohemia," *NS*, No.26 (March 25, 1986), pp.3-8.

12. Smith, Edgar W. "A Scandal in Identity," *Profile by Gaslight*, edited by Edgar E. Smith, Simon and Schuster, New York, 1944, pp.262-273.

(*The Shoso-in Bulletin* vol.7, 1997)

The Game Is Afoot!

I am always reminded of this phrase when I start to write a Sherlockian article.

We first see this famous phrase in the Canon in "The Adventure of the Abbey Grange" when Holmes tells Watson: "Come, Watson, come! The game is afoot. Not a word! Into your clothes and come!" The word "game" has two meanings. One is "quarry" or "spoils," which would be the main meaning in Shakespeare's and Holmes' words. However, the other meaning of "game" is "a diversion, pastime, or amusement; or a form of mental or physical competitive play, governed by specific rules and testing the skill, endurance, or luck of the participants."

This latter meaning is important, as Sherlockiana is a "game," like chess or Monopoly for me. "Sherlock Holmes is alive" and "Dr. Watson wrote the Canon" are rules of the game, and I do not want to change these rules. It would be impossible to play chess if you deny the rules of movement of the chess pieces. We can enjoy playing games when we adhere strictly to the rules.

I am also a member of the Arthur Conan Doyle Society, and I know there are many distinguished studies of ACD. I read these studies with great interest, but this is a different matter - this is English literature. It is one thing to play Monopoly, and another to study someone who invented Monopoly. Playing the game is not a substitute for studying history. They are completely different matters.

Recently some people have claimed that most of the problems in the Canon have already been solved, and there are no new subjects for Sherlockian scholars to discuss. They propose "Victoriana" - the study of Victorian times - as the new way for Sherlockians. I cannot accept this view. There are no problems solved with regard to the Canon. You would understand this simple truth just by seeing De Waal's massive bibliography, where thousands of pages list tens of thousands of writings about Canonical problems. Surely people would not have so much to say about problems which have already been solved.

Victoriana is required as basic knowledge for serious Sherlockians. Michael Harrison, Vincent Starrett and other Sherlockians of my grandfather's generation knew first-hand what the Victorian world was, and Sherlockians of my father's generation also have good knowledge of the era, passed down by their parents. For the third generation Sherlockians, however, the Victorian era is long-past history, and it is especially difficult for non-English Sherlockians to get - and understand - detailed information on the Victorian lifestyle. We must put forth much hard work to understand the world of Sherlock Holmes.

However, this is only an entrance, an "undergraduate course." Having gotten that far, one sees the entire, great world of Sherlockian fun stretching beyond.

I hope *The Shoso-in Bulletin* helps you to join - and enjoy the "game."

(The Shoso-in Bulletin vol.8, 1998)

John Clay's Grandfather

Sherlock Holmes said that John Clay's grandfather "was a Royal Duke, and he himself has been to Eton and Oxford," in REDH. Richard Lancelyn Green wrote in a footnote in *The Oxford Sherlock Holmes* "the grandfather would have been one of the four sons of George III (1738 - 1820) who were not enthroned." This theory is widely known in the Sherlockian world. In his *Practical Handbook of Sherlockian Heraldry*, Julian Wolff said "It is generally agreed that John Clay's grandfather was one of the seven sons of George III because they were the Royal Dukes who were in action during the epoch that his link with royalty was forged."

Jabez Wilson described John Clay as "not short of thirty." As this case occurred in 1887 (Baring-Gould), 1889 (Folsom and Zeisler) or 1890 (Bell, Blakeney, Brend, Christ, Dakin and Hall), Clay would have been born before 1860. Wilson also stated "he's not such a youth either. It's hard to say his age." Holmes called him "young John Clay." Clay would have been in his thirties, or might have been in his early forties. Namely, he was born between about 1845 to 1860.

John Clay had no titles. Holmes mentioned him as "Mr. John Clay." Inspector Jones called him "your highness," but it was a joke. His father would not have been a peer.

Firstly, as Green said, I exclude princes who were enthroned, namely, George IV (1762-1830, Prince of Wales, Duke of Cornwall and Rothesay), William IV (1765-1837, Duke of Clarence and St.Andrews) and Ernest I of Hanover (1771-1851, Duke of Cumberland). If one of them were Clay's grandfather, Holmes would have said his grandfather "was a king."

Four other princes remain. The eldest prince was Frederick Augustus, Duke of York and Albany (1763 - 1827). He was the second son of King George III. He had a mistress, Mary Anne Clarke, and married Frederica Charlotte Ulrica Katherine, daughter of Frederick William II, King of Prussia, but their marriage produced no offspring. The Duke of York and Mary Anne Clarke were involved in the Duke and Daring Scandal, and it was believed that this was the cause of the madness of King George III.

It is said that Captain Charles Hesse might be his illegitimate issue, but there is no evidence to substantiate this. Captain Hesse was killed in a duel with Count Leon, the bastard son of Napoleon I, Emperor of France.

Edward Augustus, Duke of Kent and Stratheam (1767 - 1818) was the fourth son of George III. He married Victoria, daughter of Francis I, Duke of Saxe-Coburg-Saalfield, and had Queen Victoria. Before his marriage, he had a mistress named Adelaide Dubus and their daughter was Adelaide Victoria Augusta (1789 - 1790). Edward also had a son or sons with Julie de St Laurent when he was in Canada. It is said their children were adopted at birth. John Clay had "been to Eton and Oxford." As he was educated in England, it is not probable that one of these sons was Clay's father, making Clay a Canadian.

Augustus Frederick, Duke of Sussex (1773 - 1843) had an illegitimate child by Miss Tranter of Windsor, Lucy Beaufoy Tranter. However, it is not probable that she was John Clay's mother, as she would have been too old to have given birth to John in the mid-nineteenth century. Augustus married Augusta Murray, daughter of the fourth Earl of Dunmore. This marriage was declared null by the Arches Court of Canterbury, but it did have issue. Augustus Frederick d'Este was born in 1794 and died in 1848. Augusta Emma d'Este was born in 1801 and married Thomas Wilde, first Baron Truro of Bowes, and died in 1866. It is probable Augustus Frederick d'Este had had a child in his last years. However, it is improbable that Augusta had a child when she was in her forties. John Clay had no title, and he would not be a child of peers. The Duke of Sussex married Cecilia Laetitia, daughter of Arthur Saunders Gore, second Earl of Arran in 1831, but had no issue.

Adolphus Frederick, Duke of Cambridge (1774 - 1850) married Augusta Wilhelmina Louis, daughter of Frederick III, Landgrave of Hesse-Cassel in 1818, and the couple had children. Their first son, George William Frederick Charles, the second Duke of Cambridge, (1819 - 1904) married Sarah Louisa privately in 1847. He had three sons, George William Adolphus (1843 - 1907), Adolphus Augustus Frederick (1846 - 1922) and Augustus Charles Frederick (1847 - 1933), but they were all too young to have been the father of John Clay.

Sarah Louisa had illegitimate children before her marriage to the second Duke of Cambridge. These children were not sired by the Duke, but they might have called themselves the Duke's family. Charles Manner Sutton Fairbrother (1836 - 1901) and Louisa Catherine, (b.1839?) who married a Captain Hamilton, have a slight possibility of being John Clay's father or mother.

Adolphus Frederick's second child, Augusta Caroline Charlotte Elizabeth Mary Sophia Louise, (1822 - 1904) who married Frederick William, Grand Duke of Mecklenburg-Strelitz, and his third child Mary Adelaide Wilhelmina Elizabeth (1833 - 1897) who married Francis Paul Charles Louis Alexander, Duke of Teck, were of adequate age to be mother to John Clay's mother, but they were already married when REDH occurred, and Sherlock Holmes would have mentioned that "his mother was a Royal Duchess." Mary Augusta Louise Olga Pauline Claudia Agnes, daughter of Duchess of Teck married George V in 1893.

As observed above, we have these candidates as parents of John Clay.

1. Augustus Frederick d'Este (1794 - 1848).
2. Charles Manner Sutton Fairbrother (1836 - 1901).
3. Louisa Catherine (b.1839?).

The first one is the real son of the Duke of Sussex, but the latter two are not actually children of the Duke of Cambridge. Considering all the facts, Augustus Frederick d'Este is the most probable person to be the father of John Clay, and the Duke of Sussex was John Clay's "Royal Duke" grandfather.

Bibliography;

1 Weir, Alison; *Britain's Royal Families*, Revised Edition, Pimlico, London, 1996.
2 Kiste, John Van der; *George III's Children*, Alan Sutton, Phoenix Mill, 1995
3 Mori, Mamoru; *Eikoku Oushitsu Shiwa*, Daishukan, Tokyo, 1986.
4 Doyle, Arthur Conan; *The Adventure of Sherlock Holmes*, edited by Richard Lancelyn Green, Oxford University Press, Oxford, 1994.
5 Weller, Philip; *Elementary Holmes*, Sherlock Publications, 1994.

6 Baring-Gould, William S.; *The Annotated Sherlock Holmes*, Clarkson N. Potter, New York, 1967.

(The Shoso-in Bulletin vol.8, 1998)

Tom, the "Tai-jin" Sherlockian

Note:
　　Our fellow member, Fred Levin, informed me by e-mail of the sad news of Tom L. Stix Jr. It was not unexpected news, as I heard he had been hospitalized, but I cannot believe his departure came so soon. In Japan, it is said all people who pass away become Buddhas, but Tom had the virtue of a Buddha before he passed away. I explained this as "Tai-jin" in my article published in the Baker Street Journal, as he was not a Buddhist. However, his contribution to the world of Sherlockiana and his big heart would make it possible for him to meet not only God, but also Buddha. And I believe Tom solved the big Sherlockian problem of Holmes' travel to Tibet, through an interview with the Buddha.
　　This article was first published in the Baker Street Journal, Vol.47, No.1.

* * *

Many articles and books on the Baker Street Irregulars have been published, especially during the last few years. I have enjoyed reading these books very much. Vincent Starrett, Christopher Morley, Nathan Bengis, Julian Wolff and many more Sherlockians have appeared in these pages, and they helped me, a new member of the Baker Street Irregulars, to understand the history of our society. I also attended the fiftieth anniversary weekend of B.S.I., and saw many old photographs of the annual dinners of the B.S.I.'s Golden Age. I found the historical Sherlockians mentioned above, and also found the younger faces of the famous Sherlockians of our day.

However, for me, all of them are merely history. I know Vincent Starrett and Christopher Morley only from books and photographs. I have never seen Julian Wolff or Issac Asimov. They are very famous and they made splendid contributions to the world of Sherlockiana, but they are familiar in the same sense that illustrious historical characters like Washington or Lincoln are familiar. For most young generation Sherlockians, including me, Tom L. Stix, Jr. is *the* Baker Street Irregular.

Tom's contributions to the Baker Street Irregulars have been a greater achievement than it is possible to say in these pages. I would like to concentrate my point of view to his decision to open the door of the B.S.I. more widely.

There were several foreign Sherlockians who received their investiture before Tom became Wiggins; for example: Henry Lauritzen of Denmark in 1961, Naganuma Kohki of Japan in 1962, and Stanley MacKenzie of Britain in 1967. However, until recently most of members of the Baker Street Irregulars were American gentlemen.

Tom changed this tradition. His wide viewpoint caught earnest non-American Sherlockians and female Sherlockians.

Most of living Japanese Sherlockians, such as Kobayashi Tsukasa, Ueda Hirotaka and I, received our B.S.I. investiture from Tom. Who could imagine that so many Sherlockians from the Far East would receive these shillings? It is true there are more than twelve hundred members in the Japan Sherlock Holmes Club, but because of the language barrier, it was very difficult to pay attention to this small eastern country. However, Tom did it.

But not only Japan benefited. Tom's eye did not overlook other important Sherlockian countries. It was a great joy for me to learn that my friend Alan Olding of the Sherlock Holmes Society of Australia received his investiture in 1988. Another friend, Jean-Pierre Cagnat of France was investitured in 1993, with me. Many British Sherlockians (or Holmesians) were awarded this honour during Tom's leadership of the B.S.I.

It was 1991 when I went to New York to attend the annual meeting of the Baker Street Irregulars, as a guest. Before the official schedule began, Tom kindly invited me to lunch on Thursday, at The Players. I was only twenty-eight years old at that time, and it was only the second time I had attended a foreign Sherlockian event. When I entered the building, I was overwhelmed by its splendid interiors, and moreover I was awed to find so many "real" Sherlockians. They are all some decades years older than I; they are from my father's generation. Their names are very familiar for an earnest Baker Street Journal reader. It was the first time for me to meet Tom. He was a man of dignified appearance, and I got the impression of what the Chinese call, "Tai-jin."

It is difficult to translate this word into English, but my dictionary says "a man of virtue," "generosity," or "big-hearted." However, that does not encompass the whole meaning of the term. I think it also carries a philosophical depth and conviction. A world-wide or cosmopolitan point of view is important to be a Tai-jin, too. It is essential for every leader, but few leaders possess this virtue. Tom is a man who possessed this splendid element, and only a Tai-jin can bring progress to new generations.

I still vividly remember the splendid lunch. I had brought the first volume of my magazine, *The Nezire Zanmai International* (now called *The Shoso-in Bulletin*), and presented it to all the attendees. I also asked them to sign their names to my copy so I might treasure the memory. It is in front of me now. Tom and other eminent Sherlockians received my gift, and encouraged me to continue my publication. I had not decided to continue publishing this magazine, but I made so many encouraging friends in New York that I decided to publish the second volume.

Now, *The Shoso-in Bulletin* has grown to be an international Sherlockian magazine with contributions not only from the United States and Britain, but also from many European, Asian and Oceanic countries. Thank you, Tom, for making it possible to continue our international project.

(*Baker Street Journal*, Vol.47, No.1.
and *The Shoso-in Bulletin* vol.8, 1998)

Sherlockiana in Japan

It is frequently mentioned that Japan exports everything. Your car in your garage might be a Honda or Nissan. On the other hand, the field of Sherlockiana is over-imported, because of the high wall of language. We study the English language for three years in junior high school, and three more years in high school, but there are only a few people who can speak or read English. It might be the same case as the study of Latin with British students. Most Japanese Sherlock Holmes fans enjoy reading Sherlockian books only in Japanese, and perhaps a few original books published in English or German. It is lucky for them that there are many translations of Sherlockian books: for example, *Baring-Gould's The Annotated Sherlock Holmes*; *The Oxford Sherlock Holmes series*; Edgar W Smith's *Profile by Gaslight*; Matthew Bunson's *Encyclopedia Sherlockiana*; Ellery Queen's *The Misadventures of Sherlock Holmes*; and Robert L Fish's *The Memoirs of Schlock Holmes*. This selection is only a part of books published, and one of my bookshelves is occupied entirely by Japanese books. Compared to speakers of other languages, the Japanese are lucky in this field.

In the first paragraph, I did not write "Sherlockians," but "Sherlock Holmes fans," to refer the members of the Japan Sherlock Holmes Club. You may wonder if there is any difference between them, but there is a significant gap. "Sherlock Holmes fans" are those who like to read Sherlock Holmes stories. They treat and enjoy the works of Conan Doyle as fiction. "Sherlockians" are different. They are players of "The Game," and "The Game" has rules. These rules are "Sherlock Holmes is alive," and "The Canon is the true stories written by John H. Watson, MD." That is the reason why we Sherlockians call Conan Doyle "the literary agent," who supported Dr. Watson.

You may recall in "The Pink Panther" series, Inspector Clouseau. was attacked by his servant Kato with Karate. The Inspector tells Kato that he may attack any time and anywhere, for the training of Karate. In this way, Sherlockians should say "Sherlock

Holmes is alive" at any time and anywhere, when asked "Is Sherlock Holmes a fictional character?" That attitude might cause a misunderstanding. Even a professor of English literature at a Japanese university wrote; "There WERE Sherlockians who believed Holmes was a real person." If we really believe he was a real person, we are a cult group. It is clear Sherlock Holmes *is* a fictional character, but that it is the rule to treat him as a real person to play the game. If we frequently meet and communicate with western Sherlockians, there would not be such misunderstandings of the rule, but as our country is in the Far East, it was not easy to attend Sherlockian meetings in USA or UK, and we "learned" Sherlockiana from books only. This makes for some funny misunderstandings. If the rules are strictly applied, there would be less than 25 Sherlockians in Japan. The other nearly 1200 members of the Japan Sherlock Holmes Club would be only "Holmes fans."

Another trend in Japan is "Victoriana." This might be a fate for people who do not have the tradition of Victorian cultures and societies. For Vincent Starrett, Christopher Morley, and S. C. Roberts, the first generation of Sherlockian are real Victorians. The second generation Sherlockians could ask their fathers or grandfathers about the Victorian world. Even now, in England and America, there are many Victorian buildings remain, and so much information is still available. However, in the Far East, it is not easy to find historical information on the Victorian world, and we have no Victorian traditions in our life, though the era was in progress when Japan was modernized. It is the first step to have knowledge of the Victorian world to understand the Canon, but in Japan, the means of understanding is often mistreated as the main purpose. It is a great disappointment when I read an article in *The World of Holmes,* the magazine of the Japan Sherlock Holmes Club, and find no Sherlock Holmes or Conan Doyle there.

But Japanese Sherlockiana has its own virtues, and not only in translations of western books. Even now, the most popular book for elementary school pupils is the Sherlock Holmes series. There are many children's adaptations of the Canon published in Japan with full original illustrations. Collecting children's adaptations is an important field for Sherlockian collectors in Japan. It is the main purpose for one of the Japanese members of the Baker Street Irregulars. For me, the adaptation series by Yamanaka Minetaro was my first meeting with

Sherlock Holmes. This series was first published around the 1950's, and the stories were changed for easy understanding by children. For example, Holmes and Watson use a car for their transportation. This may be due to the influence of American movies shown in Japan these days. It was not faithful to the original, but it was enjoyable and kids were so excited by the stories. It is a shame that this series is now out of print because some Japanese Sherlockians complained about changing the original stories. However, there are other adaptations available, and collectors cannot stop buying these books.

It is well known that Japan produces many animated films and cartoons, and Sherlock Holmes is no exception. The biggest series was "Sherlock Hound," produced with an Italian production company. Its Holmes and Watson are those of the dog world, and Professor Moriarty in a white cape always appears as the counter part of Holmes. Mrs. Hudson is young and beautiful, and many kids help Holmes with his detections. Its early episodes were made by Miyazaki Hayao, who is now famous for his splendid animation films, "Totoro" and "Porco Rosso." The "Sherlock Hound" series was broadcast in many nations and sold as videotapes, so that some of you might have seen some of them before. It is one of the best Sherlockian products in Japan, and will not be forgotten among Sherlockians.

These years, the number of Japanese Sherlockians who attend Sherlockian festivals in the USA or UK is increasing, and a few western Sherlockians recently visited Japan and communicated with Japanese Sherlockians. In particular, there were six guest speakers: Michael Whelan, Peter Blau, James Webb, Catherine Cooke, and Jane & Philip Weller invited to the last year's Japan Sherlock Holmes Club's grand meeting. It was the landmark convention of these twenty years history of our society. These communications will accelerate the growth of Japanese Sherlockiana, and I hope western Sherlockians also will be interested in our activity.

(*The Strand Magazine* No.7, 2001 in Italian,
& *The Shoso-in Bulletin* vol.9, 1999)

The Japanese Sherlock Holmes Statue Now

My friend Mr. Keith Webb's fine article explains the construction of the Sherlock Holmes statue in Japan so well – some of the facts Keith mentions were unknown to me until I read his article – that I shall confine myself to writing other trivial things about it.

I dare say that this statue is the most unfortunate one of the four in the world. I visited two of the others, in Edinburgh and Meiringen, both in the centre of town and both having many visitors. The new statue in Baker Street should be the most visited of all, being in the very centre of Sherlock Holmes' world. However, the Japanese statue is in the countryside, and only a few people visit it each day.

Oiwake, where the statue stands, is a country town with summer villas for long-stay holidays, and there are a few casual sightseer, most of whom stop at Karuizawa, a larger town with many hotels and shopping streets. The district is also covered with snow for half the year; and in summer, as Keith says, there is a danger of thunder. Dr Watson said of Holmes that 'neither the country nor the sea presented the slightest attraction to him' ('The Cardboard Box'), and added, 'I had never before seen him show any keen interest in natural objects' ('The Naval Treaty'). Holmes might well feel both loneliness and boredom in such a solitary place. (Incidentally, the Karuizawa area is conveniently accessed by rented bicycles. If you visit the statue by this means you are likely to be a solitary cyclist!) When my wife visited the statue during a summer holiday there were so many weeds around it that it looked shabby. She (and myself, of course) had donated towards the statue when it was erected, and it was a shock to her to see it in such a state, and with so few visitors.

There was a crisis some years ago when Dr Kobayashi told us at a meeting that there was a proposal to expand the park where the statue stands, and the town council asked him to remove it. Of course

Dr Kobayashi protested that proposal and we discussed the problem at the meeting. I do not know what the result was, but the statue still stands there, and the park has not been expanded. I suspect that the recession of the Japanese economy at that time saved our statue.

However, there is some good news about the Japanese statue. In the first week of every May several dozen members of the Japan Sherlock Holmes Club gather at the statue, to hold a meeting and to clean up the monument itself. After the cleaning up they hold a picnic at the foot of the statue. This is possible because it is in the countryside; it might be possible at Meiringen too, but not in Baker Street!

In the summer holidays there is a convention called the 'Karuizawa Seminar.' It is a two day event held at a hotel in Karuizawa and about twenty Sherlockians attend. The statue is not the main focus of the seminar, but those attending always visit it, either between presentations or after the seminar closes.

In Japan we visit our ancestors' graves twice a year, and I am reminded of these events as I write this article. These two Buddhist events are called 'Obon,' in spring, and 'Ohigan,' in the summer, and the souls of our ancestors come back to earth from the heavens to stay with us for some days. These events remind us that we do not exist without our ancestors, and we give thanks to them. Noe of the Japanese Sherlockians point out that these two events resemble visits to the statue, and I do not claim that Holmes is in the heavens; but I think the subconscious minds of Japanese visitors to the statue understand the similarities. In that sense the Japanese statue is not merely a monument, but a symbol of the affection that Japanese Sherlockians have for the Master.

(*The Ritual*, No.24, 1999, The Northern Musgraves)

"Rogues Gallery"

I, Hirayama Yuichi was born in 1963, in Tokyo Japan. My family name is "HIRAYAMA," and my personal name is "YUICHI." This is the Japanese traditional style of writing names, and my western friends call me "YUICHI." It is a joy for me to communicate and meet with foreign Sherlockians. I am a member of Sherlockian societies of many countries, and was investitured as a member of the Baker Street Irregulars in 1993.

It was twelve years old when I read *Profile by Gaslight* edited by Edgar W. Smith in Japanese and learned what Sherlockiana is. I was fascinated with it, and decided to be a Sherlockian. In high school, I founded The Men with the Twisted Konjo, and published private magazines in Japanese. This society was closed once, and in 1991 re-established for publishing an international Sherlockian magazine, *The Shoso-in Bulletin*. This magazine is still published, and includes articles by many members of the Northern Musgraves. It also includes articles from all over the world: Britain, France, Germany, Switzerland, Sweden, Spain, Italy, Russia, Lichtenstein, Belgium, Japan, India, Hong Kong, Malaysia, Australia, America, Canada and Brazil. I have no chance to publish articles from Africa or the Islamic world. If you know any Sherlockians in these areas, please introduce them to me.

Mr. John Hall and I wrote *Some Knowledge of Baritsu- an investigation of the Japanese system of wrestling used by Sherlock Holmes* published by The Northern Musgraves, as well as some articles in *The Baker Street Journal* and other magazines. But I have never published a book in Japanese before. There are six members of the Baker Street Irregulars in Japan, including the late Dr Naganuma Kohki, and I am the only member who has not published any Japanese books. Now I plan to publish a pamphlet of a Doyle work, "Jelland's Voyage," the only story situated in Japan, with annotations in English.

I am a general practice dentist. My wife Hiroko is also a

Sherlockian. Some members might remember us attending a convention held in York, for our honeymoon. It was such an enjoyable Sherlockian gathering, and it was the first time we met our good friend, Mr. John Hall. Our daughter Michiko, six years old, is a fan of quizzes and puzzles. Our son Sho-ichiro, four years old, named after Mr. John Bennett Shaw, is an earnest fan of "Mr. Bean." I do not know if they will be Sherlockians or not. Anyway, they cannot read *The Ritual* yet.

(*The Ritual*, No.26, Autumn 2000)

Dentures are the Best Disguise:
Dental Aspects of Sherlock Holmes

Charles Goodman's fine article "The Dental Holmes" is the ideal for every Sherlockian dentist. It consists of a letter from Dr. Charles S. Wilson, who treated Sherlock Holmes for years, answering questions from Dr. Goodman. In this article, he mentions Holmes' "so-called "eye" tooth, which had been knocked out by a chap named Matthews in Charing Cross Station," and notes "we in the dental profession know that under normal conditions his canine tooth could never have been easily 'knocked out.' Even the dental surgeon equipped with specially devised forceps must exert unusual leverage and force to remove that type of tooth. I am advised by one of my colleagues, who is also an official examiner of the Royal Boxing Commission, that in all his wide experience he never saw a normal canine knocked out in a boxing match. Therefore I am sure that your deduction that Holmes had pyorrhea is quite correct."

"Pyorrhea" is now called "Periodontitis," which is an inflammation and infection of the ligaments and alveolar bone which support teeth. Swelling and abscess are shown in gingival. Loss of bone causes looseness of the teeth, and in the end, the teeth are lost.

As Dr. Goodman pointed out, a canine is one of the most rigid teeth in the human mouth. A canine has the longest root of all the human teeth. Dentists often find older people's mouths with no teeth but canines. Kurokawa et al. wrote in their article that "According to the residual teeth positions, the left lower canine showed the highest value (37.9%)." Other canines also have the highest value of the upper or lower half jaw. This result means the canine lasts the longest time in the human mouth.

If one of the strongest teeth, a canine, was lost, other weaker teeth would have been lost earlier. Dr. Goodman wrote, "Holmes insisted that I avoid any display of metal. He said, 'Make me a bridge that even the keen eye of a Moriarty will fail to detect.'" For making a bridge, both the adjacent teeth should have been rigid, but it seems they were not. It is a rare case in which only a canine is lost, and the

90

other teeth are in good condition. I suspect most of the other teeth were lost when his canine was knocked out. If the anterior teeth or premolar teeth remained, they would have also been knocked out when his canine was. In addition, if his canine suffered from severe periodontitis, the anterior teeth or premolar teeth should have been in much worse condition, and would have been lost. It is well presumed that Sherlock Holmes had only four canines or less in his mouth, when one of them was knocked out by Matthews.

In the Victorian era, "Pyorrhoea Alveolaris" or Periodontitis was a common oral disease, but its cause was not well known. Sewill wrote in *Dental Surgery: Including Special Anatomy and Pathology* that "Pyorrhoea alveolaris deserves to be styled the opprobrium of dental surgery. Of its etiology virtually nothing is known, knowledge of its pathology is almost equally lacking, whilst prognosis is always unfavorable, treatment being rarely able to do more than mitigate the severity of symptoms and slightly check the course of the malady. In the majority of cases in which pyorrhoea establishes itself, it slowly progresses in spite of treatment, affecting tooth after tooth until the whole dentition is destroyed." (p.427)

Morton Smale considered in *Diseases and Injuries of the Teeth*, that "Taking all points into consideration, pyorrhoea alveolaris seems (1) to be present in many persons suffering from general disorders or diathesis; (2) to be excited in many instances by local irritants, such as the presence of tartar, debris of food, mechanical injury from abnormal articulation, such as occurs in many outstanding upper front teeth." (p.275). L. R. Meredyth said in *The Teeth and How to Save Them*, "The most of these combine to form one great cause, which does the mischief in nineteen cases out of twenty, and that is, lack of cleanliness and care about the mouth." (p.164).

They could not find the bacteria that causes periodontitis, but understood its symptoms and treatments well. Sewill said, "The treatment of pyorrhoea must be first directed to thorough removal of tartar. General antisepsis of the mouth must be assiduously practiced by the patient. A soft toothbrush and a suitable dentifrice and antiseptic lotions must be used. The spaces between the teeth, which become widened as the alveoli waste, should be frequently cleared of foreign particles with a thin quill tooth-pick. In using a lotion the mouth should be partly filled and the fluid forced to and fro between the teeth by the movement of the lips. More direct applications must be made to the necks of the teeth and within the gum pockets around. An aqueous solution of perchloride of mercury, 1 in 3,000, is one of the most efficacious agents, but others may be, of course, employed." (p.431).

These treatments are close to contemporary initial treatments, with the exception of mercury. However, "Teeth which have become so loose as to be constant sources of irritation should be extracted." (p.432) is a different case. Nowadays, most dentists take great pains not to extract patients' teeth, but in those days, or 30 years ago, extraction was much oftener done than in our times.

"Hospital Reports" from *The British Journal of Dental Association*, Vol. 31, I (1888) reports the number of patients and their treatments. In February 1888, London Dental Hospital treated 4773 cases, and 2350 cases were extractions, 1692 were gold and other fillings, 132 were advice, 169 were irregularities of the teeth, and 430 were miscellaneous and dressings. 49.2% were extractions. In this same hospital in March 1888, 48.9% were extractions. At The National Dental Hospital, in March 1888, 47.7% of all the cases were extractions. At the Victoria Dental Hospital of Manchester, in December 1881, 63.7% of all the cases were extractions. It is safe to say one in two dental treatments was an extraction, and extraction was very common treatment in Victorian dentistry.

Now we know Sherlock Holmes would have suffered from severe periodontitis. But *why* did Holmes suffer from periodontitis? Was he in one of the high-risk groups? There were no scenes in which Holmes brushed his teeth, but this is not definitive evidence, as Watson did not record all of Holmes' doings.

One of Holmes' bad habits was smoking. It is well-known fact that smoking damages the throat and mouth membranes. It is also a cause of cancers of the respiratory organs and mouth. Does smoking cause periodontitis, too? Aubrey Sheiham reports "1. Persons who smoked tobacco had more debris and calculus than nonsmokers. 2. Smokers had more severe periodontal disease than nonsmokers. There was a gradient of oral cleanliness and severity of periodontal disease from low in nonsmokers to high in smokers of 11 or more cigarettes per day. 3. Persons who stated that they smoked 1 to 10 cigarettes per day had less severe periodontal disease and cleaner mouths than those who smoked more." Jan Bergstrom reports "The results, based on adults with good oral hygiene, suggest that loss of periodontal bone is related to smoking. The smoking related bone loss is not correlated with plaque infection." Smoking not only causes periodontitis, but also causes loss of bone. Hanioka & Shizukuishi report that peculiarities of smokers' periodontitis are large amounts of alveolar bone loss and detachment, many deep periodontal pockets, lots of tartar, and while their inflammation level is the same or less than non-smokers, the amount of plaque is the same. They suggest that smoking inhibits immunity and restoration of tissue demolished by periodontitis.

The other bad habit of Holmes was cocaine. Rosenbaum writes "Hygiene in general and oral hygiene specifically, are frequently neglected by drug addicts. It is difficult to know whether this is because they have never been taught appropriate preventive measures or whether they are unwilling to take the time necessary to do an adequate job. Additionally, because the patient is taking drugs which affect normal thought processes, the pain from untreated dental problems may be masked by the drug being abused. This combination of factors results in a patient with very little dental interest practicing unsatisfactory prevention. The end result is an abnormally high decayed and missing tooth rate." Lee *et al* write, "Among cocaine users, there is a greater incidence of bruxing and, as a result, they have flatter cuspal incline of the posterior teeth. (*Bruxing is one of causes of periodontitis; Hirayama*) Cervial abrasion of the teeth has also been observed in higher frequency among cocaine users because of vigorous tooth brushing. Gingival lacerations at the corners of the mouth have also been reported among patients using cocaine. *(These injuries of gingiva also worsen periodontitis; Hirayama)* Anorexia and malnutrition are common findings in cocaine abusers, and oral manifestations secondary to malnutrition are glossodynia, angular cheilitis, and *Candida* infections. Patients abusing cocaine along with a second drug, such as alcohol, present with more serious dental problems. These patients have a higher rate of decayed or missing teeth, have advance periodontal disease, and marked xerostomia."

It is safe to say that Sherlock Holmes' bad habits, such as smoking and cocaine addiction, seriously damaged his gingiva. In addition, he was an earnest boxing player. Such physical force would do fatal damage to the teeth of periodontal patients. Most of his teeth would have been extracted in his twenties and thirties, and when he met Matthews at Charing Cross Station, which occurred before the

93

Great Hiatus, he had only a few canines in his mouth.

* * *

There are several instances of circumstantial evidence that Sherlock Holmes had only a few teeth, or he wore dentures in his mouth.

It is well known that Holmes was a master of disguise. Even Watson, who lived together with him, was frequently deceived by his fine disguises. Now there are many special make-up methods, but it was the Victorian era in which Holmes lived. Just a false mustache or a hairpiece would not be so effective.

For example, in SIGN, Holmes disguised himself as an old sailor, and

He came across sullenly enough and seated himself with his face resting on his hands. Jones and I resumed our cigars and our talk. Suddenly, however, Holmes's voice broke in upon us.

"I think that you might offer me a cigar too," he said.

We both started in our chairs. There was Holmes sitting close to us with an air of quiet amusement.

"Holmes!" I exclaimed. "You are here! But where is the old man?"

"Here is the old man," said he, holding out a heap of white hair.

"Here he is: wig, whiskers, eyebrows, and all. I thought my disguise was pretty good, but I hardly expected that it would stand that test."

Holmes took off his disguise within some seconds, and showed his normal face to Watson. In FINA, he disguised himself as "a venerable Italian priest," and

I turned in uncontrollable astonishment. The aged ecclesiastic had turned his face towards me. For an instant the wrinkles were smoothed away, the nose drew away from the chin, the lower lip ceased to protrude and the mouth to mumble, the dull eyes regained their fire, the drooping figure expanded. The next the whole frame collapsed again, and Holmes had gone as quickly as he had come.

94

Again in EMPT, Holmes was "strange old book collector," who visited Watson.

I moved my head to look at the cabinet behind me. When I turned again, Sherlock Holmes was standing smiling at me across my study table. I rose to my feet, stared at him for some seconds in utter amazement, and then it appears that I must have fainted for the first and the last time in my life.

Why could Holmes change his disguise so fast and effectively? I believe the reason was his dentures. He had several partial or complete dentures in different designs for his mouth, and changed them when he was in disguise, or completely removed them from his mouth, when he disguised himself as an old man.

For every dentist, artificial teeth arrangement is one of the most important processes in denture making. Just a few millimeters difference makes the patient's looks change. Some dentists ask patients to bring a photograph taken in youth, when they had all their own teeth. At least, we make an effort to create the same look of anterior teeth arrangements with the patients' old dentures, if there are no irreparable damages.

Some actors make use of the character given by dentures. A Japanese actor named Kamiyama Sojin, who played the villains in Hollywood films before the World War II, had no teeth. He used many dentures to change his face to be seen as evil. Japanese contemporary actor Mikuni Rentaro also has no teeth, and uses several sets of dentures like those of Kamiyama. Mikuni is called one of the best performers in Japan. In the Edo era, about 300 years ago, there was a master Ninja (a spy) named Yagyu Munefuyu. His grave was investigated by historians, and his dentures were found. He was not old enough to put on dentures when he died, and some historians believed he had all his teeth extracted, and used dentures for purposes of purposes.

Just a little rearrangement causes a complete change of face, and if Holmes took out his dentures, his face would be completely changed to that of a very old man. In the three cases above, Holmes was disguised as an old man, and that was his favorite disguise. He did not need to bring another set of dentures in his pocket to create this most effective disguise.

As we have discussed, it is obvious that Sherlock Holmes had only a few or no teeth in his mouth. However, he did not regard the loss of his teeth as handicap, but made good use of it in his detective activity as a disguise. It enabled him to make a quick change in disguise, and effectively deceived both his enemies and Dr. Watson.

Bibliography

1 Goodman, Charles; "The Dental Holmes," *Profile by Gaslight*, Edited by Edgar W. Smith, Simon and Schuster, New York, 1944.
2. Kurokawa, Hiroomi, Ezura, Akira; "Dental Examination at Geriatric Welfare and Health Care Institutes in Niigata Prefecture," *Shigaku*, 87(1): 64-70, 1999.
3. Sewill, Henry; *Dental Surgery: Including Special Anatomy and Pathology*, London, Bailliere, Tindall & Cox, 1901.
4. Smale, Morton & Colyer, J.F.; *Diseases and Injuries of the Teeth, Including Pathology and Treatment*, London, Longmans, Green, and Co., 1893.
5. Meredith, L. R.; *The Teeth and How to Save Them*, London, William Tegg, 1872.
6. "Hospital Reports," *The British Journal of Dental Association*, p396-97, Vol.31, I, 1888.
7. Sheiham, Aubrey; "Periodontal Disease and Oral Cleanliness in Tobacco Smokers," *J. Perriodontol.*Vol.42, No.5, p259-63, May, 1971.
8. Bergstrom, Jan, Eliasson, Soren, Preber, Hans: "Cigarette Smoking and Periodontal Bone Loss," *J. Periodontal*, Vol.62, No.4, p242-246, April 1991.
9. Hanioka, Takashi, Shizukuishi, Satoshi: "Shishubyou Kanja to Kitsuen Shukan," (Periodontitis Patients and Smoking Habits) *The Journal of the Japan Dental Association*, Vol.49, No.6, p17-29, 1996. (in Japanese)
10. Rosenbaum, Charles H.: "Did you treat a drug addict today?" *Int Dent. J* Vol.31, No.4, p307-11, 1981.
11. Lee, C.Y.S., Mohammadi, H., Dixon, R.:"Medical and Dental Implications of Cocaine Abuse" *J Oral Maxillofac Surg.*, Vol.49,

p290-93, 1991.

(*The Shoso-in Bulletin* vol.10, 2000)

Chinese Works
in the History of Sherlockian Pastiches

It is said the Sherlock Holmes stories, which anyone would have read in the childhood, have inspired the largest amount of parodies or pastiches in western literature. Several of them have been translated into Japanese, and even Japanese writers, for example, Yamada Futarou, Shibata Renzaburou, Hoshi Shin-ichi and many others have written their own parodies or pastiches of the Master. That phenomenon would tell how attractive Sherlock Holmes is, and how many Sherlockians there are in the world.

What is the first Sherlockian parody in the world? The first story from the Canon, A *Study in Scarlet*, was published in 1887, but it was not so popular and so no one would have been interested in creating a parody. The boom of Sherlock Holmes came after the publication of the series of short stories in *The Strand* in 1891. Several months later, in November of that year, "My Evening with Sherlock Holmes" was published in *The Speaker* under an anonymous name. It is said that this is the first Sherlockian parody. This short story makes fun of Holmes' observations and detections about his client at the first acquaintance. The first American parody was John Kendrick Bangs' fun novel, *The Pursuit of the House-Boat*, published in 1897. Later published parodies were also parodies for fun or a joke.

The French writer Maurice Leblanc choose Herlock Sholmes as a counter part of Arsene Lupin in "Too Late, Herlock Sholmes" (1907) and *Arsene Lupin VS Herlock Sholmes* (1908). This story and novel is not for just laughs. As Lupin stories, they are serious works. However, from the point of view of Sherlockian parody, Holmes' name was changed, and he was treated as a dull detective to show Lupin to advantage. It is not possible to call these stories pastiches.

The first pastiche of the Sherlock Holmes stories was, perhaps, not until 1920. In this year of the origin of Sherlockiana, Vincent Starrett published "The Unique Hamlet" privately.

However, it was not republished commercially until the anthology *The Misadventures of Sherlock Holmes* in 1944. Meanwhile, August Derleth started to write the Solar Pons series in 1929. His intention was that since the original Canon was not published anymore, he would write the new Canon instead of Conan Doyle. Though the names of the characters and the times are different from the Canon, it is the successor of the Canon in spirit. But since the names are changed, strictly speaking, it is not a pastiche.

There is a curious short story called "The Man Who Was Wanted." This manuscript was found in Doyle's library after his death, and it was believed to be an unpublished new Sherlock Holmes story. This story was first published in *The Cosmopolitan Magazine* in 1948. However, after detailed investigation, this manuscript was found to be written by an architect named Arthur Whitaker in 1910. Doyle had bought it as an idea for the Canon at ten guineas, and left it in his papers. In terms of the year of writing, it is the earliest pastiche. Whitaker wanted it to be published with himself as a co-author with Doyle, and he would not have any intention to write a pastiche when he created it.

The first introduction of Sherlock Holmes in China was in, "Ying Baotan Kan Daomiyue An (A British Detective's Stolen Treaty Case)", in *Shiwu Bao* August 1 - September 21, 1894 (The Naval Treaty). After that, Holmes stories were translated one after another in China. The Japanese mystery writer Edogawa Rampo wrote "It is common knowledge that Chinese mysteries are backward compared to those in Japanese, but it was unexpected for me to see that at least in the translation of Holmes, they were ahead of us." However, the first Japanese translation was "Kojiki Doraku" (*Nihonjin*, January 3 - February 18, 1894, The Man with the Twisted Lip), which was actually slightly earlier than that of Chinese. In any case, in the amount of translations of Holmes and other Doyle works in the 1900s and 1910s, Chinese works were not inferior to Japanese ones, and in addition, works which were still not translated into Japanese were already introduced to China.

In 1916, all 44 Holmes stories published until that time were published as the collected edition that surprised Edogawa Rampo. In Japan, the first collected edition of Sherlock Holmes was not published until Kaizo-sha's Collected Works of Doyle.

According to Nakamura Tadayuki, "After all, Sherlock Holmes had overwhelming popularity. ...... Speaking frankly, it is said that any books whose title included his name, were best sellers." This means there were good amounts of parodies and pastiches in China.

According to Tarumoto Teruo's study, there were more than twenty parodies or pastiches, most of which were published between the 1900s and 1910s. The oldest one would be, "Xieluoke Laiyou Shanghai Diyi'an ---Lengxue (Sherlock Holmes' First Adventure in Shanghai) by Chen Jinghan, *Shi Bao*, 1904.12.18."

It is unfortunate that I have not seen this work, but judging from its title it is easy to guess that it is not a real work of Doyle. I've read some of these Chinese works, but most of them were along the lines of Chinese traditional crime novels, and there is no logical detection of crime or criminals. The preface of one of them reveals its story and criminal. In another story, a criminal appeared at the end of story without any connection with the story, and is arrested. Even in the real Holmes' translations, the titles revealed their contents. It is no way that is Chinese peculiar way.

Most Chinese parodies are easy to identify as fake works, but there is one that seemed a real Holmes story, but was not:

"Yan Xu (The False Bridegroom" by Hu Jichen, *Chun Sheng* vol.5, 1916.6.1"

This seems to be a translation of "A Case of Identity" written by Conan Doyle. However, there is a preface that states, "This story is based on a western story, but I added some different parts." "A Case of Identity" continues for pages, but then Mary goes on summer holiday, and a murder case makes Holmes visit Scotland. In the end, this murder case is solved without any relationship to the main story. The story then returned to IDEN itself again, and it is also solved independently of the other storyline. So we can say that the translator inserted a new murder case pastiche into the middle of IDEN. Even in a story which is believed to be a Doyle story, there is the possibility of a parody. We need to make certain it is a Doyle work by actually reading it.

I'll give you another example:

Shenqian Yin (Deep and Shallow Impression) by "Watson", published by Xiaoshuolin Zong Faxingxuo, Shanghai, 1906

Tarumoto discussed the details about this story. He said, "It is a well done pastiche. The mistaken murder of twins, and simultaneously occurring case of theft are very interesting. The most important evidence is only the footprints, which might be too weak, but the author dropped an advance hint on this matter. More than anything else, the author used the formulas of the Sherlock Holmes stories very well."

As an introduction to the story, he wrote an observation about Watson. Holmes watched Watson return to their rooms at Baker Street, with a refreshed mood and water drops on his hat, and pointed out that Watson had been for a walk very early in the morning. A beautiful and attractive lady then appeared. He investigated the case in great detail at the scene of the murder. Holmes adopted a disguise. There is an action scene at the end of story. Most of a Holmes story's typical points are included. The author of this pastiche must have had distinguished skill.

As you can see, *Shenqian Yin* uses supreme logic and story construction which was exceptional for a Chinese pastiche of the Canon at that time. At that time in England, after the success of Sherlock Holmes, the "Rivals of Holmes" new short serial detective stories were flourishing. For example, Austin Freeman's "Dr. Thorndyke" series, Baroness Orzy's "The Old Man in the Corner" and others. Compared to them, *Shenqian Yin* is not inferior. However, if it was to be so distinguished, I could not stop suspecting there was an original western story and he simply changed the name of the detective to Holmes. I asked active Sherlockians in Japan, the USA and Britain about the story of *Shenqian Yin*, but all of them answered that they had not read such a story before.

At the beginning of *Shenqian Yin* are the words "Huasheng biji", which means "written by Watson". There might be such other examples, but this is the forerunner of Nicholas Meyer's *The Seven Percent Solution* (1974), a pastiche written seventy years later. As you know, after Meyer's work, this style became popular for Sherlockian pastiches.

In conclusion, *Shenqian Yin* is the best of the Sherlockian pastiches written in China, when pastiches were still not popular, and if it is an original, it anticipated future western Sherlockian pastiches. It holds a place of special importance in Sherlockian pastiche history.

Bibliography

1 Nakamura Tadayuki, "Shinmatsu Tanteishousetsu Shikou (1)", *Shinmatsu Shousetsu Kenkyu* No.2, P122, 1978.

2 Edogawa Rampo, "Sherlock Holmes Zenshu" *Kaigai Tantei Shousetsu sakka to Sakuhin 2*, p114, Kodansha, 1989.

3 Tarumoto Teruo, *Shinmatsu Shousetsuronshu, Horitsubunkasha*, 1992, and personal communications.

(Shinmatsu Shousetsu Kara No.61, April 1, 2001 (in Japanese) & *The Shoso-in Bulletin* vol.11, 2001)

My First Meeting
with Sherlock Holmes

As a member of a non-English-speaking culture, it was inevitable that I would read the Holmesian Canon in translated editions. However, this means that I can enjoy reading many different translations and adaptations. Even faithful translations have a different flavor and atmosphere; in addition, reading children's adaptations was great fun for me when I was a small child. This is a kind of fun that is denied to English and American Sherlockians or children, who are able to enjoy the stories in their native tongue.

I was eight years old when I found the thick volumes of children's adaptations of the Sherlock Holmes series, with their colorful dust jackets, at my elementary school's library. There were also other mystery adaptations - for example, the Arsène Lupin series and "Boy Detectives" series written by Edogawa Rampo, a famous Japanese mystery writer (whose name is a tribute to Edgar Allan Poe). All the boys in my class enjoyed reading the "Boy Detectives" series, but half of them liked Holmes, and the other half were devotees of Lupin. To me, although I do not why, the most attractive volumes were the Sherlock Holmes series.

The Japanese adaptations of the Sherlock Holmes stories were done by several writers, and there were three or four editions of Sherlock Holmes for children. The series most favored by children was written by Yamanaka Minetarou. Yamanaka was already a veteran writer of many bestsellers when he adapted the Sherlock Holmes series. His greatest success was *Tekichu Oudan Sanbyakuri* [Crossing the Enemy Camp], published in 1931. It is a documentary story of a cavalry scout team of the Japanese army during the Russo-Japanese War. Another of Yamanaka's book is *Ajia no Akebono* [Dawn of Asia], published in 1932. It is a spy novel featuring Japanese officer Hongo Yoshiaki. Japanese science fiction writer Yokota Junya claimed that he did not find the "007" series interesting at all, simply because he had read the superior *Ajia no Akebono* when he was a child.

It is said that almost all Japanese children of my father's generation read Yamanaka's books. He was an army officer in his youth, and retired from the army to support Sun Yat-sen, the father of the Chinese Republic, as a general staff officer during the Second and Third Revolutions. He also acted on behalf of a peace movement during the Sino-Japanese War, as he was a military academy schoolmate of Tojo Hideki, the Japanese prime minister and army minister, and Anan Korechika, the last army minister. Yamanaka is also said to have been a speechwriter for Prime Minister Tojo.

Yamanaka changed many lines of the Canon to make them easier for Japanese children to understand. So many changes were made that some Sherlockians believe he destroyed the Canon. For example, Sherlock Holmes, in this book, is a cheerful person with a good appetite, and some of the stories were written by Violet Hunter or even Mary Watson! Of course, many children have also read other author's versions, and so they know such liberties were characteristic of Yamanaka's version. Thus, they simply read to enjoy his vivid expression. For example, here is the opening of "Six Napoleons."

"The Great Detective Holmes!"

It is a great joy for me that all of you read the detective stories of Holmes. I am so happy!

However, I, Watson, was married to my lovely Mary, and went to practice medicine. I left Holmes after having lived with him for years. From the first day of my practice, I was surprised that there were so many patients.

"Oh my Mary, what's going on?"I asked my wife.

"Of course, we must be thankful to Mr. Holmes."

"I see. He has become famous, and everyone also knows me, too. That's the reason for my many patients?"

"It must be. Otherwise there would not be so many patients at our door."

"OK, but it is I who make Holmes famous. And readers of Holmes stories would also think Dr. Watson's treatment is good."

"You advertised yourself by writing Mr.Holmes' record?"

"Wait, wait! Not at all! Don't you believe me, Mary?" Just after one week after our marriage, we were verging on a quarrel. "All right. I declare not to write Holmes's record, forever. Never again!"

Who could tell that this is "Six Napoleons"? After that scene, many readers demand that Watson write new stories, and Mary proposes that she and her husband write the next story together. In the Yamanaka version, "Six Napoleons" is written by Mary and John Watson. Such adaptations were much more effective than any television programs or films of the Canon I have ever seen.

Children were crazy about Yamanaka's Holmes, even while understanding it was not a faithful translation. Without Yamanaka's adaptations, I would not be a Sherlockian, nor would I be interested in Sherlock Holmes and Conan Doyle. Even now, his books are in my bookcase, and I read them again and again. It brings back good childhood memories, and I still enjoy his exciting adaptations.

I am sorry his versions are no longer available and are not in school libraries. Nowadays, only a few Sherlock Holmes books are displayed at the bookshop's children's corner. These faithful but boring adaptations are still popular for children, but now these books are read because they must be. The students are not enthusiastic readers, as I was.

In my opinion, an enjoyable adaptation is essential for a first meeting with Sherlock Holmes for small children in non-European cultures. This might be one reason there are so many Sherlockians in Japan and why the Japan Sherlock Holmes Club is the largest Sherlockian society in the world. I wish every child could have read Yamanaka's books, but unfortunately they are too expensive at antique bookshops now.

It's my dream to publish Yamanaka's adaptations for my own children someday. It might be too late - they are already six and four years old - but I believe if they read Yamanaka's adaptations, they will be good Sherlockians, too.

(*The Baker Street Journal*, Vo.51, No.3, Autumn 2001)

The Idle Killers of the K.K.K.

"The Adventure of The Five Orange Pips" is a story of the assassination of two generations. It is not clear why the Openshaw family were targeted by the K.K.K., an American secret racial association, but it is assumed that Elias Openshaw had some criminal evidence against members of the K.K.K., of which he was also a member, and other important members tried to stop him from talking. This would be an urgent matter, and K.K.K. members would have been worried about it every night. However, the assassins they sent were too idle and acted mysteriously. It is incomprehensible why they sent such incapable assassins abroad, and did not choose better ones.

Elias Openshaw "emigrated to America when he was a young man and became a planter in Florida, where he was reported to have done very well. At the time of the war he fought in Jackson's army, and afterwards under Hood, where he rose to be a colonel. When Lee laid down his arms my uncle returned to his plantation, where he remained for three or four years. About 1869 or 1870 he came back to Europe and took a small estate in Sussex, near Horsham." It was in 1878 when his nephew John Openshaw first met Elias, and they lived together. On March 10, 1883, Elias received a letter from Pondicherry, India which contained five orange pips and the words "K.K.K." Elias died on May 2, 1883, in a little green-scummed pool.

Joseph, Elias's brother and the father of John, moved to Horsham in early 1884, and received a letter on January 4, 1885, with five orange pips and the message "Put the papers on the sundial." This letter was posted at Dundee, Scotland. Joseph died three days later, on January 7, 1885.

John Openshaw received his pips letter, which was sent from east London in September 1887, and died in the Thames.

The most incredible thing is why the assassins took such long holidays between their murders. Elias lived peacefully for thirteen years in England. They might not have been able to find him, as Elias was not a social person. However, they then took a one year and ten month holidays until threatening and killing Joseph. From Joseph's murder to John's, there was a two year and eight month interval. The assassins, Captain James Calhoun and two other Americans were staff of the Lone Star, but it is unbelievable that they were also part-time killers as a side job. If their first purpose in visiting England was the papers of Elias, why didn't they resign their job on ship and concentrate on their most important work? If they did not need to kill the Openshaw family so urgently, did they need to kill them at all? When they first visited Horsham to investigate Openshaw's house, why did they not steal the papers or set his house on fire after killing Elias? They must have researched Horsham very well, since they killed Elias and Joseph in very dark without any evidence, and knew that there was a sundial in their garden. The paper they wanted was just inside of the house, only some feet away. Why didn't they take it? They could kill three men, why can't they steal a small tin box? They were the most negligent assassins in the world. The K.K.K. commanders would order another assassin to kill Captain Calhoun and the others, if they were sane.

It was totally impossible for me to find any reason for them taking such long intervals between the three murders. It is easy to conclude they were idiot assassins, but such a result is not what I want. There would be something wrong there.

The only explanation after eliminating the impossible, is that there were no assassinations in Horsham. Elias died in this situation;

We found him, when we went to search for him, face downward in a little green-scummed pool, which lay at the foot of the garden. There was no sign of any violence, and the water was but two feet deep, so that the jury, having regard to his known eccentricity, brought in a verdict of 'suicide.'

If three men violently tried to kill Elias in a pool, there would be many footprints around the pool. Elias's clothing would be dirty and torn. He was not a small puppy, but a violent man. There were no signs of murder. I think Elias died of a heart attack or some other sudden illness. Even if "he winced from the very thought of death," he cannot escape the hand of illness.

Even for Joseph, "He had, as it appears, been returning from Fareham in the twilight, and as the country was unknown to him, and the chalk-pit unfenced, the jury had no hesitation in bringing in a verdict of 'death from accidental causes.' Carefully as I examined every fact connected with his death, I was unable to find anything which could suggest the idea of murder. There were no signs of violence, no footmarks, no robbery, and no record of strangers having been seen upon the roads."

There was no evidence to support that it was a murder. Sherlock Holmes himself said "It is a capital mistake to theorize before one has data. Insensibly one begins to twist facts to suit theories, instead of theories to suit facts" in SCAN. John Openshaw did not show the letters and pips received by Elias and Joseph, but just presented a letter written to himself. There is no support to prove his story.

I cannot stop suspecting the reliability of the story told by John Openshaw. If there were no letters from the K.K.K., no one would believe they were murders. John cannot show the letters themselves, but only tell his story. It is suggested that John told Holmes a falsehood. You may wonder why John told such a lie to Holmes, as he died (or was killed?) just after that by K.K.K. assassins. I'm also suspicious of this.

Benjamin Clark writes in "The Horsham Fiasco", that "Elias led a solitary life in Horsham, so the desire for company in the house was understandable; but surely it was an oddly selfish request, calculated as it was to deprive a retired widower of his only child." and "Even odder, however, was the apparently ready acquiescence of the father to this arrangement. Joseph was a rich man so, as far as the present was concerned, the boy had nothing to gain materially by the change, which none the less he was perfectly willing to make without, apparently, any regrets." Mr. Clark thought John was the only child of Joseph, but if there were a brother, the situation is changed. If John had an elder brother (we can here call him Joseph Jr.), he would inherit all the fortune of Joseph, and John would receive nothing. It would then be best if John was adopted by Elias.

If Elias and Joseph died naturally, and Elias did not make the will which was mentioned in John's story, what would have happened? Joseph Jr. would receive the fortune of Joseph Sr., and John would receive Elias'. However, if Joseph Jr. spent all the money in the stock market, or Elias' fortune was ten times larger than Joseph Sr.'s, what would Joseph Jr. think then? It would be a good motive to kill John.

I suspect it was Joseph Jr. who visited 221B, wearing John's clothes. He told a false story about the K.K.K., which he made up from Elias' old stories, to make Holmes believe there were serial murders and become suspicious of the K.K.K. John might have been already dead in the Thames. Joseph might just have thrown a large stone, and cried "Help!" from the embankment. In addition, Holmes did not research Horsham, or visit Openshaw's house. He did not know whether the story told was truth or not, and he did not know the real face of John. But Holmes believed the story, and Joseph Jr. could then inherit the fortunes of Elias and Joseph Sr., just by telling a lie to Holmes and murdering his brother.

(*The Shoso-in Bulletin* vol.12, 2002)

Sherlockiana in Japan 2001-2002

The most welcome Sherlockian item since the publication of the last issue of the *Shoso-in Bulletin* (vol.11), was the complete set of DVD disks of *The Adventure of Sherlock Holmes* from Granada Television. It consists of twenty-three disks, including three versions of each story, including the original English version, a Japanese translation version, and a version dubbed in Japanese. I have no chance to compare it with that of American DVD disks, but it is said that the Japanese version is better quality.

Old Japanese translations of the Canon also gained the attention of publishers. The third volume of *Meiji no Hon-yaku Mystery* (Translated Mysteries of Meiji-era, three volumes, edited by Kawato Michiaki, Sakakibara Takanori, Satsuki-shobo, Tokyo) contains the first translation of the Canon into Japanese (TWIS, 1894) and six other stories from the canon which were translated up to 1911. *Meijiki Sherlock Holmes Hon-yaku Shusei* ("A Collection of Translations of Sherlock Holmes in the Meiji-era", in three volumes, edited by Kawato Michiaki, Arai Seiji, Sakaibara Takanori, Kinokuniya-shoten, Tokyo) include twenty early translations. These two books received the Sherlock Holmes Award from the Japan Sherlock Holmes Club at the March convention.

The JSHC Summer Convention was held at Matsue, Shimane on August 25. Endo Takahito spoke on "Sherlock Holmes and Shimane prefecture," Nakanishi Yukata presented the paper "Lafcadio Hearn and Holmes/ Doyle". Hearn is a British man who came to Japan to be a professor of English literature. Later he married a Japanese woman and wrote many stories about Japan. Nakanishi pointed out that Hearn's great grandfather's name is "Richard Holmes." Harada Kakuko talked about "Sherlockian Drugs". Shigaki Yumiko and Amano Yaeko showed a video of the unveiling ceremony of Crowborough's Doyle stature and FMHC's Dartmoor tour cerebrating the anniversary of *The Hound of the Baskervilles*.

In "The Rockheart Castle" in Takayama, Gunma, there is a "Gentleman's Coach" used for Granada's Sherlock Holmes series. I do not know why it is there, and I have never seen it myself, but it is said there is a doll of Holmes in it, and some pictures on display.

There was a performance of a ballet about Sherlock Holmes on October 20, at Melpark Hall, Tokyo. Its title is "Sherlock Holmes: The Adventure of the Missing Great Diamond," and it was written by Kitahara Naohiko. It is the second attempt at a Sherlock Holmes ballet. I enjoyed it, though some parts were difficult to understand, and there was no speech. I needed to ask Mr. Kitahara about it after the performance. It received the Special Award of the JSHC.

The Spring Convention was held on March 17, in Tokyo. Firstly, Seki Nagaomi presented "The Canon in China". He worked as a CEO of a company in Shanghai for many years, and he reported on many Chinese translations of the Canon and parodies of the past twenty years.

To celebrate the one hundredth anniversary of HOUN, there was a panel discussion on HOUN. First, Prof. Koike Shigeru said that though HOUN was situated in the countryside, all the characters were metropolitan citizens, and it may be called a metropolitan novel, and the first distinguished metropolitan mystery. Next, there was a discussion on "Who benefited in HOUN?" Before the discussion, all the members wrote their answers on paper. After discussing these results, we considered the problem again, and finally decided that the character who gained the most benefit was Dr. Mortimer. Second place went to Henry Baskerville; third place was Beryl Stapleton. Other answers were Cartwright, the postman of Grimpen, readers of HOUN with great joy, and nearly twenty other candidates. On the other side, of the characters who were harmed in the case, the Hound, Selden, Jack Stapleton were top three. Others were Dr. Mortimer's spaniel, the kidnapped girl in the legend and others. The final result was that it is impossible to get perfectly right answers.

(*The Shoso-in Bulletin* vol.12, 2002)

Some Problems on
"Conan Doyle Syndrome"

Recently, there have been several psychological studies on Sherlock Holmes and Sir Arthur Conan Doyle published. Some of them are quite worthwhile to read, but some of them are of questionable worth, in my opinion. I have always wondered whether psychology and psychiatry are true sciences. The essential condition to be a science is that one double-checks experiments for verification. However, it is quite difficult to arrange the same conditions in two experiments for psychiatric study. Even now we cannot understand what the mind is, and it is impossible to find two people with the same mind. It is inevitable that these experiments have unsatisfactory conditions. In addition, it is impossible to do animal experiments for psychology, because it is doubtful whether any animal has the same mind as a human. On the other hand, dentistry, my profession, is the most scientific field in medicine, because dentistry is a way to change a part of the human body into an artifact. All the experiments are physically, biologically and chemically well conditioned. Double checks are essential for every experiment.

From a point of view of a scientifically trained person, I always doubt the reliability of psychology. I wonder why many people, including intellectuals and doctors, believe Freud's theories are true. Freud's work was just retrospective analysis and deduction, not proof or verification. He observed his patients and created his hypotheses, but no one has ever proven his hypotheses to be correct. It is possible all of his hypotheses are wrong. For example, cerebral physiologists have found that his assessments on dreams are wrong, and proved that dreams are not controlled by the brain. And even if Freud's hypotheses were true, he observed only Austrian middle class people. It is quite difficult to apply his thoughts to people with other cultural backgrounds. It is not easy for us Japanese to understand or predict how Freud's patients thought.

Naked is the Best Disguise is the most famous psychological work on Sherlock Holmes and Conan Doyle. The author, Samuel Rosenberg, put forward the notion of "Conan Doyle Syndrome." He "found" that:

"My accumulated notes had revealed that in almost every story I'd synopsized, the printed or written word in any form - books, book titles, magazine or newspaper articles, advertisements, signs, diaries, manuscripts, letters, words scribbled on scraps of paper, words written on the wall (even in blood) or in the floor dust of a murder chamber, or even expressions read in a person's face - was always accompanied by an allusion or some form of forbidden sexual expression, either heterosexual or homosexual, or both. This allusion was usually associated in turn with images of draconian punishment in the form of the murder or individuals or of masses of people in Sodom and Gomorrah, Khartoum, Jericho or Milan, or in the English and the American Civil Wars." (p.92)

Rosenberg gave examples as follows.

Story	Word	Sexual Expression	Murder
LAST	Bee-Book	Bee	WWI
VALL	Almanac	A man supposedly killed by his wife and her lover	John Douglas
STUD	Decameron	Decameron & ring	Drebber
EMPT	Catullus	Catullas	Ronald Adair

When I first read his book, a question rose in my mind. If his hypothesis is true, this condition would not be satisfied in another author's works, as they had different backgrounds and mentalities from Conan Doyle. However, it does not seem so for me because of the following reasons:

(1) Especially before World War II, detective fiction was written as a past time for intellectuals, and most of the characters in detective fiction belonged to the middle class or upper class. They are educated people, and it is natural for them to get close to books or magazines.

(2) For Freudians, most things are regarded as sexual symbols. For example, any long thing, such as a snake, a rocket, a knife, is a phallic symbol. A Freudian can find a sexual symbol in anything.

113

(3) In detective fiction, it is natural to find murders. That is one of the main themes of detective fiction.

If I find "Conan Doyle Syndrome" in other writers' work, it can no longer be called "Conan Doyle Syndrome." It is just a commonality in detective fiction, and it means it does not have any relationship with Doyle's psychology.

First, I checked several short stories by R. Austin Freeman (1862-1943). He is the author of the "Dr. Thorndyke" series, the most famous "rival of Sherlock Holmes." His cultural background would be near to that of Conan Doyle, and this is a reason to choose him as the first example. These short stories are the first five that were translated in a Japanese book called "The Casebook of Dr. Thorndyke."

(1) "A Case of Premeditation"

The murderer Pembury read *Chambers' Encyclopaedia* (First condition, words), and he went to buy musk. Musk is "a strong-smelling reddish-brown substance produced by a gland in the male musk deer" (*The Oxford English Reference Dictionary*), and is secreted to attract female musk deer (Second condition, sexual expression). After that, Pembury killed Pratt. (Third condition, murder).

(2) "The Echo of a Mutiny"

"The chart-rack, the tell-tale compass and the chronometers marked it as the captain's cabin." (First condition, words) Girdler's lighthouse would be called a phallic symbol by Freudians. (Second condition, sexual expression). Jeffereys killed Todd. (Third condition, murder).

(3) "A Wastrel's Romance"

Bailey stole an invitation card (First condition, words). He danced with his former lover at the party. (Second condition, sexual expression). He thought he killed her with chloroform (Third condition, murder).

(4) "The Old Lag"

Dr. Thorndyke received a letter (First condition, words). Belfield was "at home all evening and night." (Second condition, sexual expression). The Camberwell murder occurred (Third condition, murder).

(5) "The Blue Sequin"
Dr. Thorndyke received a telegram (First condition, words). Old lovers quarreled in a compartment of a train (Second condition, sexual expression). Miss Grant was stabbed with an Ox horn. "Ox" is of course, male, and "Ox's horn" is a phallic representation for Freudians. (Second condition, sexual expression & Third condition, murder).

Though I did not choose these stories intentionally, all of them can be interpreted as expressing "Conan Doyle Syndrome." Should we now call this disease "Conan Doyle - Freeman Syndrome"? Or it is a common aspect for Victorian writers?

Next, I examine a writer with a completely different cultural background. His name is Edogawa Rampo (1894-1965), the "Father of Japanese Mystery." His first short story, "Nisen Douka (Two Cent Coin)" (1922) is the first true original mystery written in Japanese. He wrote many mysteries and horror stories, and also helped young detective writers. He edited *Houseki* detective magazine, and established the Japan Mystery Writers Club. As you can see, he had no cultural relationship with Victorian mystery writers, Doyle or Freeman. Of course, he read their works earnestly, but it would not have affected his principal mindset.

(1) "D zaka no Satsujin Jiken" (Murder at D Slope)
There was a murder at an antique bookshop (First condition, words & Third condition, murder). The shop owner, the murderer, was a sadist, and the victim, his wife, was a masochist (the Second condition, sexual expression).

(2) "Ichimai no Kippu" (A Ticket)
A wife was found dead on a railroad (Third condition, murder). A ticket was found under a rock near her (First condition, words). It was found that it was a suicide, and she wanted her husband treated as a murderer, because he betrayed her with a mistress (Second condition, sexual expression).

These two stories satisfy the conditions for "Conan Doyle

115

Syndrome." Should we now call it "Conan Doyle - Freeman - Edogawa Syndrome"? No, we cannot. "Conan Doyle Syndrome" is not a distinctive feature of Doyle. It is a common aspect of every work of detective fiction. At least, it does not need to be restricted to Conan Doyle's work. You can find this symptom anywhere you want. It is a natural, normal thing, and it is not a "syndrome" or "disease." Sherlock Holmes said "It is a capital mistake to theorize before one has data. Insensibly one begins to twist facts to suit theories, instead of theories to suit facts." (SCAN). This would be a typical case of what Holmes warned against.

Bibliography:

1 Rosenberg, Samuel: *Naked is the Best Disguise*, Penguin Books, 1975.
2 Freeman, R Austin: Sondaiku Hakushi no Jikenbo (*Casebook of Dr. Thorndyke*), Sogensha, Tokyo 1977.
3 Freeman, R Austin: *Dr. Thorndyke His Famous Cases*, Hodder & Stoughton, London, 1929
4 Edogawa, Rampo: *Shinri Shiken* Shunyo-do, Tokyo 1925

(*The New Baker Street Pillar Box* No.33-34, 1999
& *The Shoso-in Bulletin* vol.13, 2003)

The Model of Sherlock Holmes

By Takata Gi-ichiro, MD

Translated and edited by Hirayama Yuichi

The translator's comment:

Takata Gi-ichiro was a doctor who graduated from Kyoto Imperial University in 1912. His specialty was forensic medicine, and he became a professor at Chiba Medical College. He was also an earnest writer on medical subjects for the usual magazines.

This article translated below was published in Hanzaigaku Zasshi *(The Magazine of Criminology), Vol.4, No.1, January 1931. It is not a magazine for everyone, but is of interest to scholars of criminology. Dr. Furuhata Tanemoto, the father of forensic medicine in Japan, also wrote articles for this magazine.*

However, this article is out of place, and left the readers with many questions.

As you will find out, this article is not true. Conan Doyle was a medical student at Edinburgh University, and it was impossible for him to visit Eton, which is near Windsor. Bell's first name was Joseph, not John, and he was not Doyle's colleague or student, but his professor. The strangest point is that Takata said he found this article and translated it for readers. I cannot believe such an article was published abroad, as if written by Conan Doyle himself. I suspect it was an original story by Takata. If my guess is right, it is one of the earliest parodies of Sherlock Holmes. Several Sherlockian parodies had already been translated into Japanese at that time, but as far as I know, there were only five original Japanese parodies published before this article.

#   #   #

(*Takata's comments*)

I was asked by the editor to write some comments on crime, but at the moment I do not have any particular opinions. However, I just found an interesting article which I now introduce for readers. It would be of interest to readers of this magazine that Arthur Conan Doyle, a mystery writer who died a short time ago, was also a doctor. In addition, it has a bearing on the study of criminology that Sherlock Holmes, the great detective who appeared in his novels, was modeled on a real person.

This article I produce below is by the late Conan Doyle, on the model for "Sherlock Holmes."

#   #   #

When I was a student at medical school, I frequently visited Eton school to listen to lectures. One time, two days after my arrival at Eton, a case occurred.

Most students of Eton lodge in dormitories which have many rooms like hotels. One morning, a caretaker brought breakfast to Will Parett's room, but there was no response to his knocking, and the door was locked. The caretaker reported it to a dormitory superintendent, and they broke through the door. Parett was dead on his bed, with a pistol in his hand. There was a paper with the words "Please do not ask any questions about my death. I commit suicide" on a table. There were no suspicious circumstances. The doctor who performed a post-mortem said the cause of death was a bullet in the chest. However, the pistol in his hand was fully loaded, with all six bullets in their chambers. The situation took on a new aspect, and Scotland Yard became involved.

Their investigation confirmed that nobody had entered or exited Parett's room. All the windows and doors were closed and locked from the inside. There was no other way to exit from the room. But nothing was stolen, and there was no question that the farewell note was in Parett's own hand. All the evidence pointed to a suicide, but it was impossible to accept that result, as the bullets of the pistol were not fired, and no other weapons were found. Furthermore, the bullet which had crashed through his chest and hit the wall was of a different caliber from the pistol in his hand! Investigation by the police was in vain; this case was wrapped in mystery.

One afternoon, I visited my friend Barnes' room and was introduced to a friend of his, a student named John Bell. When we referred to the case of Parett, Barnes said, "I believe Bell can solve that mystery." According to him, Bell was very interested in such mysteries and had solved some cases mathematically and logically before the police force, just by carefully reading newspaper reports.

As expected, Bell had already solved most of the Parett case, at that time.

Bell started to explain deliberately.

"I believe the Parett case would be solved in a short time, as it is so easy. I have been thinking on that matter, and I suppose I understand most of it. However, there are only a few facts I do not know. Barnes, did Parett have a girlfriend?" Bell suddenly asked. Barnes hesitated, but answered. "Yes, he did. His teacher's daughter, Miss Mabel Firill."

Two days later, we gathered again at tea time. The police had been totally incompetent. Barnes told us Mabel Firill had left for Africa suddenly that morning.

"I know the reason for her sudden departure." Bell said. "I told her the Parett case would be solved soon."

We were surprised to hear that, and Bell explained. "This case is basically simple. The result of investigation was, Parett did not commit suicide, but he was not killed by a villain as is shown by his last will, and the door was locked as well. It was certain there was a crime, and Parett was actually complicit in it. It might have meant Parett wanted the criminal who shot him to run away. Concerning the love affair, it is important. I did not know who she was, but the day before yesterday, you told me her name, Barnes. So, I met Miss Mabel yesterday. This proved my theory was right. Miss Mabel was deeply in love with Parett, but realized he was treating her coldly recently. On the night of Parett's death, she visited him with her pistol. They had a quarrel, and Miss Mabel in jealousy and agony shot him. Wounded Parett realized it was fatal, and wanted to help the woman he loved. After her escape, he locked the door, wrote his will, and took hold of his pistol. But he had no more strength to shoot it, and fell down. That was the result, as we know."

Later, it was revealed to be the truth.

I had the opportunity to be amazed by Bell's splendid ability of investigation again and again. There are many cases which Bell helped the detectives of Scotland Yard to solve. I asked him to give me permission to write a novel modeled on him, and he accepted. By the way, concerning the name "Sherlock Holmes," when we were walking in Piccadilly, Bell found this name on a poster at a music hall,

119

and we took it for the detective.

(The Shoso-in Bulletin vol.13, 2003)

Sherlockiana in Japan, 2002-03

As Japan has slipped deeper into recession over the years, the number of members of the Japan Sherlock Holmes Club has declined. In its best days, there were more than 1200, but it is now just over eight hundred.

There have been only a few publications on Sherlockiana, but SUZUKI Toshio's *SHERLOCK HOLMES THE CHRONOLOGY OF HIS ADVENTURES* (privately printed) is the best of this year's harvest. Suzuki compares famous chronologists' theories, and shows his original ideas, creating his own new chronology of the Canon. Though it was printed privately, serious Sherlockian scholars should need a copy for their study. Regrettably, it was mostly written in Japanese, but it also has a simple summary in English, for each chapter. I hope I can introduce Suzuki's fine works in English in the near future.

The Japanese translation of the Oxford edition of the Canon by Dr. KOBAYASHI and Mrs. HIGASHIYAMA was completed. Because of the expensive price, it is still not the most common edition of the Canon for Japanese Sherlockians, but it will be when paperback editions are available. In the translators' afterwards, the two translators argue over a Freudian analysis of the Canon and Mary Doyle's "affair" with Dr. Waller, but it is doubtful that such a theme was suitable for the translation's afterwards. More discussion would is needed about this problem, but unfortunately there is no "Don Quixote" to challenge a former professor of psychology.

Rodger Garrick-Steele's *The House of the Baskervilles*, one of the largest news items for Sherlockians all over the world, was published in Japan. (translated by SAGA Fuyumi, Nan-Undo, Tokyo, 2002) Its contents was reported as a news item in England and other countries. Most Sherlockians were surprised and angered by his claim that Conan Doyle stole the idea of *The Hound Of The Baskervilles* from Fletcher Robinson, and that Doyle and Mrs. Robinson later poisoned him, but the original manuscript has been never published in English. I do not know why this manuscript was only published in Japan, but I suppose SHIMADA Soji, supervising translator and one of the most famous mystery writers in Japan, was interested in this manuscript and recommended it to the publisher. Though Shimada wrote a Sherlockian parody in the past, it is doubtful he has much knowledge of Sherlockiana and Doyleana. There are too many elementary mistakes in this book. For example, Garrick-Steele says SOLI was published after HOUN. The author suggests Robinson's short story, "The Tragedy of Thomas Hearne" is the original of HOUN, but there are no points of resemblance between these two works, except that they are staged in Dartmoor. This short story is included in *The Chronicles Of Addington Peace* and *The Trail Of The Dead* (B. Fletcher Robinson & J. Malcolm Fraser, The Battered Silicon Dispatch Box, Shelburne, 1998). This book is still available from the publisher, one of our members, Dr. George Vanderburgh.

There is no evidence about the "murder" of Fletcher Robinson by Doyle and Mrs. Robinson. Garrick-Steele insists, but I must judge it as just a fiction. It seems Mr. Shimada was also disappointed with this situation, but he says that Garrick-Steele is writing a second work, and he hopes there would be evidence of the murder in that one. But I do not think Garrick-Steele can provide any reliable evidence in the next volume, even if he can find a publisher. I'm now finished writing a review of this notorious book in English.

The Summer Convention of the Japan Sherlock Holmes Club was held (though it was not in summer) on November 2-3, 2002 in Nara, where the Shoso-in is. Ninety-eight members attended. The Spring Convention was held in Ryogoku, Tokyo, on March 21, 2003. It was the 50th convention of the JSHC. Ninety-seven members gathered, and the special guest speaker was Mr. ASHIBE Taku, a mystery writer who also wrote a Sherlockian pastiche. He made remarks on the aspect of "adventure" in the Canon. Another special presentation was a performance of "KODAN." This is a traditional Japanese storytelling performance. Originally war stories were performed, but about one hundred years ago, there was a boom in telling mysteries. Mr. KYOKUDO Nanko, a Kodan storyteller, intends to revive the mysterious Kodans. On that day, he showed a new performance called *The Speckled Band*. It was about forty minutes of storytelling, and we were pleased to hear the story of the Master in our traditional style.

Nobody received The Sherlock Holmes Award of 2003, but the Encouragement Prize was presented to SUZUKI Toshio's *Sherlock*

Holmes: The Chronology of His Adventures.

(*The Shoso-in Bulletin* vol.13, 2003)

"The Illustrious Client"

"The Illustrious Client" (ILLU) is one of the cases in the Canon in which Sherlock Holmes was contracted by the British Royal family either directly or indirectly. It is widely believed the illustrious client represented by Colonel Damery was King Edward VII, the son of Queen Victoria, who had just succeeded to his mother's throne. I also had no reason to question this well-known theory. However, the letter from the Bootmakers of Toronto announcing a special contest about discovering the identity of the illustrious client planted a small question in my mind. That is why I started to write this article.

First, I needed to check whether Edward VII was suitable for the illustrious client or not. According to Sherlockian chronologists, this adventure occurred on September 3 (the Canon, Baring-Gould, Christ, Dakin) or September 13 (Bell, Zeisler) or October 3 (Folsom, Hall), or just some day in September (Brend) 1902.

It is a well known fact that Edward VII's coronation was scheduled on June 26, 1902, but it was postponed because of his sudden illness. He was finally crowned on August 9, 1902, at Westminster Abbey. Many kings, queens, princes and princesses gathered from all over Europe; in addition, many soldiers from British colonies all over the world attended the coronation parade. The great Imperial festival was concluded with the review of the Fleet in Portsmouth five days after the coronation, that is, August 14. According to *Edward VII: His Life and Times* by Sir Richard Holmes, "The King was not thoroughly convalescent at the Coronation, and he spent the month following the ceremony of the Royal yacht recruiting his health." This means Edward VII left England with his yacht after August 14 for one month at least, and he did not return until September 14. As I stated above, there were so many guests that he might have left much later in order to hold parties for them. Anyway, Edward VII was not in England on September 3 or 13, dates proposed by many chronologists as the date of ILLU. In addition, even on October 3, the King would have just returned from his holiday trip, and would have had not had any time to hear General de Melville's problem right before or after his coronation. My good friend the eminent Sherlockian scholar Mr. John Hall told me in our private communication that Colonel Damery could contact with the King by telegram, and he did not need to be in London. It's possible the King ordered the Colonel to lend the precious dishes to Holmes by telegram. However, in the last scene of this story, Watson wrote "A brougham was waiting for him. He (Colonel Damery) sprang in, gave a hurried order to the cockaded coachman, and drove swiftly away. He flung his overcoat half out of the window to cover the armorial bearings upon the panel, but I had seen them in the glare of our fanlight none the less. I gasped with surprise." Why did the Colonel get on such a coach? If it were the King's coach, why did the King lent it to the Colonel? If he was alone, he could have chosen a hansom cab to conceal his identity. It would be too dangerous to use the King's coach without it being necessary. If the King was on the sea, and the Colonel used the king's coach without his permission, it would be a betrayal. The only possibility was that it was the "Illustrious client" *himself* in the coach. That is the simplest answer. But the King was on the sea. As a result, we must conclude that the "Illustrious client" was not King Edward.

It is an unexpected truth, but it is safe to say that there is only a slight possibility that King Edward VII was the illustrious client.

If not he, who was the illustrious client? There were several possibilities. At least, he was a member of the Royal family. Dr Watson would not have been amazed by just Dukes or Counts. He was over middle-age, as he knew Miss de Melville from her childhood. He had a good collection of Chinese pottery. He knew General de Melville well. These are the bits of evidence we can use to find him.

King Edward had three younger brothers. The oldest one was Alfred Ernest Albert, Duke of Edinburgh and Saxe-Coburg and Gotha (1844-1900). He was already dead when ILLU occurred in 1902, and there is no possibility that it was him, though he was a collector of glass and ceramic ware. The youngest brother, Leopold George Duncan Albert, Duke of Albany (1853-1884) also died long before the case.

The last possibility was Arthur William Patrick Albert, Duke of Connaught and Strathearn (1850-1942). He was the only brother of Edward VII alive when ILLU occurred. He joined the Royal Military College in his youth, and served as an army soldier throughout his life.

He was promoted to the Field Marshall in 1902. He also served in India (1886-1890). He visited Japan with his wife privately when he was the Governor of India. He might have had a connection with General de Melville during his service in India or at some other place. It is possible he first met Miss de Melville in the community of Indian British army officers. He was fifty-two years old in 1902, long enough for an "old friend, one who has known the General intimately for many years and taken a paternal interest in this young girl since she wore short frocks." He was the only child of Queen Victoria who did not give her any trouble and was the favorite son. This would mean he was a gentle and reliable person.

Later, the Duke became the Governor General of Canada (1911-16) and many Canadian places are named after him. He is one of the most popular sons of Queen Victoria in Canada. It was a joy for me to find a Japanese and Canadian connection with my "Illustrious Client," as I started my research motivated by the Canadian competition.

In addition, concerning my country, his son Arthur Frederick Patrick Albert (1883-1938) also visited Japan in 1906 to make Emperor Meiji a knight of the Garter, in 1912 to attend the funeral ceremony of Emperor Meiji, and in 1918 to present the title of Field Marshal to Emperor Taisho.

The Duke of Connaught died on 16th January, 1942. His son had already died two years before, and his grandson Alastair Arthur succeeded his title. However, Alastair lived only for a while. He died on 26th April, 1943, in Canada. He had no issue.

(Canadian Holmes vol.26, No.4, 2003
& *The Shoso-in Bulletin* vol.14, 2004)

Book review

Title: KONAN DOIRU SATSUJIN-JIKEN
(The House of the Baskervilles)
By Rodger Garrick-Steele
Translated by Saga, Fuyumi
Afterword by Shimada, Soji
Nan-un-do, Tokyo
October 4, 2002, ISBN4-523-26412-0

In recent years, there have been newspaper articles about the accusations by Rodger Garrick-Steele claiming that Sir Arthur Conan Doyle stole the idea of *The Hound Of The Baskervilles*, one of the most famous Sherlock Holmes stories, from his friend Bertram Fletcher Robinson. Further, Garrick-Steele has charged that Conan Doyle had an affair with Mrs. Robinson and murdered Fletcher Robinson.

Garrick-Steele contacted many publishers trying to publish his book, *The House Of The Baskervilles* in England and America, but failed. Even now (May 2003), the original English version has not been published. However, to our great surprise in Japan, the Japanese version was published in October 2002 by Nan-undo, Tokyo. This publisher has a close relationship with the famous Japanese mystery writer, SHIMADA Soji, who wrote the afterwards for this book. It is thought that SHIMADA's interest in Garrick-Steele's book set the stage for publication. Though English and American Sherlockians and Doyleans can accurately determine its contents from newspaper articles, only Japanese Sherlockians can read all the details of Garrick-Steele's opinion. I think it is my duty to outline and review this book for my foreign friends.

This book review is based on the Japanese edition, and so all the quotations from this book are "double-translations" by the reviewer.

This book starts in March 13 1989, the day Garrick-Steele and his family moved to an old house named Parkhill in Dartmoor, where the Robinson family lived about 80 years ago. In the Introductory Chapter, he insisted he had the psychic ability to see ghosts, and soon after his move, many spiritual phenomena occurred. He learned that this house was owned by the Robinson family and Harry Baskerville, the model for the Baskerville family. One day he found a portrait left at the entrance of his house. It was of Arthur Conan Doyle at six years old and his father Charles, and was painted in 1865 in Edinburgh. He did not know who left it there, or why. A Sherlockian in the costume of Sherlock Holmes calling himself "Mr. North" suddenly visited Parkhill and promised to help Garrick-Steele to investigate the history of Parkhill House. He sent old photographs of the house, and Garrick-Steele was surprised to find his own face in one of these photographs taken thirty-one years ago. Garrick-Steele's psychic friends visited his house and pointed out that the ghost who wandered over his house was the ghost of a maid. This is the introduction to this book. These psychic events have no direct relationship with *The Hound Of The Baskervilles*. Fletcher Robinson did not die in this house, and the ghost was not him. The questions about the Doyle portrait were never solved, and actually, it was not a painting, but a photograph. This might be interesting for spiritualists, but is of no help to serious scholars of Sherlock Holmes and Conan Doyle.

From Chapter three, Fletcher Robinson's biography starts. It is not a large matter whether his biography is right or not, but it seems there are no points to discuss especially. Harry Baskerville, coachman of the Robinson family, also appeared as a close friend of Fletcher.

According to Green[8], Robinson "was soon engaged to write a book on Rugby (1896)...was a contributor to Cassell's Magazine...and wrote a series of articles on 'Capitals at Play' (1898), 'London Night by Night' (1899), and 'Famous Regiments' (1899-1900). In 1900 he joined the staff of the Daily Express (which C.A. Pearson had just founded) and was sent out to South Africa to establish its new service." (p85-86).

Garrick-Steele says in his book that after graduation from college, he met his uncle John Robinson, the editor of the *Daily News* at his home and became a staff member of the *Daily News*. He also mentions Doyle's "Lot No. 249" which was published two years before. That short story was published in 1892 in *Harper's Monthly Magazine* vol.85 (American edition), 24 (European edition). (Green and Gibson[2] p82). It is a great surprise that Garrick-Steele considered this short story with its cold-blooded ending the last Holmes story, (p66). As you know, it is not a Sherlockian story, but a mystery included in *Round The Red Lamp* (1894). It is a story of a living mummy who chased a college student. It is incredible to commit such an elementary mistake, if anyone is interested in Holmes or Doyle.

That is not the only example of Garrick-Steele's inaccurate knowledge of Doyle. He writes that Doyle's first book was *King Of Tolus* in 1890, and that some years later he published a mystery situated in Egypt, where a mummy attacked adventurers who sought treasure in huge pyramids (p81).

In this book, Conan Doyle visited John Robinson's house before going to the Reform Club and John introduced him to Fletcher. I do not know if this was their real first meeting or not. Green[8] says that Doyle and Robinson shared a table on their return from South Africa and "become firm friends" (p86). And Mr Green told me in our private communication that it was not their first meeting.

Garrick-Steele also mentioned that upon the knighthood of John Robinson, Doyle advised Fletcher Robinson to be a European correspondent for *Pearson's Weekly* (Mr. Green told me in our private communication that Robinson was employed by Max Pemberton at *Cassell's Magazine*.) when he had his first meeting with Gladys Hill Morris, his future wife. Robinson attended the wedding of Harry Baskerville and Alice on 17th November 1894, as a groomsman. It is curious for me that an employer's son acted as a groomsman for a coachman.

Robinson went to South Africa to report on the Boer War. Garrick-Steele wrote that Robinson's friend told him that Doyle was a cruel and violent man on the ship to South Africa. Several of Robinson's newspaper reports are reprinted here. On the return trip from South Africa to England, Robinson again met Conan Doyle on board. This is a well known fact. However, I do not know if it is fact or not that Doyle bought the NORW trick of making a false finger print with wax and blood for fifty pounds. He insists they took a photograph just after that purchase which was reprinted in the *Sherlock Holmes Journal*[8] (p87).

Garrick-Steele says Conan Doyle's pamphlet supporting the British army, *The War In South Africa—Its Cause And Conduct*, was a complete failure; though he does not mention the title, he says it was published by Smith, Elder & Co. Thus it is clear that he refers to this pamphlet. He says Doyle prepared 500,000 copies in several languages, but failed because of the illness of Queen Victoria. However, this is also incorrect. According to Green and Gibson[2], this pamphlet was printed as follows:

- first English edition—250,000 copies
- first English edition Colonial issue—22,000
- first American edition50,000
- first American edition Canadian issue—25,000
- Welsh edition—10,000
- French edition—20,000
- German edition—20,000
- Dutch edition—5,000
- Italian edition—5,000
- Portuguese edition—3,500
- Norwegian edition—3,500
- Swiss edition—1,000
- Spanish edition—10,000
- Russian edition—5,000
- Hungarian edition—8,000

Furthermore, there were second issues of the first English edition (50,000 copies), and the first Continental edition as well as a second French edition, Tamil edition, Kanarese edition, Rumanian edition, and Braille edition whose amounts of copies are unknown. Green and Gibson says that "As a result of an extensive publicity campaign, which included the use of wall posters, the pamphlet was a notable success in many countries, and was partly responsible for the offer of a knighthood, which the author accepted" (p261). A very important point is that this pamphlet was published on 16 January 1902, just one year AFTER the death of Queen Victoria.

In addition, Garrick-Steele says that Doyle was discouraged to hear of the news of the death of Queen Victoria, and decided to retire from politics and writing. Queen Victoria died on January 16, 1901. Actually he did not write fiction for magazines in the spring of 1901, but he contributed to newspapers and magazines seven times in January, once in February, twice in March and April, and three times in May.

Garrick-Steele suggested that Robinson's invitation to his country house brought back Doyle from his retirement (p154). Robinson showed his unpublished short stories to Doyle, and he advised Robinson to send them to the publisher Smith, Elder & Co. This publisher proposed that Robinson publish his stories, but change them to Holmes stories under Doyle's name. Robinson met Doyle in March 1901 (sic), at the Royal Links Hotel, Cromer, Norfolk (p191). Doyle decided also sell their new novel to the *Strand Magazine* (p193), and proposed to treat Robinson as a co-author. Doyle again visited Dartmoor on April 1901 to stay at Parkhill for eight days. Robinson and Doyle stayed at the Duchy Hotel of Princeton one night during that visit. Returning to Robinson's house, Parkhill, they took a photograph, but there was a psychic phenomenon, during which only the Robinson family and Doyle's heads were shown in a tree branch (p200). Garrick-Steele claimed that at least the first three chapters were written by Robinson alone (p200). However, there are many wrong points in this theory.

First, the publisher which published the first edition of HOUN was not Smith, Elder & Co., but George Newnes, Ltd, who also published the *Strand Magazine*. Garrick-Steele reprinted in his book a letter from Reginald Smith of Smith, Elder & Co. to Robinson, suggesting that Robinson change his story to a Holmes story and change the author's name, but as there is no relationship of this company to HOUN, the authenticity of this letter is very suspicious.

Second, according to Green[8], in March 1901, "Doyle spent several days with his mother at the Ashdown Forest Hotel ... and over the weekend of 23-25 March he was in Edinburgh to give the toast to 'The Immortal Memory' at the Edinburgh Burns Club—an occasion which had been deferred in January because of the Queen's death. Fletcher Robinson was also fully occupied. In his role as a reporter for the *Daily Express*, he covered the Oxford and Cambridge Boat Race on 30 March and visited Scotland in mid-April to cover the opening of the Glasgow Exhibition." (p86). It would be impossible for both of them to stay at Parkhill for holidays in March and April. The letter from Reginald Smith reprinted in this book is dated February 1901, which is a reply on the publication of HOUN, but February in Dartmoor is far from spring. It is bitterly cold.

Third, Garrick-Steele mentions in two different ways Robinson's unpublished story, as "The Adventure of Dartmoor" (p166) and "The Tragedy of Thomas Hearne, A Tale of Dartmoor" (p188). He also writes that Doyle read Robinson's manuscript on Harry Baskerville's ancestor who was so evil that villagers made a fence around his grave, but his ghost still appeared in the moor (p184). I do not know if this refers to "The Tragedy of Thomas Hearne," but in any event "The Tragedy of Thomas Hearne" has no relationship to HOUN. Green[9] says it "appeared in *Pearson's Magazine* (published by C. Arthur Pearson) in May 1905" (p127). Mr. Green also told me in our private communication that "A Tale of Dartmoor' does not feature Addington Peace, but Inspector Harbord. It was then changed to an Addington Peace story for the book." The "Addington Peace" series was published as *The Chronicles Of Addington Peace* in 1905 by Harper, London. It was not from Pearson.

This book was reprinted by The Battered Silicon Dispatch Box (Canada), and one can easily purchase a copy from the publisher. It is an episode told by a detective, Peace, but he is not the main character. That is Henderson, a street gang member in London. He was asked to help in the jailbreak of Julius Craig, who was in Dartmoor Prison. In accordance with their plan, Craig escaped during hard labour on the moor in the fog, and Henderson brought him to Torquay on the coast. He was disguised as "Mr. Abel Kingsley" (an American scholar) and stayed at the Princetown Arms. There was also an old guest named Thomas Hearne at the hotel. When Henderson initially investigated the moor at night, he met Hearne. Hearne told him he also wanted to rescue Craig, and suggested cooperation. Henderson accepted, and they prepared for the escape for weeks. At last, Craig escaped with the help of Henderson's cart. Their plan seemed to be a success, but Hearne then revealed his identity, Mortimer, to Craig. Craig tried to run away, but Hearne stabbed him to death. Years before, Hearne/Mortimer and his daughter had lived in Spain, and Craig had kidnapped Craig's daughter by taking her away in his yacht. She died in London. Hearne had helped him escape in order to kill him.

As you see, there are no connections to HOUN other than an escaped prisoner and Dartmoor. There are no hounds, no detectives, no mansions, and for that matter, no detection. Garrick-Steele himself writes that this story is "a story of an escaped prisoner"(p178), "a story of granite, forest and horses, escaped prisoners, watches with guns, cold mist and rain of Dartmoor"(p183). This is true, but his claim that the prisoner was chased by a black, horrible ghost which howled for blood, is wrong. It was an old man thirsting for revenge on the prisoner, not a ghost hound.

Actually, there is one reference to a hound in "The Tragedy of Thomas Hearne". That is, "You should take a walk one night when the moon is full, as it is now. Then you would understand how the stories of ghost hounds and headless riders and devils in the mires first started." (p90). It is a piece of advice given to Craig by the landlord of the hotel. That is all.

I cannot find any stories Robinson wrote about Baskerville's ancestors. This might refer to the legend of Sir Richard Cabell (1622-1672), which is frequently mentioned as the original of the legend of the hound. However, Green[8] points out that "there were no family legends known to contemporary historians...It was only after *The Hound of the Baskervilles* was published that people began to suggest that there was a connection" (p88) between Cabel and Hugo Baskerville.

However, it is true Robinson helped Doyle to create HOUN. Garrick-Steele distinctly mentioned Archibald Marshall. There is a reference by Marshall that "he gave Conan Doyle the idea and plot of *The Hound of the Baskervilles*, and wrote most of its first installment for the *Strand Magazine*. Conan Doyle wanted it to appear under their joint names, but his name alone was wanted, because it was worth so much more. They were paid £100 a thousand words, in the proportion of three to one. As I put it to Bobbles at that time, "Then if you write 'How do you do?' Doyle gets six shillings and you get two." He said he had never been good at vulgar fractions, but it sounded right, and anyhow what he wrote was worth it. (p5)

As Archibald Marshall was a close friend to Robinson, it would be correct that Robinson received one-third of payment of HOUN. There is a variety of discussion about whether Robinson actually wrote the first part of HOUN or not.

According to Green[8], Doyle and Robinson met at the Royal Links Hotel, Cromer on 30 April 1901, when Robinson told Doyle the idea of ghost dog.(p87) It was not yet a Holmes story, and Doyle suggested the double payment to Greenhough Smith of the *Strand Magazine* for changing it to a Holmes story. Doyle had not yet visited Dartmoor, and the two visited there from the end of May to June 2nd 1901. They also stayed at the Duchy Hotel of Princetown one night on June 1st. Green[9] says,

"…there is no complete manuscript. Only about 26 pages out of about 200 are known to have survived. These are entirely in Doyle's handwriting and include: the third page of Chapter One; the opening of Chapter Two; the second page of Chapter Six; the opening of Chapter Seven; the opening of Chapter Nine; the whole of Chapter Eleven, and four pages from Chapter Twelve. It is therefore impossible to prove absolutely that the entire manuscript was the work of Conan Doyle." (p128).

Marshall suggested the first installment for the *Strand Magazine* was written by Robinson. Garrick-Steele writes that there is a record of Robinson's stating that he himself wrote the first three chapters of HOUN alone (p200). But as you see above, the manuscript pages of Chapter One and Two which remain are in Doyle's hand. As they are random portions, it is not probable the other pages were in other hands. The first draft of this novel, in which Sherlock Holmes does not appear, might be written by Robinson, to help Doyle, but the truth is not known.

Garrick-Steele's incredible assertions continue. He claims that Doyle's mother Mary accused his son of breaking his promise, and that there was too much money in his bank account (p204). This would mean Doyle stole Robinson's money. I do not know if such a letter exists.

The most extraordinary claim is that the Sherlock Holmes story after HOUN was SOLI, which was ordered by Collins Co. of America. Even a small child knows that after HOUN, Doyle wrote EMPT in 1903, one year later. SOLI was written in 1904 as the fourth episode of RETURN. Furthermore, these short stories were published in the *Strand Magazine* (UK) and in *Collier's Weekly* (USA), not by Collins.

Garrick-Steele made Robinson angry in his book when Doyle received a knighthood. I do not know which newspaper article he referred to, but Garrick-Steele writes that the reason for Doyle's knighthood was his dedication to the Boer War and for writing HOUN. For Sherlockians, it is well known that the Canon was not the reason for his knighthood. Garrick-Steele's Robinson was frustrated with this news, and it is said his friends asked him why he could not also get a knighthood (p215). His wife Gladys supposedly even proposed beginning legal proceedings! (p216) As well, Robinson's friend Nevinson said that Doyle's affair was seen by his sister and her husband, Hornung, who blamed Doyle, and they got into a fistfight (p218). He also said Doyle was a "Dr. Jekyll and Mr. Hyde," who deceived the British people about atrocities in South Africa. Nevinson told Robinson that if he commenced legal proceedings, the atrocities would be revealed, and the crown's very existence would be threatened. He also said Doyle committed violence against his family, and that his secretary also beat Doyle's son Gemini (p222). I have never heard of a son of Doyle's named "Gemini" or anything like that. I wonder who he was....

After the knighthood ceremony, Doyle attended a reception, where he was called as "Sir Sherlock Holmes," and presented a shirt made in USA as a commemorative gift, (p223). As soon as he saw it, Doyle ranted and raved... Mr. Green told me in our private communication, "Doyle does say that after he had received his knighthood someone called him 'Sir Sherlock Holmes'. He was annoyed, until the person told him that he thought people changed their names when they received a knighthood - and this was bona fide mistake". However, it is hard to believe he received an American shirt as a gift. Garrick-Steele also claimed Doyle said dirty words everywhere, and that such things were reported in newspapers, especially by W. C. Stead (p224). I do not know anything about Stead actually writing such articles in newspapers. Stead died in the sinking of the Titanic. I do know that Doyle wrote a preface for a spiritualist book in which Stead sent a message after his death.

He also made Robinson say that he put all the letters from Doyle and the newspaper and magazine articles on the authorship problem of HOUN in a tin box, and buried them in the ground at Parkhill. Does Garrick-Steele want to say he found that box? There are no references to any such "discovery," but it is possible he suggested it as one of the resources of his book (p224). Robinson also said he would return to Parkhill as a ghost after his death, to tell the truth. However, Garrick-Steele's friend already said the ghost at the Parkhill was a maid!

Part 2 of the book is about HOUN, as above. The third quarter of the book is on the death of Robinson and an "affair" between Doyle and Mrs. Robinson. However, there is a fatal mistake at the beginning of Chapter Seven. Mr. and Mrs. Robinson moved to Buckingham Palace Mansions, London, found Doyle also had a room there, and the two worried about Doyle's violence (p236). It is true Doyle had a room at the Mansions for his London stay, but that was in the 1920's, long after the death of Fletcher Robinson. Mr. Green said "Fletcher Robinson did not move to Buckingham Palace Mansions, so far as I know" in our private communication. Furthermore, there is a reference to one of Doyle's plays, *The House of Temperly*, as a work of Robinson, but this play was performed at the Adelphi Theatre, 11 February - 28 May, 1910, three years after the death of Fletcher Robinson. Was the Robinson who talked about *The House Of Temperly* a ghost? This is a matter for a spiritualist. He also says savagery was in the Doyle family's nature (p237).

Steele writes that Robinson published some fiction including "The Tragedy of Thomas Hearne" in 1904 (p251), but as have seen above, this short story was actually published in 1905. If this story was the original HOUN, why did nobody refer to that "fact" when it was published? We know the answer; it does not resemble HOUN at all.

Robinson died on 21 January 1907. He had been to Paris for a holiday, and he caught typhoid there. Garrick-Steele claimed that Robinson died at a hotel in Paris where he was staying with his wife on holiday, and his body was brought to London in secret (p262). He suggests that the Paris hotel wanted to conceal the cause of death because it could be bad for the hotel's reputation. Garrick-Steele also suggests that Gladys told her family Robinson died in Paris, but he could not find any death certificate for Robinson in France. He says the death certificate for Robinson was found in England, and says Robinson died in his house after twenty-two days' struggle with typhoid. He also wonders why the name on the certificate was "Bernard," not "Bertram" (p295). He suspects a conspiracy of her Majesty's government! (p289)

Garrick-Steele's theory has a fatal mistake. First, it is a well known fact that Robinson's death occurred in London, not in Paris. Peter Ruber writes in the preface for *The Chronicles of Addington Peace*, "...on January 21, 1907, when Robinson died in London of typhoid fever." (p5). I do not know where he got the idea that Robinson died in Paris and his body was brought to London secretly. Archibald Marshall writes that Robinson "had gone over to Paris, caught pneumonia, and died in a few days at the age of thirty-six or seven[7]" (p.6-7), but it is not clear whether Robinson died in Paris or London. In addition, it is not correct to explain his cause of death as "pneumonia," rather than "typhoid." Garrick-Steele himself also writes "He was in England when he got sick" (p297).

Garrick-Steele also blames Doyle for not attending Robinson's funeral at Ipplepen or sending any messages, but Green[9] says "Among the wreathes was one from Conan Doyle that read: 'In loving memory of an old and valued friend'." (p127)

There is a reference to Harry Baskerville's ancestors. Garrick-Steele says that the great, great, great grandfather of Harry inherited a large manor house called "Heatree House" fifteen miles from Newton Abbott, but Harry's grandfather lost it all gambling (p270). I do not know if this is true. I also do not know whether it is true that W. C. Stead severely criticized Doyle about his attitude to Robinson concerning HOUN (p273).

Furthermore, there is the third part of this book pertaining to Harry Baskerville and HOUN. Garrick-Steele refers to "The Journal" 17 October, 1951. There is no such newspaper in Britain, but Ms. Catherine Cooke identified this publication as the *South Devon Journal*. Garrick-Steele referred to this article, claiming the article refers not only to HOUN, but also to SILV as being written by Robinson. However, this is not a correct quotation. According to the original article of the *South Devon Journal* on October 17th, 1951, "He (Harry Baskerville) was a coachman at Parkhill House, Ipplepen, when Conan Doyle came to stay there to gather material for his books in the area, and it was as a result of the many long journeys over Dartmoor, on which Mr. Baskerville used to drive the author, that the location and background of scenes in "Hound of the Baskervilles" and "Silver Blaze" were created." It is clear that Harry Baskerville showed Doyle the Dartmoor area which became the setting for HOUN and SILV, not claiming Robinson wrote them at all.

Garrick-Steele again misquotes this article. He writes that Harry met S.C. Roberts, the former president of The Sherlock Holmes Society of London, and the Vice-Chancellor of Cambridge University in Massachusetts, USA! Why is the president of the SHSL an American? Mr. Green said "S.C. Roberts was the President of The Sherlock Holmes Society of London, Master of Pembroke College, Cambridge - and Vice-Chancellor of Cambridge University - that is Cambridge, England" in our private communication. He also says Harry became an honorary member of the Sherlock Holmes Society of New York. I did not know such a society existed, and no such reference exists in the *South Devon Journal*. Mr. Green said "This is wrong, but Harry was offered membership of a small scion society." In his letter to me. This article also does not mention Robinson as one of the authors of HOUN. It just says, "An introduction to some of the countless legends of Dartmoor was given the famous author by Ipplepen landowner, Mr. B. Fletcher Robinson, and it was Mr. Robinson and Conan Doyle between them who decided that the young coachman's name would be ideal for the book."

Garrick-Steele also refers to an article of *Daily Express*, 16 March, 1959. However, it is easy to read the original article for earnest Sherlockian scholars, as it is reprinted in *The Sherlock Holmes Scrapbook*. In this article, Harry Baskerville said "Doyle didn't write the story himself. A lot of the story was written by Fletcher Robinson. But he never got the credit he deserved." But Harry also says "There was never such a legend. It was a story Bertie (Robinson) invented and helped to write. I don't know why he didn't get more credit. It didn't seem to worry him, though." It means Robinson did not matter on the authorship of HOUN, and it is clear he just helped Doyle. Further, this article quotes a message from "a Holmes expert" as follows: "He may have agreed with Fletcher Robinson to adapt an existing Robinson story but found it impossible to make Holmes the central figure." It would be nearer to the facts, I presume.

Garrick-Steele also refers to the *Mid-Devon Advertiser* of October 26, 1968, that also dealt the problem. However, this article entitled "The Baskerville country of Conan-Doyle (sic)" written by Arthur Wilde is a feeble one with many mistakes First of all, Wilde thought HOUN was a silent film, not a novel! He writes "...some elderly readers will recall his first silent film, "The Hound of the Baskervilles." While writing part of the film the author stayed at the Duchy hotel, Princetown..." The only reference to the Robinson problem is, "During a conversation with a friend on Dartmoor, Conan-Doyle (sic) heard about a phantom dog." There are no references to "Robinson" or "Parkhill" at all, so it is not credible to refer this as an article on this problem. In addition, Garrick-Steele also refers to an article in the *Western Morning News* of October 24, 1968 (?) by Edith Wheeler stating that Robinson rescued Sherlock Holmes and his writing ability was beyond that of Doyle. However, I could not find this article.

Garrick-Steele suspects the cause of Robinson's death to have been typhoid. He insists it is suspicious that only a well-built, healthy sportsman like Robinson contracted the disease, and not any other members of the family or fellows of his publisher. But typhoid is one of the most common diseases of past centuries. I still remember how my grandmother told me not to buy foods at stalls, because of a fear of typhoid. This was only thirty years ago. Garrick-Steele also says Robinson's body was not cremated, though typhoid was epidemic (p304), and suggests he was poisoned with laudanum by his wife Gladys. However, if Robinson was poisoned, the criminal would make sure the body was cremated to destroy the evidence. Garrick-Steele's theories contradict each other.

Garrick-Steele states flatly that Gladys Robinson was the poisoner, and Doyle assisted her to kill Fletcher Robinson. Gladys thought her husband dithering, and she was also dissatisfied about having no children. However, Garrick-Steele shows no evidence about this important suspect at all. He just says Gladys was the only person who could poison Fletcher's food, as if this is proof of her guilt. He says Gladys was attracted to Doyle who was like a father, a knight and a barbarian. But as I wrote above, the Robinsons did not live at Buckingham Palace Mansions, and Doyle only lived there years after Robinson's death. There was no chance for Gladys to meet Doyle. Green also writes "There is no evidence that Doyle ever met her" (p127).

There is also another "fiction" by Garrick-Steele. He suggests Doyle proposed that Robinson be a ghost writer of Sherlock Holmes stories, and Robinson refused. That was another reason for the murder, he writes (p318). It is not believable that Doyle and Robinson had a bad relationship after publishing HOUN. According to *A Biography of Arthur Conan Doyle*[4], Doyle joined the Crimes Club in 1904, a club of which Fletcher Robinson was also a member.

In the last chapter, the "spirit of Charles Doyle" came to Garrick-Steele, and he decided to read *The Doyle Diary*[6]. Foolishly, he thought this book was Conan Doyle's diary! He says the mysterious portrait of Charles Doyle and Conan Doyle delivered to his house ten years ago was just the same as the one on p.5 of this book (p341). Furthermore, he insists this book was published in the United States because British publishers thought such a book against Doyle's image would not be accepted by readers (p342). However, as is written

139

above, this book was published in New York and London. I do not know why he dismissed "London" which clearly printed next to "New York." He insists Conan Doyle was a brutal boy in his youth. He committed his father to a psychiatric hospital, and such a son would be the type to kill Robinson in latter days (p354).

In all fairness, *The House of the Baskervilles* is full of mistakes, errors, inaccuracies and ill will. It is hard to call it a non-fiction work, and it is even a poor work of fiction. It is said decades of British and American publishers refused to print this work, and this was the right decision. As mentioned above, there are too many mistakes, unintentional or otherwise. The general editor of the translated edition, Shimada Soji is one of the most famous Japanese mystery writers, and formerly wrote a Sherlockian parody. He would have knowledge of Conan Doyle and Sherlock Holmes at a considerable level, and it is curious to me that Shimada did not notice these errors in his book. In defense of the honor of Shimada, he points out there is no evidence of the relationship between Doyle and Gladys Robinson. In addition, Shimada says Garrick-Steele is writing his second book and the evidence might be shown in this next one.

I am thankful for the help and advice of Mr. Richard Lancelyn Green, Ms. Catherine Cooke, Mr. John Hall and the translator of *The House Of The Baskervilles*, Ms. Saga Fuyumi. I also thank Mrs. Mel Hughes for her advice on language.

References:

1 Rodger Garrick-Steele, *Konan Doiru Satsujin Jiken* (*The House of the Baskervilles*), translated by SAGA Fuyumi, general edit by SHIMADA Soji, Nan-un-do, Tokyo, 2002.
2 Richard Lancelyn Green & John Michael Gibson, *A Bibliography Of A. Conan Doyle*, Clarendon Press, Oxford, 1983.
3 B. Fletcher Robinson & J. Malcolm Fraser, *THE CHRONICLES OF ADDINGTON PEACE* and *THE TRAIL OF THE DEAD*, The Battered Silicon Dispatch Box, Shelburne, 1998.
4 Martin Booth, *A Biography Of Arthur Conan Doyle*, Hodder & Stoughton, London, 1997.
5 Ed. by Peter Haining, *The Sherlock Holmes Scrapbook*, Bramhall House, New York, 1974.

6 Ed. by Michael Baker, *The Doyle Diary* NY & London, Paddington Press, 1978.

7 Archibald Marshall, *Out And About*, John Murray, London,

8 Richard Lancelyn Green, *The Hound Of The Baskervilles*, Part One, *The Sherlock Holmes Journal*, winter 2001, p.85-91.

9 Richard Lancelyn Green, *The Hound Of The Baskervilles*, Part Two, *The Sherlock Holmes Journal*, summer 2002, p.123-128

10 Arthur Wilde "The Baskerville Country of Conan-Doyle," *Mid-Devon Advertiser*, October 26, 1968.

11 His name has gone down in mystery!" *South Devon Journal*, October 17, 1951.

(*The Shoso-in Bulletin* vol.14, 2004)

Influence of the Canon
on Japanese Detective Stories

In the late nineteenth century, a lot of western products and systems were introduced to Japan, which had been living under Samurai traditions. Japanese society was dramatically modernized and rapidly westernized. The detective story is one example of the modern Western cultural items introduced to Japan.

The first translation of a detective story into Japanese was "Waran Biseiroku," translated by Kanda Kohei in 1861. It was taken from a Dutch book called "Belangrijke Tafereelen uit de Geschiedenis der Lijfstra ffelijke Regtsplegling" by Jan Bastiaan Chritemeijer, published in 1821. The translation was not widely published, however, and the "boom" of western detective did not begin until the translations of Kuroiwa Ruikou (1862-1920). Kuroiwa was a newspaper editor and translated dime novels for his newspapers. His first translation was Hugh Conway's *Dark Days* in 1888, but he translated mainly French works, including fifteen novels of Fortune Du Boisgobey (1824-1891), the French writer of police stories, four of Emile Gaboriau, and two of William Wilkie Collins. Kuroiwa's great success influenced other newspaper editors, who also began to print detective stories. One of them was Mizuta Nanyougaishi, whose translation series, "Gushigino Tantei" ("Miracle Detective"), was published on Chuo Shinbun, in 1899. It is one of the earliest translations of *The Adventures of Sherlock Holmes*.

Kuroiwa translated nearly thirty detective stories in about five or six years, but then he lost interest and turned to romantic novels. After that, the detective story boom was over. But publishers did not stop printing translations of western detective stories, and several translations of Sherlock Holmes appeared. These translations were only published in small quantities, and were hard to find. Those who favored detective stories were an educated class of people, who could read the original English books.

142

One of the most famous Japanese novelists, who wrote several detective stories in his youth, was Tanizaki Junichiro (1886-1965). Tanizaki mentioned Sherlock Holmes and Watson in his stories "Kin to Gin" ("Gold and Silver," 1918) or "Hakuchu Kigo" ("Devilish Words at High Noon," 1918). He had studied English literature in college, and it is believed that he read Poe and Doyle in the original form.

This also applied to Edogawa Rampo (1894-1965), who is known as the "Father of the Japanese Detective Story." His first short story, "Nisen Douka" ("Two Cent Copper," 1923) is said to be the first modern Japanese detective story. For nearly fifty years, he published many "puzzle" short stories, and later, thriller novels and criticisms. He founded The Japanese Society of Detective Writers, and was the first president. He also initiated the "Edogawa Rampo Award" for new mystery writers. It is said even today that this award is a most honorable start for young mystery writers.

Edogawa wrote in a private note (published later as "Kitan," in *Extraordinaries*, 1919) of his experience with Sherlock Holmes stories. Of course, Edogawa read Japanese translations, but he was not satisfied with them. He also bought English editions and *The Strand Magazine*, and in his note, he compared them with old translations. His private translations of "The *Gloria Scott*," "The Dancing Men," and "The Three Students" still remain.

In Edogawa's detective stories, one influence of the Sherlock Holmes series is Edogawa's great detective named Akechi Kogoro. He is a private detective deeply trusted by police officers, like Holmes. In his early adventures, the storyteller is a nameless "I." This character may be Edogawa himself. There is no character comparable to Dr. Watson, and the storyteller was more like the teller of Poe's Dupin tales. Edogawa himself often confessed that the writer who influenced him most was Edgar Allan Poe, and his pen name (his real name was Hirai Taro) was taken from this famous American writer.

The clearest influence of Doyle on Edogawa's work is in his juvenile detective series. Akechi is its hero, but there is another group of heroes, the "Boy Detectives!" Their captain is Kobayashi Yoshio, Akechi's teenage assistant, and all the members of the group are boys in their early teens. Of course, the group is a reflection of the Baker Street irregulars. However, Edogawa changed one point: The Irregulars were street urchins, but members of the Boy Detectives were boys from decent homes who could ask their parents without hesitation to buy books. Readers of these books could easily identify with the Boy Detectives, and it was the fashion for boys to play the "Detective Game." The series won great success, and is still available in bookshops today.

As Edogawa did, early Japanese detective story lovers (Edogawa called them "Tanteishousetsu no Oni," or "demons of detective stories") read the Canon in English. Most of them belonged to the educated middle class. Okamoto Kido (1872-1939), who created "Hanshichi Torimonochou" ('The Casebook of Hanshichi"), was a playwright of Kabuki. "Torimonochou" is another genre of the Japanese detective story, a series of short detective stories situated in the world of the Samurai. Okamoto had a deep knowledge of English literature, and it is said that he was the best customer of the Maruzen foreign bookshop of Tokyo. He himself wrote that he bought *The Strand Magazine*, and read the Canon in English.

Another famous "Torimonochou" writer, Nomura Kodo (1882-1963), when he was a high school student, asked his teacher of English to use the Canon as a textbook. Later, Nomura studied law at Tokyo Imperial University and became a director of the Houchi Shinbun Newspaper.

The largest influence of the Canon on Japanese detective stories is the use of a "Dr. Watson" as a companion of the great detective. Conversations between the detective and his friend make a good way to explain what is going on to readers. The device is a brilliant creation, and most detective writers followed it. For Akechi Kogoro of Edogawa Rampo's works, young Kobayashi Yoshio is his good assistant, who acts as "Dr. Watson" or "Wiggins" in Edogawa's novels for adult readers. Yokomizo Seishi (1902-1981) created his detective Kindaichi Kosuke, accompanied by Inspector Todoroki or Inspector Isokawa. Yokomizo's other detectives, Yuri Rintaro and Mitsugi Shunsuke, might be influenced by Jacques Futrelle's Professor Van Dusen, "The Thinking Machine" -- Mitsugi is a newspaperman, as is Hutchinson Hatch, who reported Professor Van Dusen's cases.

The clearest examples are those of the "Torimonocho" genre. Detectives in "Torimonocho" are usually called "Okappiki" or "Goyoukiki," private assistants of "Doshin" official inspector samurais. The "Goyoukiki" worked as policemen, but because they were not samurais, they could not be given official positions.

144

"Goyoukiki" also had their assistants, called "Shitappiki," and they acted as "Dr. Watson" in the "Torimonocho" stories.

The most famous team of "Okappiki and Shitappiki" would be Heiji and Hachigoro, created by Nomura Kodo. His series "Zenigata Heiji Torimonohikae" is the longest and the most famous "Torimonocho" series ever published in Japan. He wrote 383 short stories and novels over 27 years, and the series was broadcast on television in 888 episodes using the same actors, Okawa Hashizo (Heiji) and Hayashiya Chinpei (Hachigoro).

At the beginning of most of these stories, Hachigoro visits Heiji's house and tells Heiji about rumors or new cases. One is reminded of the beginning of "The Blue Carbuncle," in which Dr. Watson visited 221B. Hachigoro's reporting news compared to Holmes always asking Watson to read the newspaper aloud. This device begins the cases easily and effectively for readers. (In this connection I may add that Japanese Prime Minister Yoshida Shigeru said he was a fan of the Zenigata Heiji series. His father-in-law, Count Makino Shinken, was one of the founding members of the Baritsu Chapter of Tokyo, the first Sherlockian society in Japan.)

In the late 1950s, a drastic change occurred in Japanese mystery writing. The era of "the great detective" ended. Matsumoto Seicho (1909-1992) and others of the new generation of mystery writers began new "realistic mysteries." In their novels, ordinary policemen or newspapermen acted as the investigators. They had no special talents, but their consistent hard work solved cases. That contrasted with old traditional mysteries and Sherlock Holmes. Traditional private detectives were criticized as "puppets" or "paper dolls," and they rapidly disappeared.

However, such "realistic mysteries" were inherently limited, with no puzzles or detections. By the 1970s, a revival of puzzle mysteries and "great detectives" occurred. There was, naturally, a demand from readers who had only had the chance to read translations of such mysteries. *Geneijou* magazine published reprints of traditional pre-World War II puzzle mysteries. Yokomizo Seishi's writing also became popular – his paperbacks selling more than a million copies – and many puzzle or "great detective" films were made.

"Great detectives" have returned to Japanese mystery writing. Under such conditions, The Japan Sherlock Holmes Club was constituted in 1978. The time of the "Great Detective" has come again.

Now in Japan, the genre known as "mystery" has a different scope than the American or British term. It includes horror novels, psychological thrillers, spy novels, love and romance tales, and science fiction. In fact, it may be translated most accurately as "fiction to read for pleasure." The "detective story" is just a part of the "mystery" genre. However, there is still a group of puzzle novels, and in 2000, The Puzzle Mystery Writer's Society was founded. Thus, the tradition of the "great detective" and unsolved puzzle stories still survives.

(*Japan and Sherlock Holmes*, The Baker Street Irregulars, 2004)

The Sherlockian Articles

by Hirayama Yuichi & John Hall

The Sporting Achievements
of Mr. Sherlock Holmes

Watson's earliest assessment of Sherlock Holmes's limits include mention of his expertise at singlestick, boxing, and fencing, and at other times in their association Watson had occasion to remark upon Holmes's knowledge – or lack of knowledge – of various sports. Our intention in this article is to survey the range of sports in which Holmes was involved, and to provide some account of his skill or success. This note will not consider 'games' or 'pastimes' as opposed to sports, although we know from cases such as "The Red-headed League" that Holmes could and did play cards. Nor will it look at such diversions as horse racing, although we know that Holmes was quite knowledgeable on that topic, as is shown in "Silver Blaze."

Our intention here is to deal solely with sports requiring more active participation. Even here, some pursuits must be excluded on the grounds that Holmes's proficiency in them cannot positively be attributed to any purely sporting inclination. In this category we must include horsemanship and the driving of a carriage, as in Holmes's day those were basic skills for any reasonably well-to-do man, just as driving a car is nowadays. Admitted, there were some people who rode or drove for pleasure rather than from necessity, just as there are now, but the indications in Holmes's case are so vague as to prevent our taking a view as to whether Holmes's skills in these areas were mainly recreational or otherwise. (Anne Jordan has advanced the theory that Holmes earned a living in his early days in practice, when cases were few and far between, by driving a cab, and this may well explain his proficiency in that area.)

Similarly, the revolver practice noted in "The Musgrave Ritual" and "The Dying Detective" may well have been the consequence of a professional, rather than a sporting, interest. However, David Landis has pointed out that Holmes did not actually favor firearms, nor did he use them regularly in his work, so there may be some grounds for thinking that the revolver practice was initially recreational. It would, of course, have come in handy on those fairly rare occasions when Holmes did go armed on a case.

On the same grounds we must rule out any detailed consideration of Holmes's cycling proficiency, though we know from "The Missing Three-quarter" that he could certainly ride a bicycle. It must be said that cycling does not immediately suggest itself as a skill which the would-be detective would diligently seek to acquire, and here again we may possibly feel justified in seeing Holmes's ability as having been acquired for fun (or as near thereto as Holmes as capable of reaching) in his childhood. Perhaps there are grounds for postulating some long cycling tour on the Continent at some stage in Holmes's youth?

"The Missing Three-quarter" does give us a pointer to the one sport which can decisively be eliminated from any list of Holmes's skills, namely rugby, for no man with an interest in rugby would have been puzzled, as Holmes was, by the telegram from Mr. Cyril Overton. (Watson had, of course, played rugby in his younger days. We know from "The Sussex Vampire" that he had indeed played with 'Big Bob' Ferguson, who was himself a three-quarter, and Watson thus must have known what the telegram meant. He probably derived considerable satisfaction from Holmes's temporary and uncharacteristic discomposure.)

June Thomson has read the fact that Holmes was unfamiliar with rugby and thus, presumably, other team sports as meaning that he could not have gone to a public (i.e. a private) school, as games would there have been compulsory. William Hyder makes a similar observation with regard to Holmes's knowledge of the violin. And WS Baring-Gould has suggested that Holmes learned his fencing from a private tutor.

This is all very tempting; it seems so logical. And yet Holmes was a proficient boxer, something we shall consider in more detail in a moment, and if indeed he did attend a public school he may well have used the obligatory gym sessions to practice in the ring. There is surely a case for suggesting that Holmes originally became interested in boxing because he was compelled to do something in those gym sessions and the team games did not appeal. Perhaps there was even some element of self-preservation in the choice of boxing at this stage, a reaction to bullying by more extroverted pupils which produced not merely proficiency in the ring, but also that sympathy with the underdog which is so evident in Holmes throughout this career. Proficiency in boxing would very effectively have prevented his being censured as a milksop by the muddied hearties of the rugger field. The use of the (unarguable) evidence that Holmes was not a team player to show that he had a private tutor must be regarded as doubtful.

Indeed, it seems clear that Holmes's remark, again in "The Missing Three-quarter," that his "ramifications stretch out into many sections of society, but never. . . into amateur sport," is intended as a summary of his professional experience rather than as a general disclaimer of any interest in sport whatsoever. That much is obvious from the general tenor of the remark, itself, from his next phrase about amateur sport being "the best and soundest thing in England" (for how could a man say that who knew nothing of it?) and from various other canonical references.

Some of those other references are tantalizingly vague, such as Holmes's recollection, in "The *Gloria Scott*," that Donnithorpe had "excellent wild-duck shooting in the fens," and "remarkably good fishing." It may have been that Holmes was speaking in a very general sense here, doing no more than assess the estate's sporting potential just as any other reasonably affluent man of the time would do. Or possibly he was looking at the sporting possibilities of the estate with the expert eye of a man whose ancestors had been 'country squires, who appear to have led much the same life as is natural to their class,' as Holmes put it in "The Greek Interpreter."

The remark does have some implications for a study of Holmes's early years. It is surely unlikely that a man who had spent all his early youth in a town, whether his ancestors had been country squires or not, would have spoken with such assurance. Moreover, Holmes never mentions his father, so it seems impossible that the two of them had been close, and thus may have visited the countryside together from a base in town, the father passing on his knowledge to the son. The logical conclusions are surely that Holmes's childhood was spent in the country, and that he had taught himself to shoot and fish.

We hear nothing more as to duck shooting, although it is possible that Holmes's marksmanship with a revolver may have owed something to his youthful fowling expeditions. The mention of a bearskin rug, onto which Dr Thorneycroft Huxtable fainted in "The Priory School" as being part of the furnishings at 221B, must be regarded as inconclusive. "The Priory School" is generally regarded as a late case (1900 or thereabouts) and that would mean that the rug could have come from almost anywhere, although one possibility must certainly be that Holmes shot the unfortunate bear on his travels during the Hiatus.

We do hear of fishing again in "Shoscombe Old Place," where Holmes and Watson "did actually use [their] fishing tackle in the millstream," and had a dish of trout for supper as a result. The fishing expedition had been intended primarily to provide a cover, an explanation for their presence in the area, but there are surely indications of some degree of skill in that dish of trout for supper, although Watson annoyingly fails to make it clear whether it was Holmes or the good doctor himself who accounted for most of the catch.

At the opening of "The Greet Interpreter" Holmes and Watson have a discussion on various topics, one of which is golf clubs. It is not clear whether the talk referred to the institution or the instrument – probably the latter-- but it is reasonable to suppose that a man must have at least a basic knowledge of golf in order to discuss any aspect of the subject intelligently. But we hear no further mention of golf from Holmes.

There is no mention at all of tennis. We know that Watson possessed a pair of tennis shoes, which he wore during the burglary of Charles Augustus Milverton's house, and it is reasonable to suppose that Holmes had provided himself with similar, if not identical, footwear on this occasion. However, even if Holmes had been wearing shoes specifically designed for tennis, that does not prove that he had any interest in the game apart from-- the shoes' noiseless maneuvering during clandestine operations.

Holmes could swim, as is clear from "The Lion's Mane" and he did so as a hobby in his retirement, so it is possible that he had also been keen on this sport earlier in his life, though again there are no other mentions of it. Swimming is perhaps something more easily learned in youth than in old age, and we may see this as another skill which Holmes had acquired during his relatively lonely childhood in the countryside. It is interesting to speculate as to where, if anywhere. Holmes might have practiced swimming in London. Many of the public baths had swimming facilities, but these would perhaps have been a trifle too public for the ascetic Holmes – a circumstance which bothered others, indeed, for the Bath Club in Dover Street was opened in 1892 precisely so that gentlemen residing in the capital might have somewhere suitable, and more exclusive, where they could swim. Even at that relatively late date, Holmes is unlikely to have joined the Bath, for he was definitely not a clubman – the Diogenes Club, noted in "The Greek Interpreter," appealed to him precisely because it catered for those who felt at home nowhere else. The most tempting possibility is some private establishment, for we know that Holmes had a weakness for the Turkish bath, and many of the better class of these also had swimming facilities. Or as an alternative, we may perhaps see Holmes as abandoning swimming altogether during his time in London, and returning to a youthful interest in it when once he had retired to the Sussex coast.

At the very outset of their acquaintance, in *A Study in Scarlet*, Watson made a list of Holmes's limits which included the observation that Holmes was 'an expert singlestick player, boxer, and swordsman.' Holmes refers to two of these three sports in "The Gloria Scott" when he says that at university he had "few athletic tastes" apart from fencing and boxing. And Watson mentions these same two again in "The Five Orange Pips" when he recalls that his list in *A Study in Scarlet* had included the note that Holmes was a "violin-player, boxer, swordsman, lawyer, and self-poisoner by cocaine and tobacco."

Let us first look at how Watson came to know of Holmes's proficiency in the early days. One possibility is that he had actually seen Holmes participating in the sports noted, and that is not unreasonable. We know that Holmes had fought three rounds with the professional, McMurdo, at Alison's rooms four years prior to *The Sign of Four*, so the bout would have been in 1883 or perhaps a year or so after, when Watson was (on the evidence of Holmes's attitude in "The Speckled Band") part of the team at 221B, and it seems quite likely that Watson would have gone along to see his friend box. And similarly Watson may have seen Holmes take part in fencing and singlestick bouts.

Another possibility is that Holmes had displayed some evidence of his prowess at 221B, cups or trophies, or perhaps equipment, and that Watson had very naturally inquired as to Holmes's interest in the sports concerned. Watson does not mention any such paraphernalia, but that is not conclusive proof that none existed. Some reconstructions of the sitting room at 221B have displayed a pair of boxing gloves on the wall, and, although there is no canonical evidence that such was the case, by the same token there is nothing in Watson's accounts to suggest that it was not. And it may perhaps not be too fanciful to suggest that the patriotic 'VR' in bullet holes mentioned in "The Musgrave Ritual" might have been inspired by the 'V' shape of a pair of fencing foils over the fire, but this is pure speculation.

The third and last of the most likely possibilities is that Watson's list was based on anecdotal evidence only. It would be perfectly natural for the two men to engage in conversation in the early days, equally natural for Watson to ask what Holmes's hobbies and interests might be. However, this is perhaps the least satisfactory possibility, for Watson does make a point of referring in *A Study in Scarlet* to Holmes's reticence as to himself.

(There are fringe possibilities for some of the skills noted. For example, it may have been that Watson had noticed some thickening of Holmes's ears, indicative of a boxing man. But this is a remote possibility: Holmes's amateur bouts would have been unlikely to produce any such trophies, and more to the point, Watson was not really that observant.)

We do know for certain that Watson must have seen Holmes box in person at some stage, for in "The Yellow Face" Watson tells us that Holmes "was undoubtedly one of the finest boxers of his weight that I have ever seen," which is specific enough. As noted above, the bout with McMurdo may well have been one occasion on which Watson was a spectator, although we cannot be certain of that. But what is certain is that Watson must have seen Holmes in the ring at some time or another, and there is nothing to rule out his having done so in the very earliest stages of their acquaintance.

It is not immediately apparent just when Holmes's interest in boxing first began. The quotation from "*The Gloria Scott*," noted earlier, makes it clear that he was already keen on the sport in university days, but he may have been introduced to it even earlier by one of those country squires whom he reckoned among his ancestors. This is perhaps unlikely, though, for Mycroft does not give the impression that he was of a similar athletic inclination, which might tend to rule out tutelage by a relation, and that in turn may mean that Sherlock began boxing at school, as already noted, or at university.

He certainly seems to have boxed fairly regularly whilst he was at university, and, that being so, we might wonder just why he seems to have had so few friends at this stage in his life. It might be thought that a keen boxer would have fitted quite well into the university sporting circle. On the other hand, Holmes may well have had a considerable acquaintance among the 'fancy' without having very many really close friends, particularly among those whose tastes ran to the cricket field or the river rather than the ring, so there is nothing there to strain our belief too greatly.

Holmes seems to have had some considerable degree of skill in boxing, in the early days at least. Apart from Watson's laudatory remark, which we might be inclined to dismiss as typical of the good doctor's praise of his friend, there is the independent evidence of McMurdo in *The Sign of Four* that Holmes had wasted his gifts and 'might have aimed high, if [he] had joined the fancy.' We might perhaps again be inclined to treat this remark with caution, to put it down to the tendency of the professional (or exprofessional) to let the amateur down lightly, but McMurdo does not immediately strike the casual observer as being prey to this chivalrous propensity.

Moreover, there are other, more unambiguous, examples of Holmes's boxing skill throughout the canon, such as his defeat of the 'slogging ruffian' Woodley in "The Solitary Cyclist," or his fight with the knife wielding Harrison in "The Naval Treaty." And there are usually believable explanations for the few occasions on which Holmes did not do so well, such as his struggle with the Cunninghams in "The Reigate Puzzle," when Holmes was just recovering from a near-total breakdown of his health.

It is once again interesting to speculate as to how (and indeed if) Holmes kept his boxing skills honed when he started in practice as a detective. Watson tells us in "The Yellow Face" that Holmes "seldom took exercise for exercise's sake," but kept in training with a diet which "was usually of the sparest." It is difficult to accept this absolutely literally, and when we remember that Watson had undoubtedly seen Holmes in the boxing ring, we might well feel justified in supposing that Holmes had, in the early days at least, been in the habit of working out at some gymnasium.

There were several boxing clubs in London, but the two most important were one in Clapton, possible, but a fair distance from 221B, and the West London Boxing Club which met at the 'Bedford Head' in Maiden Lane, off the Strand. The latter is within easy reach of Baker

154

Street, and must surely have some claim to having seen Holmes in action. In addition to these two, the London Athletic Club ran boxing classes during the winter months at Mr Waite's, 22 Golden Square, while the German Gymnastic Society (two-thirds of whose members were English) also had winter time boxing classes at 26 Pancras Road, King's Cross. There was thus no shortage of facilities.

The "Alison's rooms" referred to as the venue for the bout with McMurdo in *The Sign of Four* may have been a private boxing club or gymnasium, but are perhaps more likely to have been a private room, or rooms, let out for any public function in some inn or pub owned by Mr Alison. (Or, just possibly, Ms Alison Someone, though this is far less likely.) And pubs which specialized in the 'fancy,' with a boxing ring for the entertainment of patrons, still survived, although according to the anonymous compiler of the 1880 edition of Dickens's *Dictionary of London* they were becoming rare, so that is yet another possibility.

The mention of fencing, in "The *Gloria Scott*" makes it clear that this too was a sport which Holmes was keen on during his university days. And again, there is nothing too difficult about accepting that he would have acquaintances, but not close friends, in the fencing club. It is even possible that Reginald Musgrave had been a fellow member of the university fencing club, for the sport is one which may well have appealed to that languid aristocrat, and this shared interest could have been the origin of the friendship between the two men, though there is no hard evidence.

Once again, we cannot tell whether or not Holmes's interest predates his attendance at university. There is no further mention of fencing later in his career, which may perhaps indicate that he more or less dropped it completely later on, though here again we cannot be sure. (Dramatizers of the canon have been similarly shy of incorporating swordplay into their offerings, which is a pity, for Jeremy Brett or Basil Rathbone would surely have done full justice to the occasional bit of swashbuckling, and there would have been – for once! -- a sound canonical basis to justify its inclusion.) Holmes may have dropped the fencing in later life because – unlike boxing – there were relatively few places in London where he could have practiced fencing.

The omission of any mention of singlestick fighting from Holmes's own remark in "The Gloria *Scott*," and again from Watson's recollection in "The Five Orange Pips" is interesting. Singlestick (sometimes spelled with a hyphen, single-stick) may not be as immediately familiar as boxing or fencing, so it is perhaps worth stating that it was a sport carried out with, quite literally, a single 'stick,' similar to a quarterstaff, a five foot (or so) pole with which each of the two participants attempted to 'break the head' of the other, i.e. to draw blood from the scalp.

Singlestick fighting was particularly popular in the West Country, so that if Holmes had been interested in this sport when he was very young there may be implications there regarding his place of birth. On the other hand, the omission of any mention of this sport in "The *Gloria Scott*" may mean that Holmes acquired his interest in it after his university days.

That too is an interesting possibility, for the sport was also particularly popular with army and navy officers, and if Holmes had learned the skill from his father, that might be a pointer to the latter's occupation, and that in turn might be an explanation for the somewhat distant relations which seem to have obtained between the Holmeses, father and son. But this is speculative, and it is interesting that the one army man with whom Holmes definitely came into contact was none other than Watson. But again, if Watson had introduced Holmes to singlestick fighting, he would surely have mentioned the fact in *A Study in Scarlet*, so that seems to be ruled out. And Watson also fails to mention singlestick in his recollection of his old list of Holmes's limits in "The Five Orange Pips," so perhaps it did not stick in his mind (no pun intended) as securely as the boxing and fencing.

That in turn may indicate that Holmes's proficiency in singlestick was not particularly great, but that reading conflicts with Holmes's own claim, in "The Illustrious Client," to be "a bit of a single-stick expert." It might be asked why an expert should be so badly beaten, but there is a world of difference between a sporting contest using the correct equipment, and an assault by not one, but two, opponents who possess no sporting inclinations. Moreover, at this fairly late stage in Holmes's career, his neglect of his skills may have been a contributory factor. The question of Holmes's expertise thus need not concern us too greatly, and there is no need to subscribe to the theory put forward by Asano Yoshiaki that Gruner's hired thugs were actually Japanese martial arts experts, interesting though that suggestion undoubtedly is.

Mention of Japanese martial arts leads us naturally to the last of Holmes's accomplishments, that knowledge of "baritsu, or the Japanese system of wrestling," to which he laid claim in "The Empty House." This topic is one which has very naturally aroused a good deal of interest among Japanese Sherlockians, and there are quite considerable ramifications to it which cannot be adequately covered in a short general note such as this one. The authors of this note have produced a full-length study of the subject, and (without wishing to reveal too much detail to prospective purchasers of that!) have concluded that Holmes's skill was in jujitsu, probably acquired between 1887 and 1891, with the balance of probability favoring late 1890 for the precise date, and that to Tokyo judo teacher Kano Jigoro was Holmes's tutor. It also seems most improbable that Holmes was ever a true master of the skill, despite his easy defeat of Moriarty at Reichenbach.

References

1) Anon (Charles Dickens the younger?), *Dicken's Dictionary of London, 1880 (Second Year): An Unconventional Handbook* London: Charles Dickens, 1880, p.40.
2) Asano Yoshiaki, personal communication to The Red Circle of Niigata.
3) WS Baring-Gould, *Sherlock Holmes of Baker Street: The Life of the World's First Consulting Detective* (New York,: Clarkson N Potter, 1962)
4) Hirayama Yuichi and John Hall, *Some Knowledge of Baritsu* In press: to be published by The Northern Musgraves in 1996.
5) William Hyder, *From Baltimore to Baker Street* Toronto: Metropolitan Toronto Reference Library, 1995, p.24.
6) Anne Jordan, 'Was Holmes a Cab Driver?' *The Ritual*, No.11 Huddersfield: The Northern Musgraves, 1993, pp.8-12.
7) David Landis, 'Holmes the Marksman: A Man and his Mettle,' *The Shoso-in Bulletin*, Vol.5 (1995), pp.94-96.
8) June Thomson, *Holmes and Watson: A study in friendship* London: Constable and Co., 1995.

(*The Baker Street Journal*, March 1996)

Did you know LeBrun,
the French agent?

One of the many writers of Sherlockian pastiche and parody was the Frenchman, Maurice Leblanc (1864 – 1941). Leblanc was a journalist and novelist who, in the early years of the new century, began to write detective stories at the request of his friend Pierre Lafitte, a publisher and the owner of the magazine, *Je sais tout*.

Leblanc took an interesting approach to his pastiche: he put Holmes at the periphery of the tales, instead of at their centre. The true 'hero' of Leblanc's books is the noted French criminal, Arsène Lupin, and Holmes is cast as a relatively minor character. He does not even appear in all the Lupin stories, and when he does it is under an alias which changed almost from day to day, being sometimes rendered as Herlock Sholmes, but later as Holmlock Shears. (Although the Japanese – who esteem Lupin as highly as Holmes – simply use 'Sherlock Holmes' in their translations.)

The search for minor parallels between Holmes and Lupin is an interesting diversion: Lupin's dog, for example, is called 'Sherlock' (in *813*); there is an early morning encounter between a blackmailer and his victim at the blackmailer's house, recalling the fatal meeting in *Charles Augustus Milverton* (in *Le Bouchon de Crystal*); and so on. And as far as overall style is concerned, the Lupin stories are broadly similar to the Holmesian canon in that a narrator writing in the first person gives us most of the information about Lupin; but in the Lupin stories there are switches into the third person for whole blocks of the text. The narrator is a friend of Lupin's and is clearly a man; but he remains anonymous, positively self-effacing by comparison with the garrulous Watson. Even when Lupin and the narrator meet Holmes at a cafe, Lupin merely, 'Allow me to introduce my friend,' but he does not name the friend. The narrator is close to Lupin, for he tells us, 'My excuse [for writing the accounts] is that I can supply something new: I can furnish the key to the puzzle. There is always a certain mystery about [Lupin's] adventures: I can dispel it.' We may safely assume that the narrator is none other than Leblanc himself.

Perhaps the most significant work from the Sherlockian viewpoint is the novel first published in 1908 as *Arsène Lupin contre Herlock Sholmes*, which was initially translated into English as *Arsène Lupin versus Holmlock Shears*, and then retitled as *The Arrest of Arsène Lupin*, the form in which it is perhaps best known. (The various editions of Lupin demand a bibliographical monograph of their own; the quotations from *The Arrest* in this article are taken from the English translation – the translator is not named – published by Newnes in their 'Sevenpenny Series,' no date but *circa* 1910.)

In some ways, Lupin may be regarded as a Gallic version of Professor Moriarty. Lupin has a large criminal organisation at his disposal; there is always a car waiting at just the right place and just the right time to whisk Lupin out of the grasp of the official police force. Perhaps the most telling instance of Lupin's forward planning in *The Arrest* is that he had – a full five years before the story opens – inveigled his way into the business of an architect, M. Destange, and, whilst ostensibly carrying out repairs and alterations to various properties, had constructed several secret doors and passages in the houses concerned. It was when Lupin began to use these clandestine entrances and exits to effect the removal of various portable valuables that Holmlock Shears (whom we shall here generally call Holmes, for convenience, so long as it causes no undue confusion to do so) was called in, and the book proper begins. Even Moriarty never planned anything quite that elaborate, or that far in advance!

Lupin certainly has no lack of self-esteem: 'I search history in vain for a destiny to compare with mine . . . Napoleon? Yes, Perhaps . . .' and there is surely a fairly heavily stressed parallel here with that other Napoleon of crime, Moriarty. It would, however, be a mistake to identify Lupin with Moriarty without qualification. True, Lupin 'speaks, writes, warns, orders, threatens, carries out his plans, as though there were no police, no magistrates, no impediment of any kind in existence. They seem of no account to him whatever. No obstacle enters into his calculations.' At first glance, this may seem to parallel Moriarty's own disregard for the forces of law and order quite closely, and so far as indifference to any moral code but his own is concerned, Lupin is not so very different from the Professor.

But, unlike Moriarty, Lupin is no shrinking violet, depending for his success on secrecy, on the facade of respectability. On the contrary, Lupin positively enjoys notoriety, and he gets it – 'The name of Arsène Lupin alone was a guarantee of originality, a promise of amusement for the gallery. And the gallery, in this case, was the whole world.' And that phrase about speaking and writing as though there were no police, etc, must be taken very literally, for Lupin's exploits – it seems churlish to label them mere 'crimes' – are known to, and admired by, the public, in France at any rate. (After the event, not before, of course!) Indeed, Lupin has some connection with a newspaper which publishes laudatory accounts of those exploits, the *Echo de France* 'which has the honour of being [Lupin's] official organ and in which he seems to be one of the principal shareholders.'

Lupin is altogether a more human, more likeable figure than Moriarty, and – being French – Lupin has one little human weakness which Holmes can use against him, namely affection for the 'fair-headed lady.' Mlle Clotilde Destange, daughter of the architect, who will be noted in more detail in a moment.

Notoriety is two-edged. We have seen that 'no obstacle enters into [Lupin's] calculations,' but, for all that, 'the police struggle to do their best. The moment the name of Arsène Lupin is mentioned, the whole force, from top to bottom, takes fire, boils and foams with rage. He is the enemy, the enemy who mocks you, provokes you, despises you, or, even worse, ignores you. And what can one do against an enemy like that?'

Lupin's chief adversary in the official force is Ganimard, who is perhaps not so very different from Lestrade – 'Ganimard is not one of those mighty detectives . . . whose name will always remain inscribed on the judicial annals of Europe. He lacks the flashes of genius that illumine a Dupin, a Lecoq or a Holmlock Shears. But he possesses first-rate average qualities: perspicacity, sagacity, perseverance and even a certain amount of intuition.' But Ganimard is no match for Lupin, and so Holmes is consulted by Lupin's victims.

The treatment of Holmes (or 'Holmlock Shears,' or whatever he happened to be called) is rather curious: fidelity to, and respect for, the Doylean canon is combined with elements of caricature or parody, verging almost on resentment.

From the general initial description we learn that

Holmlock Shears is a man . . . of the sort one meets every day.
He is about fifty years of age and looks like a decent City clerk . . . He
has nothing to distinguish him from the ordinary respectable Londoner,

with his clean-shaven face and his somewhat heavy appearance, nothing except his terribly keen, bright, penetrating eyes. ......And then, of course, he is Holmlock Shears, that is to say, a sort of miracle of intuition, of insight, of perspicacity, of shrewdness. It is as though Nature had amused herself by taking the two most extraordinary types of detective that fiction had invented, Poe's Dupin and Gaboriau's Lecoq, in order to build up one in her own fashion, more extraordinary yet and more unusual. And upon my word, any one hearing of the adventures which have made the name of Holmlock Shears famous all over the world must feel inclined to ask if he is not a legendary person, a hero who has stepped straight from the brain of some novel-writer, of a   Conan Doyle, for instance.

The Doylean connection is thus explicitly indicated at the very outset; and – with the possible exception of the description of Holmes's physical appearance, which contrasts with that almost unnatural tallness and thinness noted by Watson in *A Study in Scarlet* – there is little that need trouble us about the similarities between Leblanc's 'Shears' and the Doylean Holmes. The fact that the Holmes of *The Arrest* is aged fifty would set the tale somewhere in the early years of the new century, which might bother the Sherlockian chronologists slightly, but is not unacceptable; and Leblanc notes the keenness of Holmes's eyes accurately – and even leaves him 'clean-shaven' when many Continental illustrators had saddled him with moustaches that would do credit to Baron Gruner.

....

Yet the respect for Holmes is not entirely unmixed, and there are hints of old and deep-seated geographical antipathies in Lupin's musings - ' Arsène Lupin *versus* Holmlock Shears! France *versus* England . . . Revenge for Trafalgar at last!' and this rather chauvinist view is evidently shared by the readers of the *Echo de France*, who relish the prospect of the local hero trouncing the representative of perfidious Albion. (Note also in this context that the 'two most extraordinary types of detective that fiction had invented' were both French! In passing, there is surely more than a hint of homage to Poe in the 'Dupin/Lupin' similarity?)

Certain aspects of Holmes are sometimes seen from a viewpoint which could not be anything other than French, as when,

161

suspecting an accomplice of Lupin's to be lurking in the shrubbery, Holmes 'felt to see if the cylinder of his revolver worked, loosened his dagger in its sheath and walked straight up to the enemy with the cool daring and the contempt of danger which made him so formidable.' Nobody could argue with the last sentiment, and we know that Holmes occasionally carried a revolver; but that 'dagger in its sheath' is an unquestionably Gallic touch.

The dagger apart, the character of the Holmes of *The Arrest* sometimes owes more to pure invention than to Conan Doyle. Thus, after Lupin has confined him to an empty house overnight, 'Shears' remarks -

"Pooh! . . . Schoolboy tricks! That's the only fault I have to find with Lupin . . . He's too childish, too fond of playing to the gallery . . . He's a street Arab at heart!"

"So you continue to take it calmly, Shears?"

"Quite calmly," replied Shears, in a voice shaking with rage. *"What's the use of being angry? I am so certain of having the last word!"*

(In the event, he did, as we shall see.) The Holmes of the Doylean canon has sometimes been portrayed as exhibiting fairly wide mood swings; and in the stories he occasionally shows exasperation at official incompetence, or criticises himself for not seeing the truth earlier: but he never spoke to Watson 'in a voice shaking with rage' because of some personal affront by some villain. This is exaggeration to the point of burlesque, and a similar burlesque element is apparent in the conclusion of that 'dagger in its sheath' episode just noted – the enemy in the shrubbery is, of course, Watson!

Watson (or 'Wilson' in the Lupin stories) is treated with similar disdain, if not downright contempt. Both Lupin and the narrator refer to him as 'the unspeakable Wilson,' but then that is probably accurate enough and understandable enough, considering that Lupin is, when all is said and done, a criminal – the less cultivated members of the Moriarty gang, for example, probably alluded to both Holmes and Watson as something rather less genteel than 'unspeakable' on more than one occasion.

More significant – and less satisfactory – than this mere vulgar abuse is the parody of Watson's character. Not merely the ' "Let's go!" cried Wilson, tossing off two glasses of whiskey in succession,' or his inevitable catch-phrase, 'Cigarette ashes?' at every mention of the word 'clue,' but a display of buffoonery that would put Nigel Bruce to shame: after being caught in the shrubbery, Watson allows Holmes to search the empty house, and inspect:

certain hardly perceptible chalk-marks, which formed figures which he put down in his note-book.

Escorted by Wilson, who seemed to take a particular interest in his work, he studied each room and found similar chalk-marks in two of the others. He also observed two circles on some oak panels, an arrow on a wainscoting and four figures on four steps of the staircase.

After an hour spent in this way, Wilson asked:

'"The figures are correct, are they not?"

"I don't know if they are correct," replied Shears, whose good temper had been restored by these discoveries, "but at any rate they mean something."

"Something very obvious," said Wilson. "They represent the number of planks in the floor."

"Oh!"

"Yes, as for the two circles, they indicate the panels sound hollow, as you can see by trying, and the arrow points to show the direction of the dinner-lift."

Holmlock Shears looked at him in admiration.

"Why, my dear chap, how do you know all this? Your perspicacity almost makes me ashamed of myself."

"Oh, it's very simple," said Wilson, bursting with delight. "I made those marks myself last night, in consequence of your instructions . . . or rather Lupin's instructions, as the letter I received from you came from him."

I have no doubt that, at that moment, Wilson was in greater danger than during his struggle with Shears in the shrubbery. Shears felt a fierce longing to wring his neck. Mastering himself with and effort, he gave a grin that pretended to be a smile and said:

"Well done, well done, that's an excellent piece of work; most useful. Have you wonderful powers of analysis and observation been exercised in any other direction? I may as well make use of the results obtained."

"No, that's all I did."

"What a pity! The start was so promising!" '

The attempts to make Watson look silly sometimes backfire, as when, after meeting Lupin in the restaurant, Holmes asks –

163

"Tell me, Wilson, what's your opinion: why was Lupin in that restaurant?"

Wilson, without hesitation, replied:

"To get some dinner."

"Wilson, the longer we work together, the more clearly I perceive the constant progress you are making. Upon my word, you're becoming amazing."

Wilson blushed with satisfaction in the dark; and Shears resumed:

"Yes, he went to get some dinner and then, most likely, to make sure if I am really going to Crozon, as Ganimard says I am . . . "

Holmes was wrong, and Watson was right: Lupin had indeed originally gone into the restaurant to dine, and for no other reason: he could not, and did not, know that Holmes would choose the same place in which to eat. The emphasis on burlesque is occasionally, as here, at the expense of logic.

As far as it goes, this parody element is quite funny; far more so than many deliberate attempts at humorous pastiche have been. But there is a hint not merely of parody but of downright contempt for Holmes: the worst aspect of the distorted relationship between Holmes and Watson in *The Arrest* is arguably Holmes's utter indifference when the two of them are involved in a small (and quite innocent) dispute with three young workmen, who refuse to step aside:

Shears, who was in a bad temper, pushed them back. There was a short scuffle. Shears put up his fists, struck one of the men in the chest and gave another a blow in the face, whereupon the two men desisted and walked away with the third.

"Ah," cried Shears, "I feel all the better for that! . . . My nerves were a bit strained . . .

He then realises that Watson's arm is injured

[Watson] tried to lift it, but could not. Shears felt it, gently at first, and then more roughly, "to see exactly," he said, "how much it hurts." It hurt exactly so much that Wilson, on being let to a neighbouring chemist's shop, experienced an immediate need to fall into a dead faint.

Watson is taken to hospital, where Holmes holds the broken arm, and tries to console his friend:

"That's all right, that's all right . . . Just a little patience, old

chap . . . in five or six weeks, you won't know that you've been hurt . . ." . . . He interrupted himself suddenly, dropped the arm, which gave Wilson such a shock of pain that the poor wretch fainted once more . . .

Later yet, Holmes calls to see how Watson is going on:

"Oh, when I think that, just now, in the street, those ruffians might have broken my arm as well as yours! What do you say to that, Wilson?"

'Wilson simply shuddered at the horrid thought . . .

Holmes then starts to leave:

"Take care of yourself old chap. Your task, henceforth, will consist in keeping two or three of Lupin's men busy. They will waste their time waiting for me to come and enquire after you. It's a confidential task."

"Thank you ever so much," said Wilson, gratefully. "I shall do my best to perform it conscientiously. So you are not coming back?"'

"Why should I?" asked Shears, coldly.

"No . . . you're quite right . . . you're quite right . . . I'm going on as well as can be expected. You might do one thing for me, Holmlock: give me a drink."

"A drink?"

"Yes, I'm parched with thirst; and this fever of mine . . ."

"Why, of course! Wait a minute . . ."

He fumbled about among some bottles, came upon a packet of tobacco, filled and lit his pipe, and suddenly, as though he had not even heard his friend's request, walked away, while old chap cast longing glances at the water-bottle beyond his reach.

Some commentators have insisted on taking Holmes's apparent forgetting Watson's existence in *The Dying Detective* quite literally, although many do not; but again Holmes's indifference in *The Arrest* is exaggerated to the point where it ceases to be funny. It also contrasts unfavourably with Holmes's reaction to Watson's injury in *The Three Garridebs*. (Although that particular story was not published until 1924, and it is tempting – though it may be quite incorrect – to see the uncharacteristic slipping of the mask to reveal the human face as being Conan Doyle's trying to counter the inaccuracies of such pastiches as *The Arrest*.)

. . . .

If *The Arrest* were a humorous pastiche and nothing more, it would work quite well, despite the exaggerations; but in fact it has a serious, and quite well constructed basis, the elaborate forward planning by Lupin, and the struggle between him and Holmes, which is for the most part blessedly devoid of the worst elements of excessive jocularity which characterise the early chapters.

Holmes's strategy for the actual arrest of Lupin might raise some eyebrows: Holmes has to threaten to implicate Lupin's accomplice, the more or less innocent Mlle. Destange. This might strike some readers as ungentlemanly conduct, not the sort of thing we expect of Holmes. Lupin is handed over to the official police, and, as one might expect, promptly escapes!

In the second section of *The Arrest*, subtitled *The Jewish Lamp*, Holmes is once more in a position to arrest Lupin, but Lupin neatly turns the tables. This time it is Lupin who threatens to expose a lady's honor. It turns out that she had written some injudicious letters to a persuasive villain, and been blackmailed into helping with the theft. (Shades of *Charles Augustus Milverton*, here!) Holmes, though he had been happy enough to implicate Mlle. Destange, cannot possibly see the wife of a nobleman pilloried in the press, and allows Lupin to go free, thereby to some extent redeeming himself from the earlier suspicion of caddish behaviour.

There is no record in the study of Conan Doyle by Hesketh Pearson – arguably the best of the biographers – that Leblanc and Conan Doyle ever actually met. Leblanc knew about Conan Doyle and Sherlock Holmes; and Conan Doyle knew about Leblanc and Lupin, for in the article, 'Some Personalia about Sherlock Holmes,' Conan Doyle tells how he was once taking part in an amateur billiards competition, and was handed a small packet which had been left for him. The packet contained an ordinary cube of billiard chalk, which Conan Doyle used for some months, until 'the face of the chalk crumpled in, and I found it was hollow. From the recess thus exposed I drew out a small slip of paper with the words, "From Arsène Lupin to Sherlock Holmes." Imagine the state of mind of the joker who took such trouble to accomplish such a result!' It is tempting – though probably wildly inaccurate – to think that the present was from Leblanc himself, for he seems to have possessed a somewhat pawky sense of humour.

It is unclear how Conan Doyle regarded the Lupin parodies: it is known that Conan Doyle felt that the Holmesian canon detracted from his literary reputation, and the various pastiches and parodies emphasised Holmes at the expense of Conan Doyle's other creations. It is said that imitation is the sincerest form of flattery, and Conan Doyle would surely have been more (or less) than human if he did not feel at least some pride at the compliment paid by Leblanc and Lupin; but this emotion may not have been entirely unmixed, and there is an interesting incident in *The Illustrious Client* when Gruner asks Holmes, 'did you know Le Brun, the French agent?' and Holmes replies, 'I heard that he was a beaten by some Apaches in the Montmartre district and crippled for like.' There is an interesting parallel here with the attack on 'Shears' and 'Wilson' in *The Arrest*; but is there anything more? 'Le Brun' is, after all, not so very different from 'Leblanc'; did Conan Doyle consciously (or otherwise) perhaps feel that the 'joker' Leblanc deserved a jolly good thrashing? It is an interesting thought, but at this distance in time it must remain merely speculative.

Leblanc certainly had a high regard for Conan Doyle and the genuine Holmes; in an obituary in *Les Annales Politiques et Littèraires* in 1930, he wrote of Conan Doyle (in Dr Kai-ho Mah's translation):

Conan Doyle had a lot of [talent], and of the best and most literary kind . . . But he has a still more than talent; he has the power of creation, since he created so representative a type as Sherlock Holmes . . . I defy any reader . . . not to be taken in by a Conan Doyle story from the very first pages, and not to read it to the last lime. . . The Master has a hard grip. . . It is very much due to him that the adventure story has regained a place of honour. . . Let us be grateful to the writer, Conan Doyle. Let us salute the great lesson of energy and mastery given us by the extraordinary Sherlock Holmes. And let us not forget all that is enjoyable and profoundly comic in the ineffable Watson. The man who has just died is not about to die in the memory of men.

Lupin, too, admired Holmes; in the last section of *The Arrest* – now entirely devoid of those elements of parody which mar earlier chapters – Lupin addresses Holmes almost in terms of affection, and constantly refers to him as 'maître' in a manner which recalls le Villard's praise in *The Sign of Four* - 'stray magnifiques, coup-demaîtres and tours-de-force . . . "He speaks as a pupil to his master," said I.'

It is perhaps not too difficult to believe that if Holmes – the real, the Doylean (the only!) Holmes – had actually met Lupin, he would have done exactly what 'Holmlock Shears' did, and let the lovable French rogue go free to fight another day.

References

1 Arthur Conan Doyle, 'Some Personalia about Sherlock Holmes,' (Peter Haining, [ed.]

2 *The Final Adventures of Sherlock Holmes: Completing the Canon* (London: Star, 1981), pp.160-168.

3 Hamada Tomoaki, private communication.

4 Hasebe Fumichika, 'Maurice Leblanc', Oubei Suirishousetsu Honyakushi [A History of Translations of Western Mysteries], Tokyo, Hon no Zasshi Sha, 1992, pp156-169.

5 Hall, Trevor H., 'Sherlock Holmes and Arsene Lupin', *Sherlock Holmes and his Creator*, London, Duckworth, 1978, pp56-69.

6 Leblanc, Maurice, 'A propos de Conan Doyle,' *Les Annales Politiques et Littèraires*, No.95 (1 August, 1930), p.111.

7 ---------, (trans. Kai-ho Mah), 'Apropos of Conan Doyle,' *BSJ*, vol.21, No.2, (June, 1971), pp. 100-102.

8 Redmond Donald A., *Sherlock Holmes: a Study in Sources*, Kingston and Montreal, McGill-Queen's University Press, 1982, p217; and private communication.

9 Steinbrunner, Chris, Penzler, Otto, Lachman, Marvin, Shibuk, Charles (eds), *Encyclopaedia of Mystery and Detection*, San Diego, New York, London, Harcourt Bruce Jovanovitch, 1976, pp242; 253-355.

40 Takehara Seichi, private communication.

(The writers with to thank Kasahara Seiji, who not only drew their attention to the French film of *Les Aventures*, but also generously provided some memorabilia connected with it; Hamada Tomoaki and Donald A. Redmond, for their comments, and Takehara Seichi for his original suggestion.)

(*The Ritual* No.19, Spring 1997)

Dr Watson's Title

'Being a reprint from reminiscences of John H Watson, MD, late of the Army Medical Department' is the first line of *A Study in Scarlet*, the first volume of the Canon. This is the first time we, the readers, encounter John H Watson, MD. Watson also wrote clearly that 'In 1878, I took my degree of Doctor of Medicine of the University of London.'

However, there is an interesting opinion in the latest Japanese translation of A Study in Scarlet by Dr Kobayashi Tsukasa and Mrs Higashiyama Akane.[1] These translators considered that John H Watson did not take his MD, and they consequently changed the sub-title to the story to 'being a reprint from the reminiscences of John H Watson, MB . . .' Throughout the Canon, Holmes and other characters address Watson as 'Dr,' but Kobayashi and Higashiyama contend that his was merely a courtesy title, such as James Mortimer, MRCS, honestly refused (in *The Hound of the Baskervilles.*)

It is obviously a serious matter to change one of the basic tenets of the Canon in this major fashion. Kobayashi and Higashiyama's decision was made on the basis of an article published in Japan. 'Watson no Keireki [Watson's Career]' by Ikoma Hisaaki, MD, who was assistant professor in the Medical Department of Tottori University, and who studied for a year at London University.[2] Ikoma describes medical education in the late Victorian era, pointing out Holmes's reference to Watson as being 'only a general practitioner with very limited experience and mediocre qualifications,' in 'The Dying Detective,' and noting that experimentation on animals for the degree of MD was severely restricted by law from 1876. We (HY and JH) consider the second point a minor one; but Ikoma's point about 'mediocre qualifications' needs some response.

Helen Simpson[3] also considered that Watson 'Took the degree of MD of London, an extremely difficult one to obtain.' (Of course Simpson does not deny Watson's claim to MD; indeed, if she is correct, he was well qualified rather than the reverse.)

However, David Young's opinion is 'an MD was not given away in 1878 but it would be wrong to bestow upon it the status and level of difficulty that it has today.' [4]

There are thus two schools of thought as to the sheer difficulty of Watson, or anyone else, being able to qualify as an MD. In an attempt to judge the level of difficulty, HY examined the titles and qualifications of all the physicians and surgeons in the hospitals in London in 1888, as listed in *Dickens's Dictionary of London, 1888.* (5; and see Tables I and II.)

There were 372 physicians, of whom 225 (60%) had an MD, some with other qualifications, and 124 (33%) had 'Dr,' again some with other qualifications. The total with either 'Dr' or MD is thus 93%; it is possible that some of those styled 'Dr' did not in fact possess an MD, but that 'Dr' was a courtesy title. However, the Dictionary is fairly detailed, so it seems unlikely that 'Dr' was a courtesy title in every case. Even if it were, a majority of physicians definitely had an MD.

There were 348 surgeons, including anaesthetists, oculists and surgical registrars. Of these, 157 (45%) had no style or title, 122 (35%) had FRCS or FRS, sometimes with other degrees, etc; 25 (7%) had MRCS; 12 (3%) had MB or MS or BS; 6 (2%) had 'Dr'; and 27 (8%) had MD. (And again, in all cases some had other degrees, etc.) The total with either 'Dr' or MD was thus 33 (10%).

And if we exclude those whose titles and degrees are not specifically listed, the total with an MD is 14%, and with 'Dr' or an MD 17%. So where the title or degree is listed, nearly one in five surgeons is 'Dr' or an MD.

In an attempt to ensure that the figures were as representative as possible, JH submitted the 1881 listing to a similar, though somewhat less rigorous, analysis, and found that 69% of physicians and 11% of surgeons had an MD.[a]

These figures show that taking an MD was quite common in the Victorian era for physicians, and it was by no means uncommon for surgeons. Young[4] pointed out that 'whilst it is relatively uncommon to find British General Practitioners with an MD today, this was not the case in the 19th century.' The routes to an MD were the same in London as Scotland, ie two years hospital experience and a thesis, or five years general practice and thesis or dissertation. Sir Arthur Conan Doyle graduated from Edinburgh with an MB in 1881, and after

170

general practice for five years he took an MD from Edinburgh with 'An Essay upon the Vasomotor Changes in Tabes Dorsalis.'[6] The Literary Agent could gain an MD, so why not our Watson? There were only 4% of physicians and 3% of surgeons who worked with an MB. Contrary to the opinion of Ikoma and others, doctors with an MB were scarcer than those with an MD.

Holmes's statement in 'The Dying Detective' about Watson's 'mediocre qualifications' was intended to keep Watson at arm's length, or further, and not to be taken literally; Holmes also says, in *The Hound of the Baskervilles*:

'Come, come, we are not so far wrong after all. . . And now, Dr James Mortimer - '

'Mister, sir, Mister, a humble MRCS.'

'And a man of precise mind, evidently.'

'A dabbler in science, Mr Holmes. . . I presume that it is Mr Sherlock Holmes whom I am addressing and not - '

'No, this is my friend Dr Watson.'

James Mortimer honestly refused to be called by the courtesy title 'Dr,' but at the same time Watson as called such by Holmes, almost in the same breath as Holmes's implied praise for a 'man of precise mind,' and nobody objected to 'Dr Watson.' If Watson's title 'Dr' were merely a courtesy title, he would surely have been arrogant and pompous not to do what Mortimer did and complain? And that does not match our image of Watson as an honest man.

There is an apocryphal reference to Watson's title in 'The Field Bazaar,' which might on the face of things tend to support Kobayashi and Higashiyama's point of view. Holmes says, 'I gathered from the use of the word 'Doctor' upon the address, to which, as a Bachelor of Medicine, you have no legal claim. . .' William Baring-Gould referred to this when he said that 'Doubts that Watson was, in fact, a *Doctor* of Medicine have been cast by many commentators – not the least of them Conan Doyle' in 'The Field Bazaar.'[7] However, John Hall wrote: 'Even if Watson had graduated with an MB from Edinburgh. . . then if the Edinburgh authorities were so scrupulous as to titles [as Holmes is suggesting in the story] they would surely be inclined to style him 'Dr' on account of the later (London) degree. . . the entire episode may safely be dismissed a invention.'[8] (And moreover Young, in the article already noted[4], makes the point that the London university regulations required that candidates for an MD should have taken their first

171

medical degrees at London, further reinforcing the apocryphal nature of 'The Field Bazaar.') It is rather odd that Baring-Gould should ignore the rule that the Canon is the first, and perhaps the only, source; 'The Field Bazaar' is interesting, but we cannot legitimately regard it as evidence of anything.

Hall also discussed Watson's experience at Bart's. 'Why did Watson, after having been a house-surgeon[b] at some point, then take the medical degree, MD, instead of a Master of Surgery, MCh? This takes us into the realms of speculation rather than reasoning, but there are surely enough acceptable reasons for us not to worry about it too much. Perhaps he had originally intended to specialise in surgery, but found medicine more congenial – he may have preferred his patients vertical rather than horizontal. Or perhaps he realised that an army doctor would need to be master of all trades, and thus took in surgery almost in passing, as it were. In the latter event, it would say much about his medical abilities, which are sometimes underrated.'[9]

This assumes that it was an uncommon thing for a house-surgeon to take an MD. However, as we have seen, this is incorrect; one in two Victorian surgeons had 'Dr' or MD. Even if Watson had originally intended to specialise in surgery, he may well have taken and MD. In 1888 there were 12 surgeons with MD alone after their names, but they may well also have had FRCS or MRCS, etc, and so may Watson! The latter titles may well have been omitted from the title page of A Study in Scarlet as it was not a formal medical paper. Even in our Table II, every surgeon ought to have BCh or similar, but not all of them claim this. Some write FRCS, some MB, FRCS, etc. Conan Doyle himself was Arthur Conan Doyle, MB, CM, MD, but he frequently wrote 'Arthur Conan Doyle, MD.' His own fashion of writing his qualifications changed with time:

A Conan Doyle, MB, CM (*The Lancet,* November, 1884)

A Conan Doyle, MD (*Portsmouth Evening News,* May, 1886)

A Conan Doyle, MD (*Light,* July, 1887)

A Conan Doyle, MD, CM (*Portsmouth Evening Mail,* July, 1887)

A Conan Doyle, MD (*Daily Telegraph,* November, 1890)

A Conan Doyle, MD (*BMJ,* July, 1900)

Arthur Conan Doyle, MD (Edin), LLD (*Journal of the Society for Psychical Research,* March, 1930) [10]

Conan Doyle took his MD in 1885, and this was added to his MB, CM; but Conan Doyle seldom wrote his degrees in full, even when writing to the *BMJ*. (The 'LLD' noted in 1930 was 'an honorary doctorate. . . from his Alma Mater'[11].) Watson must have had an MB from London, in order to take the degree of MD, as noted by Young[4]. Watson would also take a first degree in surgery, as a matter of course, and he may very well have had for example, MRCS as well, but simply not recorded the fact, any more than Conan Doyle listed all his entitlements.

Let us now consider Watson's army career in terms of 'real life' army men. Our good friend Major John Whitehouse kindly sent us some photocopies of publications of the Army Medical Corps, and these give the names of some army doctors. The author of 'Personal Recollections of the Afghan Campaigns of 1878-79-80. . . etc' is 'Surgeon-General GJH Evatt, MD'[12], while in another paper we find 'Surgeon-General T Crawford, MD, Principal Medical Officer, Her Majesty's Forces in Bengal.'[13] These two men fought in the second Afghan War in which Watson was injured, and both were surgeons with an MD. There is clearly nothing out of the ordinary in Watson's also being an army surgeon with an MD. As Young pointed out, the reason why Watson chose to join the Army Medical Department was just that he 'did not have the capital to buy into a good practice, and life as an assistant to another doctor was likely to be boring and not very renumerative.'[4]

Ikoma[2] also thinks that Watson could not have practised surgery at all, as he was not FRCS. Ikoma concluded that Watson was not a surgeon but a general practitioner. Again, we can look at examples from real life. The following is a fairly typical career of a surgeon who studied in London. He was Takagi Kanehiro (1849-1920), the first commander of the Japanese Royal Navy Medical Corps. Takagi was a son of a samurai, and studied medicine privately in Japan under an English doctor. Takagi was sent to Britain by the Japanese Government to study the latest medical techniques for the Royal (Japanese) Navy. He was a distinguished student, and received many awards.

1875, Sept: Entered St Thomas Hospital
1877: Clinical Clerk
1878, Jan: Secretary of Obstetrics
     April: MRCS

June: LRCP (Licentiate of the Royal College of Physicians); house physician

1879: house surgeon

1880, May: FRCS, returned to Japan

Conan Doyle's own career may be summarised:

1876, Oct: Entered Edinburgh Medical School

1878, summer: Student Assistant to Dr Richardson, Sheffield, and Dr Elliot, Shropshire

1879, summer: Student Assistant to Dr Hoarse, Birmingham

1880: Ship's Surgeon on Arctic Whaler *Hope* for seven months

1880: Student Assistant to Dr Hoare, Birmingham

1881, August: Graduated MB and CM

1885, July: MD, Edinburgh[14]

Ikoma wrote that FRCS was given to only a few outstanding surgeons, and only those who were FRCS or FRCP could be consultants. As we have seen, only 35% of hospital surgeons were FRCS in 1888 (43% in 1881). As for the 'outstanding' aspects, Takagi graduated FRCS a mere two years after his MRCS and LRCP, and only one year after his appointment as house surgeon. True, Takagi was an indeed an outstanding man, but Conan Doyle's own career is not so very far behind. One of the important rulings of the General Medical Council was that 'medical education should not be less than your years.'[14] If Takagi had studied at London he would have graduated MB in 1879, the year he became house surgeon and Conan Doyle's MB, CM was caused by 'time taken out to earn money.'[10] Conan Doyle worked as a student assistant in the summer holidays, and was a ship's surgeon on the Arctic whaler *Hope* for seven months in 1880, a year before he graduated.[15] Hall thought that Watson studied eight years at London[16], and thus it is perfectly possible for him to have taken his MD after taking, say, FRCS. (Although Hall's 'eight years' is based on the classic view that Watson took his MD by purely hospital work; Hall is now inclined to follow David Young and credit Watson with four or five years for the first degree, and five in general practice thereafter. This, however, does not alter the general argument here.)

Again, we could argue from Conan Doyle's own surgical experience. Although the sign on his door read, 'Dr Conan Doyle, Physician and Surgeon,' he was a general practitioner.[17] And we know that Conan Doyle performed some simple operations; he wrote in his biography: 'I went up country once, and operated upon an old fellow's nose which had contracted cancer through his holding the bowl of a short clay pipe immediately beneath it. I left him with an aristocratic, not to say supercilious, organ, which was the wonder of the village and might have been the foundation of my fame.'[18]

Rodin and Key wrote: 'This account indicates a good knowledge of cancer causation and surprising surgical skills for a recent graduate.'[19] Just as his sign indicated, Conan Doyle worked as a surgeon. Ikoma makes the point that there are no accounts of Watson's performing any operations in the Canon, but the stories are detective, not medical, tales. Watson was an army surgeon, faced with a blood thirsty enemy in Afghanistan, and it is legitimate to enquire whether his experience was really limited to ladling out cough syrup, or dispensing brandy for ladies who had swooned with the heat. It is surely clear that Watson would have performed surgical operations where these were needed. If David Young's theory that Watson gained his MD by five years in general practice is correct (and there are good reasons for thinking it is, as it enables us to explain some otherwise odd episodes in Watson's life, eg his visiting Australia) then commonsense alone suggests that the probability that Watson had some surgical experience becomes even greater, particularly if we do locate some part of his eventful like in the wilds of Australia, say, where there would be little other medical aid available.

In any event, we know that Watson spent some time as a house surgeon at Bart's, that is unless we disregard that part of the Canon as well. Note also that whether Watson was a house surgeon as part of his hospital studies for the MD, or just working on a temporary basis as Young suggests, still the authorities at Bart's chose Watson from however many applicants there may have been; scarcely an indication of mediocre qualifications or experience there!

Whether we look at the evidence of the Canon itself, or at the statistics of Victorian medical qualifications, or at the life of his creator, the answer is the same. It is safe to say that Watson as an army surgeon and general practitioner with and MD and other qualifications, though we can only speculate as to these. The Canon is right, as always.

(a) The figures of course reflect the fact that these men (and a few women) were on the hospital staff; it would be wrong to imply or infer that the proportions were necessarily reflected amongst general practitioners. However, the staff listed include relatively junior registrars, etc, so the figures may reasonably be regarded as a fair cross-section. (And it may well have been that the juniors with MRCS or MB were working towards Fellowship and MD respectively!

The fall in the % with MD between 1881 and 1888 is intriguing; it is tempting to see it as reflecting an increase in the examiner's standards, but this is almost too facile.

(b) There seems no dispute on this point, although the 'classic' view has been that it was part of Watson's two (or more) years hospital work; while Young [4] considers that it may have been merely a short-term post as part of his (five years) general practice.

TABLE I; Physicians at London hospitals, 1888

No qualifications noted	4	4	1%
MA, MD, MRCP	1		
KCB, MD, FRCP, DCL,	1		
MD, KCB	1		
MD	140		
MD, MRCS	4		
MD, MA	3	225	60%
MD, FRS	11		
MD, MRCP	12		
AB, MD, MRCP	1		
BA, MD	1		
MD, MRCP, DCL	1		
MD, FRCP	33		
MD, KCSI	1		
MD, KCMG	1		
MD, FRCP, FRS	8		
MD, FRCS	2		
MD, BS	2		
MD, CB	1		
MD, LRCP	1		
Dr	113		
Dr, MRCP	3	124	33%
Dr. FRCP	4		
Dr. FRS	4		
MB	11		
MB, MRCP	1		
BA, MB	1	15	4%
MB, BSc	1		
MB, FRS	1		
MRCP	1		
FRS, FRCP	1		
LKQ, CPI	1	4	1%
LRQ, CPI	1		
	total 372		

TABLE II;   Surgeons at London hospitals, 1888

				disregarding 'no title'
No title, etc, listed	157	157	45%	
Dr	6	6	2%	
MD	12			
MD, FRCS	7	27	8%	17%
MD, MRCS	5			
MD, CM	1			
MD, CB	1			
MD, BSC,	1			
FRCS	83			
FRCSE	1			
MB, FRCS	10	105	30%	55%
BA, MB,	1			
MA, FRCS	3			
FRCS, FRS	5			
MB, MS,	1			
BM, BS,	1			
FRS	14			
FRS, FLS	1	16	5%	8%
DCL, FRS	1			
MRCS	18			
MRCS, LRCP	2	25	7%	13%
MB, MRCS	4			
MA, MRCS	1			
MB	4			
MB, CM	1			
MB, MC	4	12	3%	6%
MS	2			
BS	1			
Total	total 348			

178

References

1 Arthur Conan Doyle, *Hiiro no Shusaku*, translated by Kobayashi Tsukasa and Higashiyama Akane (Tokyo: Kawade Shobo Shinsha, 1997.) [Translation of *A Study in Scarlet* in the OUP edition, 1993.]

2 Ikoma Hisaaki, 'Watson no Keireki {Watson's Career],' *Sherlock Holmes Sanka*, ed. Kobayashi Tsukasa and Higashiyama Akane (Tokyo: Rippu Shobo, 1980), pp.153-171}.

3 Helen Simpson, 'Medical Career and Capabilities of Dr John H Watson,' *Baker Street Studies*, ed H W Bell (New York: Otto Penzler Books, 1995), pp.35-62).

4 David Young, 'John H Watson: Medical School and Beyond,' *The New Baker Street Pillar Box*, No.29, Feb, 1997.

5 *Dicken's Dictionary of London, 1888* (Moretonhampstead: Old House Books, 1993.) [A facsimile of the 1888 edition.]

6 Christopher Redmond, *A Sherlock Holmes Handbook* (Toronto: Simon and Pierre, 1993), p.71.

7 William S Baring-Gould, *The Annotated Sherlock Holmes*, Vol.1 (New York: Clarkson N Potter, 1967), P.74.

8 John Hall, *Unexplored Possibilities* (Leeds, Tai Xu Press, 1995), P.12

9 Hall, *ibid*, p.18.

10 Arthur Conan Doyle, *Letters to the Press*, eds. John Michael Gibson and Richard Lancelyn Green (London: Secker and Warburg, 1986.)

11 E Alvin Rodin and Jack D Key, *Medical Casebook of Doctor Arthur Conan Doyle* (Malabar: Robert E Krieger, 1984), p.302.

12 GJH Evatt, 'Personal Recollections of the Afghan Campaigns of 1878-79-80: The "Death March" through the Khyber Pass in the Afghan Campaign,' *Journal of the Royal Army Medical Corps*, Vol.10, 1905, pp.276-291.

13 T Crawford, 'Special Report on the Hospital Organisation, Sanitation, and Medical History of the Wars in Afghanistan, 1879-79-80,' *Army Medical Department Report for the Year 1880*, Vol.22, 1882.

14 Rodin and Key, *op cit*, p.7.

15 Rodin and Key, *op cit*, pp.353-354.

16 Hall, *op cit*, p.83.

17 Naganuma Kohki, *Sherlock Holmes no Chie* (Tokyo: Asahi-shinbun-sha, 1961.)

18 Arthur Conan Doyle, *Memories and Adventures* (London: Hodder and Stoughton, 1924.)

19 Rodin and Key, *op cit*, p.27.

(*The World of Holmes* No.30, 2007, in Japanese)

Questions on Holmes

This is a project devised by HY, whereby each participant asks up to three questions and the other tries – tries! – to answer them; the first then comments on the answers, etc, until (with luck) some consensus in reached.

1: "A SCANDAL IN BOHEMIA"

Hirayama Yuichi (HY): Why did Holmes not know that Watson intended to go into practice after marrying Mary Morstan?

John Hall (JH): This is a difficult one, especially if we believe that the two men had been in partnership in Holmes's detective business. The logical reading is that the two men were <u>not</u> as close as is sometimes imagined, and thus Watson did not discuss his financial state with Holmes. But even that is not the whole story, for if Holmes were such a brilliant detective, then he would surely have deduced that Watson intended – and in fact <u>needed</u> – to go back into practice in order to make a living. The logical conclusion from that is that Holmes believed that Watson could support himself and Mrs Watson <u>without</u> going into practice.

How could that have been? Holmes must have been aware that Watson had some other source of income than medical practice, but what source? Holmes, in common with Watson's readers, knew that Watson had a 'wound pension' of some sort; but Watson had complained at the opening of *A Study in Scarlet* that the pension was inadequate even for an unmarried man, so it is reasonable to suppose that it would be pitifully inadequate for a married man and his wife (and possibly children, if things turned out that way.)

I have long believed that Watson supplemented his army pension – from the earliest days of his acquaintance with Holmes – by writing. Watson himself labels *A Study in Scarlet* as a reprint from his reminiscences, and that alone suggests that he was already working on an autobiographical opus. Then we have the hints of possible press reports of Holmes's cases: Mycroft speaks of hearing of Sherlock everywhere since Watson became his chronicler and this at a time when only *A Study in Scarlet* and *The Sign of Four* had been published.

But Another possibility is that Watson was a <u>paid</u> full partner in Holmes's detective business up until 1887 or '88 and the marriage to Mary Morstan. Ian MacQueen (*Sherlock Holmes Detected*) thinks that Watson became a partner after 1894 and the Return, when Watson sold his practice to Dr Verner, at Holmes's request. I think that Watson as already a partner before his marriage, and the money from that enabled him to buy the first practice in Paddington.

If that were so, then Holmes would know Watson had some money in the bank, and so he might think that Watson had enough to 'retire' and write his books, instead of going into medical practice.

JH: Why did Holmes and Watson lose touch after Watson's marriage?

HY: It reads very much as if the relationship cooled off to some extent when Watson married Mary Morstan. Had that not been the case, Watson would surely have sent an invitation to the wedding to Holmes; and Watson would also have sent a note to Holmes to say that he (Watson) as going into practice, if only because Holmes was a prospective patient. The almost total lack of contact suggests that the friendship as not then as strong as it had once been.

When Holmes heard of Watson's intention to marry Mary, he said, 'I really cannot congratulate you.' He then tried to excuse this coldness with, 'love is an emotional thing, and whatever is emotional is opposed to that cold reason which I place above all things. I should never marry myself, lest I bias my judgement.' But it was Watson's marriage that was at issue, not Holmes's; nobody was suggesting that Holmes should get married! And Watson was not one for 'cold reason.' It seems clear that Holmes did not want Watson to get married. It is possible that Holmes felt, as he later felt in 'The Blanched Soldier,' that Watson had 'deserted' him.

Watson wrote of Holmes's reaction when Watson returned to 221b that 'His manner was not effusive. It seldom was; but he was glad, I think, to see me. With hardly a word spoken, but with a kindly eye, he waved me to an armchair, threw across his case of cigars, and indicated a spirit case and a gasogene. . . Then he stood before the fire and looked me over in his singular introspective fashion.' This is surely the manner of a man who regretted his previous churlishness, but could not bring himself to say 'Sorry.' Watson showed his magnanimity and accepted Holmes's wordless apology. Holmes would have been relieved at his friend's reaction. When he said, 'Wedlock suits you,' that was his blessing on Watson's marriage.

It may be that Mary's attitude to Holmes was less than friendly. In 'The Stock-broker's Clerk,' Holmes visits the Watsons, but Mary does not come to see him; and odd way for her to behave. However, in 'The Boscombe Valley Mystery,' Mary actively encourages Watson to take an interest in the case, so perhaps Mary too had second thoughts?

I think that perhaps Watson's remark that 'There was but one woman to [Holmes], and that woman was the late Irene Adler' was Watson's small revenge for Holmes's talk about emotion biasing one's judgement.

HY: Why did Irene marry Norton with such haste and apparent lack of preparation?

JH: Of all the many problems associated with 'A Scandal in Bohemia,' the whole question of the circumstances of the wedding between Irene Adler and Godfrey Norton must be one of the most puzzling.

Let us begin at the end, and look at the ceremony itself. Sherlock Holmes stated that he had gone into the church after Irene

Adler and Godfrey Norton. 'There was not a soul there save the two whom [Holmes] had followed and a surpliced clergyman, who seemed to be expostulating with them.' Godfrey Norton then seized Holmes, and insisted that he act as a witness. 'It seems that there had been some informality about their licence, that the clergyman absolutely refused to marry them without a witness of some sort, and that [Holmes's] lucky appearance saved' the day. It had to be done quickly, even then, for it was approaching noon, and the wedding would not be legal were it not celebrated before twelve.

Now, this is utter rubbish. Informality or no informality, the clergyman could not marry them without two witnesses. If Holmes were one, who then was the other? We might suggest Irene's coachman, or the cabbie who drove Norton to the church; or perhaps some minor church official, the sexton or gravedigger might have been present? Might: but we know they were not, for Holmes said as much: 'There was not a soul there save' the three we know about. Moreover, as a witness, Holmes would not have to '[mumble] responses and [vouch] for things of which [he] knew nothing,' as he claimed.

The mention of the time of day is also significant. Watson says that 'A Scandal in Bohemia' took place in March 1888, although some chronologists might favour 1889. Up until 1886, marriages did indeed have to be celebrated before noon. But in that year the rules were changed, and the cut-off time was 3 pm, except for Roman Catholic church (and the name is fictitious so it is possible) then Holmes might have had to mumble responses, not as a witness but as an acolyte, assisting the priest. This seems promising, but there are two powerful objections to it. The first is that of the witnesses, for if Holmes were assisting the priest there would not even be one, let alone the requisite two; and the second is the sheer implausibility of a priest's being so ill-prepared that he did not have his own acolyte ready and waiting.

The same lack of preparation seems to have extended to the bride and groom, for their sudden departure smacks of complete ignorance not merely of the structure and content of the ceremony, but of the very fact that it was taking place at all! Watson is sometimes accused of not knowing what day it was, or whether he was married or not, but presumably even he managed to turn up on time for his own wedding! Are we seriously to believe that Norton, a lawyer, failed to remember the time of his?

It surely looks very much as if the wedding were a complete fake. If so, for whose benefit was it staged? One possibility is that Norton, for whatever reason, wished to fool Irene. How believable is that? Norton is a curious character: a successful lawyer who yet could abandon his practice at a moment's notice and catch the 5.15 am train from Charing Cross to the Continent, never to return. There might be more to Norton than at first appears, and we shall consider him again in a moment; but would Irene be so easily fooled? Remember that she had set her sights on a king. She wanted to marry the King of Bohemia; and then she changed her mind and married – if she did indeed marry – Norton. Would anyone so marriage-oriented be satisfied with a pale simulacrum? Remember too that Irene was an 'adventuress.' She relied upon her feminine charms for her living, and experience tells us (or at least it tells me! I cannot of course speak for my distinguished and happily married Japanese colleague) that such ladies are not the sort to be easily fooled.

No: of the four people present in the church, only one had so little knowledge of marriage that fooling him was easy, and that one was the confirmed bachelor and misogynist, Mr Sherlock Holmes.

Hard to believe? Consider, then, the beginning of the episode, and that very hasty departure for the church. Norton charges out of Irene's house, calls a cab at the top of his voice, roars out his destination – 'Gross and Hankey's [presumably a jeweller's, so Norton had not even bothered to buy the ring at this point, if you believe that!] . . . and then to the Church of St. Monica' – and thunders off. Before we can collect our scattered wits, here comes Irene herself, also in a bit of a rush – and also announcing 'The Church of St. Monica,' just in case anyone missed it first time.

It would look good on television, would it not, or perhaps in Technicolor on the big screen? And that it what it is: pure theatre. Not merely dramatic, but melodramatic, indeed positively transpontine. Again we must ask: for whose benefit was this performance? The answer is surely obvious. It was for Holmes' benefit, to pique his curiosity, and ensure that he would follow the happy couple to the church and witness (in every sense!) their wedding.

Unlikely? This is what Irene Adler herself wrote to Holmes: 'I had been warned against you months ago. I had been told that if the King employed an agent it would certainly be you.' And then Holmes himself had been none too discreet. He had gone along to the mews stables and made enquiries about Irene. Of course, Holmes himself thought that he was being very clever! But it is not at all out of the question that one of those cabbies who 'had driven [Norton] home a dozen times from Serpentine-mews' had mentioned the inquisitive stranger to Norton later that morning – 'Bloke asking about you earlier today, sir' – or indeed that John, Irene's coachman, was present and taking careful note, and that he alerted Irene to Holmes's presence.

Irene herself might easily have checked to see if the house was under observation. In one of her disguises, she might very well have been watching the watchful Holmes, who saw merely Norton 'in the windows of the sitting-room, pacing up and down, talking excitedly, and waving his arms. Of her [ie Irene] I could see nothing.' [Emphasis added.] Holmes did not see Irene because she was not there! She was outside, watching Holmes. (In passing, note again the very over-the-top performance by Norton. What on earth did Holmes image the lawyer to be saying that needed wavings of arms, excited talking, and all the rest?)

If the wedding were a fake, then the clergyman must have been in on it. That is not a real problem. He might have been a friend of Norton's, one professional man might quite easily know another, who had been persuaded to take part in a 'joke.' Or he might not have been a clergyman at all, but an actor hired for a couple of hours, just as Holmes himself later hired a whole streetful of people to fool Irene. (If fool her he did.) The church was a quiet one, Holmes himself said that only three people were in there when he entered it. It may well have been that Irene and Norton selected that particular church because they knew the clergyman would be away visiting the sick, or some similar parish duty, at the time in question.

Given that the whole performance was for Holmes's benefit, what was the object of it all? Clearly, to put him off, to make him, and the King, believe that the case was closed, the problem solved.

If so, it failed, for Holmes staged his own little performance with the smoke rocket. There are two possibilities here. One is that Irene really as inept as she seems; having gone through the 'marriage' ceremony she may indeed have believed that she would then be safe from Holmes's unwanted attentions; and she may have been taken in by his disguise. But the second possibility is that Irene was expecting something out of the ordinary (though she could not be expected to predict just what) and thus that her reaction was also part of the act, carefully calculated to fool Holmes. Irene's own daring salutation to Holmes at the very door of 221b may have been her way of letting him know that she had seen through his own disguise.

That the second possibility is the more likely is surely demonstrated by Holmes's own reaction to Irene. Watson says, 'It was not that he [Holmes] felt any emotion akin to love for Irene Adler,' which is unambiguous enough. And yet it is surely difficult to explain Holmes's admiration for Irene purely on the basis of her behaviour during the course of the case. All Irene did, if we take Watson's account at face value, was to reveal almost immediately the hiding place which Holmes sought, and then make a run for it when she realized that Holmes was involved. I have long thought that Watson was wrong, and that Holmes was indeed smitten – although he refused to accept the fact – by Irene's charms. But this conflicts with Watson's own assessment of the situation rather badly, and the explanation just given is a far better fit. If Holmes realized belatedly just how thoroughly he had been fooled, that would explain his admiration for Irene very neatly.

Although Irene may very well have fooled Holmes, there is a hint that things did not turn out well for her. Watson, writing two years after the case, speaks of 'the late Irene Adler,' which indicates that she had died relatively soon after that 'marriage' which Holmes witnessed. This may, of course, have been purely bad luck; but it may not. We must look more closely at the character of Mr Godfrey Norton: ostensibly a successful lawyer, he did not hesitate for a moment to throw up his career, his home and his friends in order to leave for the Continent, never to return. Just how believable is that? Possibly Norton was independently wealthy; possibly he even had a house in Paris or a villa in Italy, and there was no difficulty involved in his leaving England as he did.

But there is another possibility, and one connected with that curious figure of two years mentioned by the King: 'I must begin by binding you both to absolute secrecy for two years; at the end of that time the matter will be of no importance.' Now, why not? We might perhaps think that if the relatives of the King's prospective bride, Clotilde Lothman von Saxe-Meningen, objected to the King's amorous dalliance with Irene before he became engaged to Clotilde, they would equally object to it after the wedding. Of course, once Clotilde was the Queen of Bohemia it could be argued that the matter was settled; any moral scruples would be irrelevant. But that applies equally well two minutes after the last 'I will' as two years after.

Was it, then, political? The union of the houses of von Ormstein and von Saxe-Meningen was presumably of some significance to the political situation; more might be at stake than the marital bliss of the happy couple who were the centre of interest. But again, why the so specific time limit of two years? A treaty signed immediately after the signing of the marriage resister would be valid as soon as signed; it is unbelievable to suppose that there was a clause invalidating such a (purely hypothetical, of course) treaty in the event that it was discovered that the King had been putting it about before the wedding! In the improbable even that there were such a clause, why would the passage of two years invalidate it? Immorality is immorality, however long may elapse until it becomes public knowledge.

We can understand Watson's publishing his story immediately after the expiring of the two year limit. Watson knew a good yarn when he heard one, and he was naturally eager to share this one with his public. It is the fact of Irene's becoming 'the late Irene Adler' before the two years were up which is the sticking point. Did the King know that at the end of two years Irene would be 'the late Irene Adler,' and thus no danger to him?

Put together the curious character of Godfrey Norton and the death of Irene within the space of those two years so casually mentioned by the King, Irene's death may, of course, have been purely accidental, and Norton may have been heart-broken as a consequence. But similarly he may not: the King may have employed not just Holmes as an agent, but Norton as well, in an attempt to ensure that Irene was eliminated. That is not so fanciful as it might at first appear, for we know for certain that Holmes was not by any means the first, or the only agent whom the King had employed: 'Five attempts [to recover the photograph from Irene] have been made,' the King told Holmes and Watson. 'Twice burglars. . . ransacked her house. Once we diverted her luggage. . . Twice she had been waylaid.' So there is nothing to say that the King had not employed both Holmes and Norton to use more subtle techniques.

The fake wedding may have been intended to fool both Holmes and Irene; or it may have been purely for Holmes's benefit. If for Irene's benefit as well as Holmes's, Norton's intention may have been to play the jealous or injured husband, to persuade Irene to give up or destroy the incriminating photograph – it would not, after all, be too odd if a newly married husband asked his wife to destroy a picture of herself with a former lover. When that failed, Irene not being quite that stupid, did Norton take more extreme action?

If the fake wedding were to fool only Holmes, then Norton must have been playing a very deep game. Possibly he pretended to Irene that they would then be safe, that Holmes would withdraw. That would give Norton more time and opportunity to make his own plans. Or perhaps Norton intended from the outset that they would leave the country – it might have seemed to Norton that the police of another country might not be so quick to investigate a suspicious death as the English force.

It is difficult to be sure about all this. We may be maligning Norton, who may indeed have been doing only what he thought best for Irene; and we may also be maligning the King. But if that is so then there is much which needs explaining somehow.

JH: Why did Holmes refuse payment from the King; and what happened to the unspent balance of the 1,000 pounds expense money?

HY: It is by no means clear that Holmes <u>did</u> refuse payment. It is true that he seems to reject the King's generosity at the end of the case, and in a very brusque and unmannerly fashion; but that does not mean that Holmes did not send in a bill. We sometimes forget that Holmes was running a business; like any other Victorian professional man he would send in an account, and the client would pay when it was convenient. (Holmes says in 'The Speckled Band' that Miss Stoner is 'at liberty to defray whatever expenses [he] may be put to, at the time which suits [her] best.')

We may compute the cost of hiring the various actors and actresses who were seen in the road at perhaps ten or fifteen pounds; this leaves a considerable balance of expense money, but Holmes would naturally render a full account to the King, and return any unspent balance after deducting his (Holmes's) fee.

When Holmes refused the emerald snake ring which the King offered him, Holmes thought that he had made a hash of the case, and that the ring was too great a reward for what he had done. The photograph of Irene was another matter, although I think that it was not mere sentiment, or affection, but Holmes's desire to have a photograph to add to his criminal collection; Irene was the only woman to have bested him and it would be natural for Holmes to want to remember her for that alone. He perhaps added the photograph to that collection of portraits of criminal which decorated his bedroom wall.

The snuffbox seems to have been an extra payment, a token of appreciation, from the King, who was well satisfied with the outcome of the case.

HY: Why did the King bind Holmes and Watson to silence for a period of two years, after which the matter would be of no importance?

JH: One explanation has been suggested in a previous answer, but there is another possibility. The King may have wanted the two years in order to ensure that he had an heir (or, better, two, the traditional one heir and one spare) to the throne. Presumably Clotilde came of good breeding stock, and the King's experience with Irene (and perhaps others) would have shown him that he personally had nothing to worry about in that department. Once there was a Prince (or two) it didn't matter what Clotilde and her family might think. Those were not days of instant divorce, so perhaps the King expected Clotilde to accept matters; and she probably did.

2." CASE OF IDENTITY"

HY: Is it believable that Miss Sutherland could not recognize her stepfather?

JH: Holmes himself asked Miss Sutherland: 'Do you not find that with your short sight it is a little trying to do so much typewriting?' To which Miss Sutherland replied: 'I did at first, but now I know where the letters are without looking.' Miss Sutherland's shortness of sight is thus established.

As a further point, her step-father took care to project the image of 'a very shy man... He would rather walk with [Miss Sutherland] in the evening than in the daylight, for he said that he hated to be conspicuous... Even his voice was gentle. He'd had the quinsy and swollen glands when he was young... and it had left him with a weak throat and a hesitating, whispering fashion of speech... his eyes were weak... and he wore tinted glasses against the glare.' Miss Sutherland did not mention - but her printed advertisement did - the 'bushy, black side-whiskers and moustache' which Windibank had also assumed as part of his disguise.

Further, Windibank had acted 'with the connivance and assistance of his wife,' according to Holmes - and Windibank verified this. So if Miss Sutherland had entertained any suspicions that she had seen 'Hosmer Angel' before, Mrs Windibank could easily have dismissed them, perhaps saying that Angel had once worked with the late Mr Sutherland, let us say. (For Angel - had he been genuine - must have been associated in some way, however loosely, with the trade, or he would hardly have appeared at the gasfitters' ball, surely an event with a limited appeal, in the first place?)

Windibank himself claimed that 'It was only a joke at first,' and there is no real reason to disbelieve him here. If the joke had fallen flat, if Miss Sutherland had recognized her step-father, then the scheme to defraud her would never have come to fruition. As it was, she did not recognize him.

HY: Indeed, Holmes says as the end of the case that there is no point telling Miss Sutherland the truth: 'If I tell her she will not believe me.' An odd statement, this, on the face of it; why should she not believe the truth? Miss Sutherland, Holmes seems to be saying, is so very convinced, not by 'Hosmer Angel' but by the abstract notion of loyalty to him, by 'love' as an ideal, that she cannot accept anything which detracts from that ideal. Perhaps a century later she would have joined some religious cult, have found another focus for her idealism? Her conviction certainly has a sacred quality to it that is worthy of a better object.

JH: Miss Sutherland said she offered to type her letters, but 'Hosmer Angel' refused because 'he felt that the machine had come between us.' Why didn't Miss Sutherland feel the same about his typed letters?

HY: As noted above, Miss Sutherland was totally convinced by 'Angel.' She perhaps also saw him as being her last, only, chance for marriage (although Holmes tends to disagree here: 'it was evident that with her fair personal advantages, and her little income, she would not be allowed to remain single long.' She may have been worried that, if she complained about something, even the typewritten love letters, she would lose 'Angel.' She wanted to see only his positive aspects.

HY: Why was Holmes involved in the Dundas case?

JH: Holmes does not seem to have been much interested in 'domestic' (divorce, etc) cases, or in mundane cases of any sort. He tells Watson at the start of ' A Case of Identity' that he has 'ten or twelve' cases in hand, 'but none which present any feature of interest.' And Watson mentions elsewhere that Holmes preferred bizarre problems. It is thus not too difficult to picture Holmes being reluctant at first to handle the Dundas case; but when the details were explained to him, he would seize eagerly at the opportunity to investigate something so out of the ordinary as a husband who 'had drifted into the habit of winding up every meal by taking out his false teeth and hurling them at his wife.'

It seems clear that it was Mrs Dundas (or perhaps a solicitor or a friend of the family acting for her) who consulted Holmes. It is not clear whether Holmes actually managed to account for the odd behaviour of Mr Dundas; Holmes himself claims to have been 'engaged in clearing up some small points in connection with' the case, but he fails to mention what the points were, or what the reason for the strange conduct might have been. Perhaps Holmes simply failed to clear up the small points? His remark is ambiguous, so perhaps it was too odd even for Holmes to work out? Mr Dundas's behaviour does not seem that of a wholly sane man, but if it were madness and nothing more, why did Holmes not mention that to Watson, who was a doctor? The true explanation must remain obscure, but there are intriguing possibilities. For example, if Mrs Dundas wished to get rid of her husband, to control his money, let us say, she might have given him some hallucinogenic drug to make it seem he was mad?

JH: Why did Holmes think Miss Sutherland would not believe the truth?

HY: It is a commonplace that members of extreme cults do not abandon their beliefs easily. For example the members of Aum Supreme Truth continued their activities long after their founder had been indicted for mass murder. Similarly Miss Sutherland had convinced herself that 'Angel' was genuine, and simply would not accept anything to the contrary. Only later would the truth dawn on her, and make her life miserable.

HY: To whom did Miss Sutherland write a letter before her departure for 221b to consult Holmes?

JH: There seem to be two possible intended recipients of the letter. Miss Sutherland was puzzled; and she was angry. She planned to consult Holmes, whose name had been mentioned to her by 'Mrs Etherege, whose husband [Holmes] found so easy when the police and everyone had given him up for dead.' Miss Sutherland wrote the letter 'in a hurry and dipped her pen too deep,' so it seems likely that the letter was somehow connected with Miss Sutherland's determination to see Holmes.

The two likeliest possibilities are thus that Miss Sutherland had written a note to her mother, to say that she was going out (to see

Holmes); or that Miss Sutherland had initially meant to write to Holmes to ask for an appointment, but then changed her mind and decided to go in person. Since Miss Sutherland does not say that she had changed her mind, the more likely of the two is that the note was written to her mother, who must thus have been out of the house when Miss Sutherland left it; most likely Mrs Windibank was out with her husband, for if Mr Windibank had been in the house, and Miss Sutherland had said that she was going to consult Sherlock Holmes, then Mr Windibank would surely have tried to talk her out of it?

JH: How did the Sutherland family fare after this case?

HY: Badly! James Windibank himself may not have risen 'from crime to crime until he does something very bad, and ends on a gallows,' as Holmes predicted, but it is clear that Windibank was a sneaky scoundrel of the worst sort, and he seems likely to have been destined for a life of petty crime, if nothing worse. Then Miss Sutherland would drift into old age still moping about her wretched 'Hosmer Angel' (and how the devil could any self-respecting woman associate with anyone of that name in the first place?) So Mrs Windibank faced a fairly bleak future; but since she had connived at and assisted Windibank in the shabby deception in the first place, that was only what she deserved.

3. "THE RED-HEADED LEAGUE "

JH: Would there really be so many red-headed men applying for the vacancy as Jabez Wilson's account suggests?

HY: The salary offered in the advertisement was a generous one, four pounds a week, or slightly over two hundred a year. This compares favourably with the '£4 a month in my last place with Colonel Spence Munro,' which Miss Violet Hunter earned in 'The Copper Beeches,' and is pretty well exactly what Hall Pycroft was to have been earning with Mawson's, the stockbroker for whom he almost acted as clerk - and this was an increase on the £3 a week he had actually earned at Coxon's, his old employer. Two hundred a year was therefore good money; it would attract the attention of men from both working and middle classes. Furthermore the advertisement stressed that the duties were 'purely nominal,' though it did not specify just what these duties were to be, so for all the readers knew, the duties might have been such as to be carried out in the evenings or at weekends, and so would not conflict with what we now call 'the day job.' It was worth taking a half day off work to look into it.

It is worth remembering that when the Stoll Film Company filmed 'The Red-Headed League' in 1920, they advertised in the *Times* for 'twenty CURLY, RED-HEADED MEN... Those who have served in HM forces and have some knowledge of acting preferred.' Forty men turned up who satisfied almost all the conditions (though there were more conditions than in the original advertisement!) and the studio hired them all for the day. (See Leslie S Klinger, *The Sherlock Holmes Reference Library The Adventures*, Gasogene, 1998, p. 35.) This shows just how effective the agony column was, so it is easy to believe that there were indeed many red-headed men attracted by the original, intriguing advertisement.

HY: Why, if April 27 was 'just two months ago,' did the notice on the door read October 9?

JH: There have long been two schools of thought as to the date

194

of 'The Red-Headed League,' one favouring a starting date for the scheme of April and a date for the case as a case of June; the other favouring a winding-up date for the League (and a date for the case as a case) of October. In each instance, the duration of the League is held to be the two months which Watson mentions.

However, there is a third possibility, which does not appear to have been mooted before, and that is that both dates are correct but the computation of elapsed time is adrift. Watson would have retained the newspaper clipping with the original advertisement, and the note dissolving the League, they would be in front of him as he wrote his account. But the mention of 'two months' comes from Watson's mouth in the course of a reported conversation; but there were no tape recorders, and Watson did not - according to his own account - actually note the conversation verbatim. Is it then possible that April and October are correct, and that Watson mistook six months for two? Possibly Watson never even mentioned any time, but added it later to give colour to his story.

We can estimate how long Jabez Wilson spent on his nominal duties from his own words: 'I had written about Abbots and Archery and Armour and Architecture and Attica, and hoped with diligence that I might get onto the B's before very long.' Tom Stix ('Concerning "The Red-Headed League",' *BSJ* 4,2 , 1954, pp. 93-99) said, 'the *Encyclopaedia Britannica* [1875 ed.]... has 928 pages in Volume One, and doesn't reach the article on Attica until page 794 of Volume Two.' Wilson thus had to copy 1,722 pages, in longhand. If he worked two months only, that is almost 36 pages a day; if he worked from April to October, the average is about 12, a far more manageable total.

A further point concerns the tunnel itself. During WWII French POWs dug a tunnel at Colditz Castle. The number of prisoners digging the tunnel was initially nine, but later there were thirty. They worked twenty-four hours a day for eight months, and produced a tunnel 40 metres long, 0.7 m high and 0.6 m wide. Could John Clay and 'Archie' dig a tunnel into the bank in a mere two months? It seems unlikely. Indeed, for HY the five and a half months from April to October seems hardly sufficient; there is a strong case for thinking that the April was in one year, and the October the following year, a total of seventeen and a half months. In that event, Watson must have shortened the time span to 'improve' the dramatic content of the story. (Although JH points out that the French gold was only borrowed; a long time span would involve the possibility that the gold would not actually be there when Clay and Archie reached the vault; JH thinks April and October of the same year - with perhaps a fairly short tunnel - more likely.)

JH: Why did Watson offer to wait in the next room?

HY: JH thinks that Watson had been a partner (paid, or rather sharing the profits) before he got married to Mary Morstan. That is why Holmes did not know that Watson was going into general practice (in 'A Scandal in Bohemia') - because Holmes thought Watson had plenty of money in the bank from the detective work!) Watson did not want to push himself into Holmes's case after leaving the partnership.

HY: What did Spaulding's accomplice do whilst Spaulding was digging the tunnel?

JH: Archie must have helped with the digging! There was too much for one man; but perhaps one man took a rest after an hour's work, say, to have some fresh air?

HY: Why did the criminals close the offices of the League before the burglary?

JH: The closing of the offices is the one serious flaw in the plan. If the office were open, Jabez Wilson would have gone to work as usual, and Holmes would not be called in until it was too late! There was no reason to close the office, it was silly, and put the robbers' scheme at risk. John Clay was obviously not a clever crook! (And it seems unlikely that Prof. Moriarty planned the robbery, as some have suggested, because Moriarty would not do anything so stupid.

4: "THE BOSCOMBE VALLEY MYSTERY"

JH: Does the cry of 'Cooee' not give the solution at once? James McCarthy and his father used the cry of 'Cooee,' which 'is a distinctly Australian cry,' according to Holmes; the only other Australian in the district was John Turner, and since the father thought the son was in Bristol, it must have been Turner for whom the call was intended!

HY: It was Sherlock Holmes who pointed out that 'Cooee' was a specifically Australian usage. The newspaper report of James McCarthy's testimony said that it was 'a usual signal' between the McCarthys, father and son; while the coroner said only that he understood that the cry was 'a common signal' between the two. Outsiders reading this may well have thought that it was merely a family thing, and been unaware of the Australian connotations - the world then was not so small a place as it has since become, and Englishmen, particularly in rural areas, might well be unaware of the habits of Australian. Even had the general public known the call to be Australian, the newspaper did not make a point of reporting the presence on the district of the other Australian, Turner. Even Lestrade could not really be expected to know the significance of the call, - although one might perhaps argue that, like Holmes, Lestrade should have known!

HY: If McCarthy junior loved Miss Turner, and not the 'wife' he had in Bristol, why did he spend three days in Bristol with the 'wife'?

JH: The most probable answer here is that McCarthy junior had originally intended to discuss the possibility of divorce with his wife. (Agreed, there was in fact no need, since the marriage was not legally valid in the first place; but McCarthy did not know this – indeed, had he done so, he would not have needed to visit Bristol at all.) However, the relationship seems to have been of a fairly basic physical nature, and it seems rather as if McCarthy junior succumbed yet again to the charms of the barmaid with the Bristols, and that caused him to stay longer than he had at first intended. (This if correct, would indicate that McCarthy junior was a somewhat weak character; but that is surely how he comes across anyway? A fact which does not augur well for the future happiness of Miss Turner.)

As a further point, the nature of the relationship between Miss Turner and McCarthy junior is surely a trifle ambiguous. Miss Turner herself said that they had loved each other as brother and sister; scarcely a grand passion there. It may have been that McCarthy junior was not whole-heartedly devoted to Miss Turner, and quite enjoyed his three days dalliance in Bristol – again indicative of weakness of character?

JH: James MacCarthy's 'right hand and sleeve were observed to be stained with fresh blood. However, the stone which Holmes identified as the murder weapon had 'no marks' on it. Why was James's sleeve stained?

HY: James said in his evidence that when he found his father dying, 'I dropped my gun and held him in my arms,' so that accounts for the blood on James's hands and clothing.

The real problem is the absence of any blood on the stone which Holmes identified as the murder weapon. Possibly Turner wiped off any blood there may have been? Incidentally a far more satisfactory way of hiding the 'weapon' would have been to hurl the stone into the Boscombe Pool, where any blood would be washed off, even if the stone happened to be recovered. But then Turner was under something of a strain.

HY: James did not say what he and his father had talked about. Everyone knew about the problem of the marriage between James and Miss Turner, so it seems unlikely that the conversation was about that. What was it about?

JH: Although everyone connected with the families concerned

198

may have known of the problem of the prospective marriage, old Mr McCarthy did not know of his son's 'marriage' to the Bristol barmaid. It is thus highly likely that the conversation did indeed concern McCarthy senior's desire that his son marry Miss Turner. Naturally, James would not at first want to reveal this fact.

JH: When Holmes returned from talking to McCarthy junior, he said, 'And now let us talk about George Meredith.' Why George Meredith?

HY: Although the works of George Meredith were popular in Victorian Britain, it is difficult to find a believable point of contact between the love stories he wrote and Holmes and Watson. Meredith's other main theme, however, that of natural selection considered as Nature's method of perfecting mankind, may be more to the point. Earlier in the same case, Holmes had been reading Petrarch, who has been called 'the earliest of the great humanists of the Renaissance,' and this may indicate that Holmes was in a somewhat philosophical mood; possibly the contrast of idealized humanity with the tangled affairs of McCarthy junior struck him forcibly just at that moment.

However, there is yet another possibility; Watson's memory may have let him down, and Holmes may actually have said not 'George' but 'Owen' Meredith. This was the nom de plume of Edward Robert Bulwer, 1ˢᵗ Earl of Lytton (1831-91; and son of the writer EG Bulwer-Lytton), who was Viceroy of India from 1876-80. *Chamber's Biographical Dictionary* says that he 'effected reform but failed to prevent the Second Afghan War (1878),' and it is noteworthy that his was the very war in which Watson fought and was wounded. Perhaps Lytton had consulted Holmes? Or perhaps Holmes just wanted to talk about a man in whom he knew Watson would be interested?

HY: As old Mr Turner was not dead, Holmes could not mention the real killer's name when he gave evidence which would clear James. How did he prove James was not guilty?

JH: This is another real problem. I think that there was nothing else that Holmes could have done but lay the facts before the prosecution lawyers, saying that it would be pointless to arrest or charge old Mr Turner, who would never survive to come to trial; and presumably the prosecution saw the sense of thirst. Why, then, did Watson claim otherwise? In the first place, Watson may not have been closed associated with the actual process of the trial, and thus may have assumed that Holmes had indeed discovered some other facts material to the case. Or Watson may have known the truth, but decided that it was a bit of an anti-climax to say that Holmes had done what he had promised not to do, and revealed the truth about old Turner.

5: "THE FIVE ORANGE PIPS"

HY: Holmes said: 'I have been beaten four times – three times by men and once by a woman.' Who was this villainous but capable lady? And who were the men?

JH: There are several problems with this one. One problem is that Holmes handled a great many cases which Watson never documented – Watson and Holmes between them refer in passing to over a hundred according to my own count (John Hall: *The Abominable Wife*, Calabash, 1998), and there may very well have been more which are not even mentioned in passing; so Holmes might easily have been referring to cases which we cannot possibly identify, or which we know only by the titles which Watson so tantalizingly mentions; the old Russian woman, for example, may perhaps have fooled a very youthful Holmes.

If we consider only canonical cases, then a second problem is that of chronology. For example, if we take Watson's own date of 1887 for 'The Five Orange Pips,' then it is unlikely – though not impossible! - that the woman referred to is Irene Adler; if, however, we accept Watson's statement that he was married at the time of 'The Five Orange Pips' (and, by implication, that 1887 is probably too early), then it could well have been Miss Adler who bested Holmes. (Miss Adler would probably be the first choice of most Sherlockians when asked this question, though I have always thought that Holmes was too easily impressed by Miss Adler's criminal abilities anyway.)

Again, different chronologists put different cases before 'The Five Orange Pips,' so that the possibilities change according to the chronology we select.

A further complication arises when we ask just what Holmes may have meant by the word 'beaten': did he consider that Mrs Grant Munro in 'The Yellow Face' had 'beaten' him? She certainly fooled him, at least up to a point, and this case occurred before 'The Five Orange Pips' according to many chronologists; but that is not necessarily what Holmes meant.

Similarly, when Holmes speaks of men defeating him, the identities of the men concerned are far from clear. In 'The Resident

Patient' (placed before 'The Five Orange Pips' by many commentators), Holmes was arguably 'beaten' in the sense that the man whom he should have protected was murdered.

Then TS Blakeney puts 'The Greek Interpreter,' in which Watson saves the eponymous interpreter's life, but Holmes failed to act quickly enough to save either Mr or Miss Kratides, before 'The Five Orange Pips,' so the villains there might be said to have beaten Holmes.

And similarly HW Bell puts *The Valley of Fear* – in which Holmes failed to prevent Moriarty committing murder – before 'The Five Orange Pips.' These three might well be the cases to which Holmes refers; but this must remain speculative.

JH: Why does Watson speak of his wife being on a visit to her mother's? At this time he should not have been married, and anyway Mary Morstan had no relatives!

HY: In some editions 'mother' appears, but in others it is 'aunt.' The obvious answer is that 'mother' is a misprint, and 'aunt' is correct.

Mary says in *The Sign of Four* that 'My mother was dead, and I had no relative in England.' If 'aunt' is correct, this statement certainly means that her mother was dead, but it may mean not that she had no living relatives whatsoever, but that that her other relatives were simply not in England. At that date it needed not only money but time to go round the world. Even if Mary's aunt, and perhaps also other relatives, were alive and well, the fact that they were not in England would make it difficult for Mary to seek her (or their) advice when her father died. But it would be perfectly logical for Mary to invite such relatives to her wedding, and given enough notice, they would probably return to England if they were able to do so.

As a final point about the date, it is possible that Watson was not actually married at the time of the case. He may have meant 'wife' in the sense that Mary later became his wife. It is possible (though at that time frankly unlikely) that Watson and Mary were sharing a house though unmarried – a more likely possibility is that Mary had moved into their future home, and Watson was still at 221b, and Watson may not have wished to state this in print.

In any event, the fact that Mary (then still Miss Morstan) was away on a visit meant that Watson did not have to think about the forthcoming wedding ceremony, or look for a suitable house etc; he had nothing to distract him from taking an interest in Holmes' work.

HY: Why did Captain Calhoun waste so much time between the murders of Elias, Joseph and John Openshaw?

JH: Calhoun was on board a sailing ship; he was obliged to wait until he reached land before he could act. After killing Elias, Calhoun would wait to see what effect produced on Joseph; and similarly the killing of Joseph might have the desired effect (desired, that is, by Calhoun) on John. In each case Calhoun waited to see what would happen; what with that, and with the circumstance of his being at sea for much of the time, delay was inevitable.

On the other hand, Calhoun did manage to visit England in order to kill Elias Openshaw and later Joseph. Why then did Calhoun not use those 'visits' to search the house? It seems very much as if Calhoun were not really serious about the papers? Perhaps his motive was mostly revenge against the Openshaw family, rather than a desire to recover the papers?

JH: How did the villains decoy Openshaw to the Embankment, which was out of his way?

HY: The easiest way would be for one of the villains to pose as a cab driver and wait for Openshaw. As it was the proverbial dark and stormy night, and as he was naturally in a very nervous state, Openshaw might well take a cab, and could then be driven wherever the villains wished.

As an alternative, perhaps they did not actually 'decoy' him, but merely overwhelmed him by sheer weight of numbers, knocked him unconscious and carried him to the Embankment?

HY: Why did Elias destroy his KKK papers and so cause his own death?

JH: There are two separate, though related, issues here. One is that the destruction of the papers may not actually have caused Elias's death; when the first letter with the orange pips arrived, Elias 'shrieked. . . "My God, my God, my sins have overtaken me!"' and when John asks "'What is it, uncle?"' "'Death," said he.' It was only after realizing that he was under sentence of death that Elias burned the papers, as a sort of act of defiance - "'They may do what they like, but I'll checkmate them still,"' he says. It seems likely that Calhoun and his associates intended to kill Elias, not so much for the sake of the papers, as for what they considered his betrayal of them, or their cause – a possible explanation, again, for Calhoun's failure to pursue actively the acquisition of the papers when he had killed Elias, and later Joseph?

Calhoun then asked Joseph, and then John, for the return of the papers. Calhoun did not know that Elias had burned the papers; Calhoun would be afraid that the papers contained evidence which might incriminate himself and others as members of KKK. (And perhaps Calhoun intended to use the information about those others for blackmail, and was acting in self-interest more than from motives of 'justice'?) Had John been able to do as Holmes suggested, and convince Calhoun that the papers had been destroyed and were thus no danger, then John might have lived.

JH: Should Holmes have blamed himself for Openshaw's death?

HY: John Openshaw had waited (wasted?) two days after receiving his 'KKK' letter, posted in London. The killers would be either in London, or lurking near Horsham when Openshaw visited Baker Street. In addition, it was a stormy night. The killer might be following Openshaw closely, might easily be seated next to him, without Openshaw's being aware of the fact. The killer or killers were evidently not without skill, for Openshaw's uncle and father had been killed easily enough.

Openshaw had a gun in his pocket, but considering the ease with which Openshaw's father and uncle had been killed, Holmes should at the very least have called a cab to take Openshaw to Waterloo Station, and it would have been even better had Watson gone along with him. Ideally, Openshaw should have remained at Baker Street overnight, and returned – with Holmes and Watson – next day. As it was, there was insufficient time for Openshaw to convince the killers that the 'KKK' papers were destroyed.

Some commentators detect the shadow of Professor Moriarty in this case, but there is no real evidence for this. Even if Moriarty were involved, the case predates Holmes' investigation into the Moriarty gang, and so Holmes could hardly blame himself for not knowing that Moriarty had a hand in the case.

Gavin Brend says 'John Openshaw had the melancholy distinction of being one of the only two clients to be murdered after they had consulted Holmes, the other unfortunate being Hilton Cubitt of 'The Dancing Men.' (*My Dear Holmes*, p.85) Holmes had a pride in his profession, as he says; and he did not lose many clients. Even if Watson, and Watson's readers, do not blame Holmes, there seems little doubt that he blamed himself.

6. "THE MAN WITH THE TWISTED LIP"

JH: What was the real 'Theological College of St George's' of which the late Elias Whitney, DD, was Principal?

HY: According to Baring-Gould's *Annotated Sherlock Holmes*, 'This would be St Joseph's College.' Owen Dudley Edwards agrees with this (OUP edition, p.347) – 'perhaps based on the theological college of St Joseph,' but no source is listed. Baring-Gould adduces no evidence in support of the suggestion, so perhaps it was based merely on similarity of the names?

It is difficult to determine the actual college. For example there was a College of St Mark in King's Road, London. According to the *London Encyclopaedia* (Macmillan, London, 1983) 'In 1840 the whole site became the College of St Mark, a training college for Church of England teachers. The first principal was Derwent Coleridge, son of the poet, and the Assembly Hall still bears his name. In 1923 the College of St John was transferred here from Battersea,' and the school is now called the College of St Mark and St John.

The relations between Watson and Isa Whitney are odd: Watson says 'I was Isa Whitney's medical adviser,' but Whitney's reaction – 'My God! It's Watson,' and 'But you've got it mixed up, Watson,' are more like those of a personal friend. I suspect that Watson and Whitney were old friends, perhaps having been at school together. The Canon does not mention Isa Whitney's profession, but he would not be a doctor. It seems probable that Whitney was a student at the same school as that attended by both Watson and Percy Phelps (see 'The Naval Treaty'), and since Phelps was a member of the British upper classes, this was probably a Church of England School, not a Catholic one. It would be natural for the Whitney brothers to share the same religious beliefs, so that the fictitious 'St George's' would be a Church of England establishment. That would rule out St Joseph's, and in my view makes St Mark's the more likely.

JH: I think that the clue is in the saint's name; as George is patron saint of England, so David is of Wales, and St David's College at Lampeter is a well-known theological institution. I therefore suspect that Isa Whitney may have had a Welsh lilt in his voice.

HY: Why did Holmes stay at St Clair's house?

JH: Watson asks the selfsame question: 'But why are you not conducting the case from Baker Street?'

And Holmes replies. 'Because there are many enquiries which must be made out here.'

Holmes has already given Watson such information as he has about St Clair: 'a gentleman. . . who appeared to have plenty of money. . . He had no occupation, but was interested in several companies, and went into town as a rule in the morning, returning by the 5:14 from Cannon Street every night. . . ' (Holmes uses 'interested' in the City sense, meaning that St Clair was a shareholder in various companies.)

Now, Holmes knew that St Clair was last seen in the opium den; the logical course would be for Holmes to ask how St Clair got there. Holmes would naturally make enquiries of those who regularly used the 5:14 pm. train, and of those who were St Clair's companions on the morning trains which he used. And Holmes would find either that none of these fellow-travellers knew which companies St Clair visited, or that St Clair had bandied about names which Holmes would subsequently find to be either dummies, or of firms which had never heard of St Clair. As a further point, an ordinary investor might attend the Annual General Meeting of a company in which he has shares, but does not normally visit that company, or others in which he has shares, every single day. Mrs. St Clair might be sufficiently financially naive as not to know this; Holmes would not. As a further point, Holmes talks of St Clair's debts as amounting to '£ 88 10s, while he has £ 220 standing to his credit in the Capital and Counties Bank,' so Holmes had evidently made enquiries of St Clair's bankers; and these gentlemen would vouchsafe the quite astonishing information that St Clair had never in his life paid in a single dividend! More, that all his deposits, and quite substantial deposits at that, were in cash. This would surely make Holmes suspicious.

The London end of the case having proved a very dead end,

Holmes had no alternative but to make more detailed enquiries at St Clair's home. Or at any rate, to say to Mrs St Clair that he had to make detailed enquiries, whilst actually engaging her in the sort of apparently innocuous conversation that he used in order to gain information that the other person was unaware that they possessed. (See e.g. 'A Case of Identity,' for an example of this.) Holmes would be hoping for some clue, something which Mrs St Clair said in the course of general conversation which would give Holmes some insight into St Clair's odd life after he left home, or something at least that would give Holmes some kind of staring point.

JH: Where was the real 'Upper Swandam Lane'?

HY: Many candidates have been advanced as the original, such as 'Lower Thames Street' and 'Whapping High Street' (CEC Townsend), 'Upper Thames Street' (Alan Wilson) and 'Stoney Lane' (HW Bell.)

D Martin Dakin (*A Sherlock Holmes Commentary*) says 'There is an alley called Swan Lane leading down to the river from Upper Thames Street, which, given the building changes in seventy-five years, might well be the one: although, as it is only a narrow passage leading down to the water, Mrs St Clair could not have walked along it looking for a cab, but only past it; and anyway it was too near to Cannon Street [rail] station for her to have needed a cab.'

Which is all very well, but Watson does say that 'Upper Swandam Lane' was 'north of the river' and 'to the east of London Bridge,' and Upper Thames Street is to the west of the bridge, so it can't be that. There are, however, many names to this west side which are tantalisingly close, Swan Lane, Old Swan Lane, Old Swan Pier, Old Swan Yard, and it seems logical to assume that these provided ACD with much of the inspiration for 'Upper Swandam Lane.'

As for actual locations on the ground, a glance at the street plans of the time shows that Lower Thames Street is the obvious starting point, although Lower Thames Street itself is too far from the river to be the actual location. Between Lower Thames Street and the river, and between the bridge and the great fishmarket of Billingsgate, however, as seen on plans of the time there was indeed a mass of wharves and buildings, exactly as Watson says. 'Upper Swandam

Lane' is clearly meant for one of these – perhaps Lyons Quay or Somers Quay would be a good choice, not too far from the (probably inaptly named) Fresh Quay or Steam Packet Quay.

JH: I wonder if the widely known ceremony of 'swan-upping' might have suggested the street name to Conan Doyle? (And, by the way, a swan's 'dam' (mother) is a 'pen,' so it may just be a joke at the reader's expense?)

HY: Why did Mrs St Clair visit Upper Swandam Lane alone, a very odd thing for a respectable Victorian lady to do? Why didn't she ask the Aberdeen Shipping Company to send her the parcel by post?

JH: This is an interesting point, and again one difficult to explain satisfactorily. Holmes says that it was 'a small parcel of considerable value,' and one possibility is that Mrs St Clair did not trust the postal service, although this seems unlikely. Nor is it probable that she wanted the parcel in a hurry, since in Victorian times there were six or seven deliveries per day, and a parcel posted in central London in the morning would reach her in the afternoon.

As a further complication, the offices of the Aberdeen Shipping Co. are stated to be in 'Fresno Street,' but most of the big shipping firms in this general area had offices in Cannon Street (Wells, Fargo or Pitt & Scott) or Gracechurch Street (Continental Daily Parcels Express) or similar well-known thoroughfares, and none of these would have taken Mrs St Clair anywhere near the river. Aberdeen Shipping may have been a very small firm with its offices right on the river.

Another possibility is that the parcel came from abroad and that Mrs St Clair had to pay duty on it and collect it from the Customs House, just east of Billingsgate, and it may be that Aberdeen Shipping had a small office near the Customs House, for precisely this sort of eventuality. However, in either of these cases, it is surely very odd that some gallant clerk of the Aberdeen Shipping Co. did not offer to walk with Mrs St Clair to the station, no great way off, or summon a cab for her?

There are all sorts of <u>possible</u> explanations, most of them scurrilous or idiotic or both, but surely the most logical assumption is that Mrs St Clair was simply lost, that she took a wrong turning on coming out of the shipping office and quickly found herself in very insalubrious surroundings? This would explain her looking for a cab, when the station was so very close.

JH: Why was the opium den, 'The Bar of Gold' known as 'the vilest murder-trap on the whole riverside'? It would surely be better for the owners to keep customers alive so that they could buy more opium!

HY: Even the villainous lascar would not wish to kill perfectly good customers, or he would have to close down his establishment! However, opium is a well-known addictive drug, and many addicts lose all their property as a result of their addiction. But even without money, they would turn up demanding more of the drug, and that would be a nuisance for the lascar, who would not have hesitated to dispose of such unfortunate wretches.

Moreover, gullible people who had money but were not addicted may well have been inveigled to The Bar of Gold on the classic pretext of 'having a good time,' and there supplied with enough opium to lower their resistance, robbed, and thrown, drowsy but alive, into the river, to take their chances. The police would not treat any deaths which occurred as a result as being murder, as there would be no marks of violence on the bodies; suicide or accident would be the likely verdict. If the victim survived, he would probably be too embarrassed to make a fuss.

HY: St Clair said; 'All day a stream of pennies, varied by silver, poured in upon me, and it was a very bad day upon which I failed to take £ 2.' Is this figure realistic?

JH: Holmes says of Hugh Boone, St Clair's *alter ego*: 'He is a professional beggar [who sits in an angle of the wall in Threadneedle Street]. . . I have watched the fellow more than once. . . and I have been surprised at the harvest which he has reaped in a short time. His appearance. . . [marks] him out from amid the common crowd of mendicants, and so, too, does his wit, for he is ever ready with a reply to any piece of chaff which may be thrown at him by the passer-by.'

Holmes's own observations, then, confirm (in general terms) that Hugh Boone is successful at accumulating cash. Let us look for a moment at the copper coins found in St Clair's coat, recovered from the river bank, which represent the non-silver part of his earnings, and which may reasonably be assumed the be fairly typical of the 'copper' part of his average takings.: '421 pennies,' says Holmes, 'and 270 half-pennies,' a proportion of 3 to 2, almost exactly (3:1.924 for the pedants.) Hugh Boone's daily take of £ 2, then (remembering that the £ had then 240 pence (d) to it), is represented by 360 pennies and 240 half-pennies. Assume that each donor gives one, and only one, coin, and we need six hundred (less than generous) donors, which is a lot. However, should each donor give copper to the value of, say, 2 ½d or 3d, that cuts the number needed quite significantly. Hugh Boone's pitch was carefully chosen, right in the heart of the financial district: a City gent (no ladies in those non-PC days!) might well grab whatever copper was in his pocket without bothering to count it, particularly if he had had a profitable day's trading.

As a further consideration, Hugh Boone himself says later on that: 'a stream of pennies, varied by silver, poured in upon me.' Regrettably we do not know the amount of this variation, but even a few of the smaller silver coins, 3d and 6d, would again soon cause the total to mount up.

And there may have been larger silver coins, too; in the summer of 2003, the *Daily Mail* newspaper, investigating suggestions that modern beggars earn enormous amounts, paid several actors to pretend to be beggars and report back. The highest earner was an elderly man, a 'character' actor, who earned a respectable £ 60 or £ 70 in a day, and who said, significantly, that his 'clients' seemed to like his repartee. As Holmes specifically noted Hugh Boone's gift in that regard, it is surely not too much to assume that Hugh Boone, a trained actor with a talent for picking up cues, overheard a good deal of financial gossip and used it in his patter: 'Did well with those gold shares, did we, Mr Fanshaw?' to which Fanshaw, who perhaps (as the City is a superstitious place) thinks that Hugh Boone is some sort of human talisman, replies: 'We did, and here's your share of it!' as he throws the cheerful beggar a florin or half-crown.

But let us assume that all this is nonsense; that Hugh Boone did <u>not</u>, in fact earn £ 2 a day. Perhaps he exaggerated, not wanting Holmes and Watson to think that he was an unsuccessful beggar; or perhaps Watson, as so often in these instances, misheard or misremembered. Let us assume that Hugh Boone earned for St Clair not £ 2 per day, but £ 2 per week. Very well: but Mr Hall Pycroft, 'The Stock-broker's Clerk,' the sort of a man who was working in the very buildings outside which Hugh Boone sat, was earning £ 200 a year at Mawson's, or £ 4 a week; Watson himself had, on his return to London from India, 11/6 a day, again around £ 4 a week. Our £ 2 a week is thus fairly respectable, more than a working man might expect; a man could live (though admittedly not in any great style) on it, and it would not take too much good luck for Hugh Boone to equal the income of a Hall Pycroft or a Dr Watson – at the very least.

We may thus assume that St Clair spoke the truth, and that Hugh Boone's earnings were as he says, £ 2 a day.

7. "THE BLUE CARBUNCLE"

HY: What did Henry Baker do in the British Museum? Was he a clerk in the library, or did he perhaps study like Karl Marx?

JH: Henry Baker himself says, 'There are a few of us who frequent the Alpha Inn, near the Museum – we are to be found in the Museum itself during the day, you understand,' which suggests that Baker was in the Museum full-time, in whatever capacity. He was not a rich man, and he was too old to be a student, which suggests that he was employed by the Museum itself. It has been suggested that Baker earned his living as some sort of researcher, working for those who wished to consult the Museum's resources, but could not visit the Museum personally. However, there would surely be other sources of information, record offices, other museums and libraries, where such a researcher might be found? Why would Baker be always at the one place, were he not an employee? The logical conclusion is surely that he was employed in a fairly humble capacity at the Museum.

JH: When Watson first calls on him, Holmes has 'a pile of crumpled morning papers, evidently newly studied, near at hand.' Why? Holmes has already deduced that Mr Henry Baker has suffered a 'decline of fortunes,' and thus could hardly be expected to advertise for the goose's return; and the theft or loss of a goose is hardly the sort of thing to make the front page! So, what was Holmes looking for in the newspapers?

HY: As noted throughout the Canon, the newspapers were a fertile source of information for Holmes in a general sense; the newspapers noted by Watson might have been Holmes's normal morning reading, and have no relation wt all to the Baker case.

Again, Holmes might initially have expected that Baker would advertise for the goose, the loss of which would be a blow to Baker. His 'I am at a loss to know now why you did not advertise' may have been intended to draw the answer, 'Shillings have not been so plentiful with me as they once were,' thereby confirming his own deductions.

Another possibility might be that Holmes expected a further altercation between Baker and the gang of roughs who first attacked him. The attack itself might, for all Holmes knew, have had nothing at all to do with the goose, but be connected with some other matter altogether, and the in that case 'roughs' might well have sought out Baker, intending to do him further harm, when once the fuss had calmed down. Holmes may well have been looking in the newspapers for an account of an injured, or dead, man in Tottenham Court Road or nearby.

HY: What was Henry Baker doing with a goose in Tottenham Court Road at 4 o'clock in the morning, leaving his wife at home? Why didn't he go straight home with the goose immediately he got it from the landlord of the Alpha Inn? And was the Alpha Inn open on Christmas Eve?

JH: What he was doing was going home! True, 4 am. is a trifle late; but we must remember that the licensing laws were not then so strict as they later became. (Indeed, the licensing laws which governed Britain for a century were instituted during the First World War precisely because the liberal opening hours previously in force were seriously damaging wartime production, or, rather, the absenteeism they induced was.)

Add to that the fact that Baker liked his glass of something – the evidence of Baker's hat, says Holmes, 'seems to indicate some evil influence, probably drink, at work upon him.' And later on Watson notes in Baker 'A touch of red in nose and cheeks, with a slight tremor of his extended hand,' all of which seems to confirm Holmes's surmise. As long a Baker had money to spend, he would be likely to stay in the Alpha; while as long as the Alpha had paying customers, it would remain open, particularly on Christmas Eve, when trade would be sure to be good.

As a last point, we do not know for certain that Baker had not left the Alpha much earlier; he may have set off for home, forgetting all about his goose, only remembered it when his shaky hand put his key in the lock, and been obliged to return for it!

JH: Mr Henry Baker says: 'a Scotch bonnet is fitted neither to my years nor my gravity.' So why did he buy the thing?

HY: Goose is not a popular dish in Japan, but according to the Granada TV version of 'The Blue Carbuncle,' it is much larger than a chicken, if smaller than a turkey. I am not too familiar with the English appetite, but a goose seems to me to be too much for two people. I suspect there were also young Bakers, sons and daughters, perhaps grandchildren. As Baker himself says, a Scotch bonnet is not fitted for an older gentleman, but it is for young people. I think that as a rule this bonnet was put on Henry Baker Junior's head, and his father simply borrowed it temporarily.

HY: Ryder ran away, but what of the Countess of Morcar's maid, Catherine Cusack? Holmes presumably did not give her away to the Countess, so did Cusack perhaps continue a life of crime?

JH: Perhaps. But then perhaps Holmes dropped a hint to the Countess – without actually giving away Ryder, or naming Cusack specifically – which would lead the Countess to dismiss Cusack?

We do not know the exact relations between Ryder and Cusack. Ryder himself says 'It was Catherine Cusack who told me of [the carbuncle],' which suggests that Cusack was pretty amoral to begin with. (Though, in fairness, Ryder comes across as the sort of little creep who would take refuge in 'The woman made me do it,' anyway.) It may possibly be that Holmes <u>did</u>, after all, tell the Countess directly that her maid was untrustworthy; or perhaps Holmes, still full of Christmas spirit, had a quiet word with Cusack, told her to watch her behaviour in future, because Holmes would certainly be watching it closely?

As so often in the Holmes stories, one is left wondering just what became of Ryder and Cusack after the story closes.

JH: What was the real 'Hotel Cosmopolitan'?

HY: The Countess of Morcar, who stayed at the Cosmopolitan,

owned the blue carbuncle, whose value was estimated at £ 20,000. It is improbable that she stayed at some B&B, or the Victorian version of the YWCA.

Gavin Brend suggested Claridge's, with honourable mentions for the Ritz, Carlton, Berkley, and the Cecil, all first-class accommodations in Victorian London. Brend also suggested that the Savoy was unlikely, as it had just opened in 1889, and was unlikely to need repairs. In view of the Countess's wealth, few Sherlockians would dispute Brend's choices.

There is, however, one problem. James Ryder took the stone from the Countess of Morcar's room, and hurried with it to his sister's house in Brixton Road, which is south of the Thames. Ryder told Holmes that 'I made up my mind to go right on to Kilburn,' where a friend, Maudsley, a former crook, 'would show me how to turn the stone into money.' Now, Kilburn is north of the Thames, near Hampstead, in the north-west London.

Ryder, in association with Catherine Cusack, the Countess's maid, had stolen the stone, and, according to the newspaper report, he 'gave his evidence to the effect that he had shown Horner [the innocent handyman framed for the crime] up to the dressing-room of the Countess of Morcar upon the day of the robbery, in order that he might solder the second bar of the grate, which was loose. He had remained with Horner for some little time, but had finally been called away. On returning, he found that Horner had disappeared, that the bureau had been forced open, and that the small morocco casket in which, as it afterwards transpired, the Countess was accustomed to keep her jewel, was lying empty upon the dressing-table. Ryder instantly gave the alarm, and Horner was arrested the same evening.'

Ryder, confronted by Holmes, said that he did not know what to do after he had taken the stone. This is unbelievable. Holmes himself says that Ryder 'knew that this man Horner, the plumber, had been concerned in some such matter before, and that suspicion would rest the more readily upon him. . . You made some small job in my lady's room. . . and you managed that he should be the man sent for. . . when he had left, you rifled the jewel-case, raised the alarm, and had this unfortunate man arrested.' And Ryder denies none of this. Ryder, then, had planned the whole thing well in advance, from the choice of fall-guy to the loosening of the bar of the grate. It is surely inconceivable that Ryder had made no plans for the disposal of the

216

stone? His logical course would have been to go to Kilburn at once, rather than cross the Thames, and later re-cross it, all the while leaving himself open to being stopped by the police for further questioning – or it would have been logical if the hotel were north of the river.

The difficulties with getting to Brixton are lessened if the Hotel Cosmopolitan were south of the river. At that time, there were few really good hotels on the south bank. Prices here at the turn of the century are in the range 3/6 (York Hotel, Waterloo Hotel) to 4/6 (Bridge House Hotel, Queen's Hotel at Upper Norwood) per night. This is comparable with places like the railway hotels (Charing Cross hotel, 4/6; Great Western Hotel, from 4/-), but considerably less than Claridge's at 10/6, Carlton at 7/6, or even the Cecil, from 6/- a night. The hotels on the south bank would all be perfectly satisfactory, but the Countess would surely want something a touch more expensive?

There is one outstanding candidate for the hotel patronized by the Countess. It is not actually south of the river, but is very near Blackfriars Bridge. De Keyser's Royal Hotel was 'well situated on the Victoria Embankment, Blackfriars, and largely patronized by Germans, Frenchmen, and other foreigners; 400 rooms, electric lights, lifts, large marble hall and lounge pens. [pension] 12s 6d – 25s per day,' according to Baedeker (1905).

It would not be too surprising if the Countess were not British. Even if it were a British title, she might be the daughter of a French or German aristocrat. [See also the question on the identity of the Countess, below.]

De Keyser's Royal Hotel was about one-and-a-half miles from the Brixton Road. Ryder would cross Blackfriars Bridge, then via Blackfriars Road, Lambeth Road, and Kennington Road. He probably planned – had the scheme with the goose not gone horribly awry – to go back to Victoria Station, from where an omnibus to Kilburn started.

JH: Note that the fact that Ryder had deliberately loosened the bar of the grate means that the Savoy cannot be excluded, despite Brend's observation noted above. But my own candidate for the 'Cosmopolitan' might have been the 'Metropolitan,' on the grounds that the names are so similar; the Metropolitan stood near Liverpool Street Station, again north of the river, though, and I agree that the thought of a quick getaway might appeal to Ryder.

217

But had he in fact intended all along to take the stone to his sister's? Ryder does seem very inept – Holmes says 'He's not got blood enough to go in for felony with impunity,' and this seems to me to understate the matter quite considerably. Ryder tells Holmes that when Horner was arrested 'it seemed to me that it would be best for me to get away with the stone at once,' which is a very odd statement; had he not thought that before stealing the stone? Perhaps not. Perhaps he had originally planned to conceal it somewhere in the hotel but it then – belatedly – occurred to him that that was not such a good idea after all. In a word, he panicked.

Fearful of a search, he fled precipitately, running for shelter to the familiar surroundings of his sister's house, with no real notion as to what to do next. It was only when he got to the Brixton Road that he thought of his old friend, Maudsley – 'I went into the back yard and smoked a pipe, and wondered what it would be best to do. I had a friend once called Maudsley, who went to the bad. . . I made up my mind to go right on to Kilburn. . . and take him into my confidence. . .' [Note in passing that his sister must have been an early recruit to the anti-smoking brigade, making him take his pipe out into the yard. I sympathize.]

Two other points of interest: the first is that Ryder's employers must have had a very lax attitude, they never seem to have queried his being away on 'some commission' for what must have been – whether the hotel were north or south of the river – a considerable time. (Although there would be, presumably, a very considerable fuss when once the loss of the stone were discovered, which might cover Ryder's long absence.)

The second point is that Ryder says that he will leave the country, then the charge against Horner 'will break down,' which makes very little sense; Ryder had not, after all, seen (or, rather, pretended to see) Horner steal the stone. Perhaps this is another case where we must postulate Holmes having a discreet word with the authorities as to the true facts? (And perhaps also with the Countess regarding her maid, as noted elsewhere here?)

HY: Who was the Countess of Morcar?

JH: A sneaky 'bonus' question! And an interesting one. There is

– obviously – no real title corresponding. The name sounds Scottish to me, so that will be the starting point; and, although I generally disapprove of pulling names to bits to deal with individual elements (since it does rather denigrate the writer's powers of creative imagination), the results are interesting in this case. Conan Doyle's use (over-use?) of the *mor*. . . element in Sherlockian names has been widely noted, though I personally cannot see any deep and sinister significance in it. A logical candidate might be 'Moray'; James Stuart, illegitimate son of James V of Scotland, was created Earl of Moray (and, by the way, also Earl of Mar, another name not a million miles away from our target) by his half-sister, Mary. Moray was involved in the death of Rizzio, and various other adventures, and it is impossible that Conan Doyle should not have known the name and history.

For the . . .*car* element the glaringly obvious candidate is Carlyle (incidentally a one-time mathematics teacher who later became a private tutor – sound familiar?), who later yet became a noted writer (and translated Goethe, a writer quoted by Holmes), and was Lord Rector of Edinburgh University in the 1860s; again, it is impossible that Conan Doyle would be unaware of the man. (Doesn't Holmes quote him somewhere or other? and as yet another of these trivial asides, Carlyle accepted the Prussian Order of Merit, but when offered a GCB by Disraeli, he refused it.)

A Scots title, then Morcar. The Countess was wealthy: the reward offered for the return of the blue carbuncle was £1,000, and that, says Holmes, 'is certainly not within a twentieth part of the market price.' Holmes goes on to say, 'I have reason to know that there are sentimental considerations in the background which would induce the Countess to part with half her fortune if she could but recover the gem.' The last bit may be mere hyperbole, and even if it isn't the calculation is complex, but it does seem as if the Countess's fortune was at least £ 40,000.

There may not have been an Earl of Morcar; the title may, in one of those odd quirks of aristocracy, have descended in the female line. (And it is interesting to note that of the five 'Countesses in their own right' still extant, four are Scottish titles, the fifth being a very recent (1947) creation.)

It there were an Earl of Morcar, then – Scots lairds being proverbially as poor as kirk mice – we may perhaps postulate another trans-Atlantic alliance of new money and old names similar to that planned in 'The Noble Bachelor'; in a word, the Countess may well have been an American heiress. If that were the case, then it seems probable that the Earl had died, since the Countess appears to have been travelling on her own; evidence of a young wife and old husband, perhaps?

Be she Scots or American, with a fortune and a title and no husband to be seen, the Countess is surely an interesting character in her own right. And perhaps with something of a past: when Holmes speaks rather prissily of 'sentimental considerations' he may indeed mean that the stone was a legacy from dear old Auntie, but the phrase does seem to hint at something a good deal racier. It is a great shame that we never actually get to meet the Countess.

8. "THE SPECKLED BAND"

JH: Watson opens his tale with: 'On glancing over my notes of the seventy odd cases in which I have during the last eight years studied the methods of my friend Sherlock Holmes. . . ' Is it believable that Holmes had only seventy cases in eight years? Or does 'odd' mean 'strange and noteworthy'?

HY: It is unclear whether Watson's 'eight years' means the interval between *A Study in Scarlet* (1881) and 'The Speckled Band' itself (1883); or that between 'The Speckled Band' and 'The Final Problem' (1891); or that between the case of 'The Speckled Band' and Watson's publishing his account (1892). If the former, it is 'two' years and not 'eight.' I don't know the reason for such a misprint (it might be, as usual, a typesetter's mistake), but it is believable that there were seventy cases in the first two years of Holmes' and Watson's association, ie around one case per week. However, as noted in *A Study in Scarlet*, Holmes was widely consulted by detectives as Scotland Yard, and also by private clients; Holmes would not necessarily have been an active agent in these 'cases,' but a consultant, a true armchair reasoner, giving his opinions or conclusions without having visited the scenes of the crimes. Watson would very likely not include such cases in his tally, particularly since he hand Holmes might not even be sure of the correctness of the deductions, or of the outcome of the cases.

Taketomi Koh estimated the number of Holmes' cases, and he accepted the figure of two years. (Taketomi Koh, 'Iraikensu-u (Number of Cases of Sherlock Holmes)' *Sherlock Holmes Zatsugaku Hyakka*, 1983, Tokyo Tosho, pp 44-47). He estimated that Holmes had accepted five hundred cased by 1888 (on the evidence of *The Hound of the Baskervilles*), and over a thousand by the time of the Great Hiatus. In all, he estimates Holmes dealt with a total of 2,872 cases. Frank Walters ('Upon the Probable Number of Cases of Mr Sherlock Holmes') estimates Holmes' cases at around 1,700.

However, this means changing the Canonical figure from 'eight' to 'two.' Henry T Folsom considers that when these words were written, Watson was looking at his notes after Holmes' death. In that case, seventy cases is too small a figure for almost nine years of activity on Holmes' part. 'Odd' might thus mean 'strange and noteworthy.' But it means such remarkable cases occurred only once every seven weeks or so, which in itself seems a very small figure. Taketomi estimates the average length of a case at 3.28 days, so it seems odd that Watson did not take note of any case for an average of 45 days, merely because there were no cases worthy of note!

My preferred solution is the former, the seventy cases are those between *A Study in Scarlet* and 'The Speckled Band,' in which Watson attended investigations with Holmes.

JH: I think there is a misprint, but of the number of cases, not the number of years.; I think Watson jotted down '700' and this was transcribed or misread as '70' then polished up to 'seventy,' or perhaps our printer's devil (axiomatically if not proverbially inept) thought that seven hundred was impossibly high and 'corrected' it. Seven hundred cases in eight years is around two per week which approximates to Taketomi's estimate of around three days per case.

HY: Some scholars think it impossible that Helen Stoner could get to London in the early morning, and indeed suspect that Helen herself may have killed both her sister and father. What do you think?

JH: We must remember that railways in Victorian England were somewhat more reliable than they are nowadays. There is no difficulty in believing that Helen could have got and early train!

What is harder to accept is that Helen – who had already claimed to be in a very nervous frame of mind – did not notice her step-father get into, or out of, the same train as she herself took. (He must have taken the same train in order to follow her so closely.) However, if it were dark (and it was 7:15 am. in April when Watson was roused from his slumbers, by which time Helen was already seated in the sitting-room at 221b, so it would be dark when she set out); and more particularly if there were activity at Leatherhead station (and there would most likely be workmen setting out, milk or post being loaded, etc, so that is not too hard to accept either), then she – not expecting Roylott to be up and about at that hour – may well have failed to spot her step-father.

There are three serious arguments against Helen as the murderer of her sister and Roylott. The first is the mere fact of Roylott's visit to Holmes; why should Roylott threaten Holmes if Roylott had nothing to hide?

The second is the problem of the mechanics of the thing: Helen might have killed Julia with no difficulty, but how could Helen, not even being in the house, possibly arrange for the snake to (i) lurk in the ventilator until it was time to be thrashed by Holmes; and then (ii) crawl back to kill Roylott? True, it might have been trained; but in that case it was damned well-trained! (And there remains the metallic clang, the whistle, etc to be explained as well.) And arising from this is the third objection, namely why on earth should Helen ask Holmes to investigate a number of which she herself was guilty? As with Roylott's visit, it simply makes no sense at all, unless the explanation given by Watson and Holmes is correct.

JH: Speaking of their requirements of a night at Stoke Moran, Holmes tells Watson 'An Eley's No.2 [revolver cartridge] is an excellent argument. . . That and a tooth-brush are, I think, all that we need.' When did Holmes think that Watson would want, or need, to brush his teeth?

HY: Such a combination would perhaps not be a usual one for a Victorian gentleman; Watson would surely have needed a razor and a clean collar, at the very least.

However, Holmes clearly considered that a tooth-brush was the essential item of a personal nature for Watson to carry with him. Such a recommendation might lead us to suspect that Watson was actually a woman; but in that event (s)he would also require a large amount of cosmetics. [JH: No western man would have dared to write that! And I even fear for HY should Hiroko read it.]

As I have noted elsewhere, Sherlock Holmes suffered from periodontitis, and lost most of his teeth. Holmes might be conscious of this condition, and this may point to Watson's also suffering from the same disease.

Watson would be a little over thirty years old at the time, and that is the sort of age when one might expect the initial stages of the disease. However, Watson may have first suffered from periodontitis during his service in Afghanistan. On the battlefield it is not always easy to find the time or place to clean one's teeth properly, and 'In a large number of instances pyorrhoea is associated with disturbance of the general health,' (Henry Sewill, *Dental Surgery*, Bailliere, Tindall and Cox, London, 1901, p 427). Watson was healthy enough before the battle of Maiwand to control bacteria in his mouth, but after is injury his condition was critical, and it might be that his mouth condition was not of the best either.

In those days the cause of periodontitis was unclear, but it was known that one main cause was 'lack of cleanliness and care about the teeth.' (LR Meredith, *The Teeth and How to Save Them*, William Tegg, London, 1872, p 164.)

'The treatment of pyorrhoea must be first directed to thorough removal of tartar. General antisepsis of the mouth must be assiduously practised by the patient. A soft toothbrush, and a suitable dentifrice and antiseptic lotions must be used. The spaces between the teeth, which become widened as the alveoli waste, should be frequently cleared of foreign particles with a thin quill tooth-pick.' (Henry Sewill, *Dental Surgery*.)

Holmes would have been told by his own dentist that brushing was essential for suffers from periodontitis, and might have recommended this self-treatment to his good friend Watson.

HY: Why did Dr Roylott go to India to work, rather than buy a practice in England?

JH: Helen states that Roylott 'obtained an advance from a relative, which enabled him to take a medical degree and went out to Calcutta.' It is marginally possible that Roylott had already shown some character flaws, and consequently that this 'relative' made the advance conditional upon Roylott's leaving England. However, if Roylott had become an embarrassment to his family, they would perhaps have insisted that he leave England at once, rather than stay for the long time it took to obtain a medical degree, so that is probably not what happened.

The real clue might lie in Roylott's destination: Calcutta was for a long while the most prosperous city in India under the Company and the Raj, it was the place to which all those 'loungers and idlers of the Empire' (or at any rate those of them who did not gravitate to London!) were irresistibly drawn. It is perhaps true that the pickings were not quite so rich as they had been when Charnock, Clive, or Hastings strolled arrogantly about the Maidan; but there were still good pickings in the mid-1800s. Roylott was simply making what was, in truth, a sound financial or business decision when he opted for India.

JH: '"You see it, Watson?" . . . But I saw nothing.' Why? Why did Holmes see the snake, where Watson did not?

HY: Lionel Heedleman ('Unravelling "The Speckled Band",' *BSJ*, 34, No3, Spring 1986, pp 5-13) argues that 'if the snake had been on the bell-pull when Holmes struck, Watson would have seen it. A snake had coiled round a ripe cannot suddenly disappear. It could, of course, have fallen on to the floor, in which case Watson would have heard it fall, or it could, as Holmes believed, have crawled back up the bell-pull, when again Watson would have observed it.' But a Japanese Sherlockian and zoologist, Saneyoshi Tatsuro, points out that a snake cannot turn back on a rope.

Needleman also notes Watson's 'the sudden glare flashing into my weary eyes made it impossible for me to tell what it was at which my friend lashed so savagely.' But Leslie Klinger (*The Adventures of Sherlock Holmes*, Gasogene Books, Indianapolis, 1998) argues 'But the eye adjusts to the glare of a match in a fraction of a second. Watson's loyalty to his friend forbade him to protest that there had been no snake on the bell-pull, but his honesty prevented him giving the reassurance that Holmes had sought.' If Klinger is right, where was the snake? I suspect that there was a second hole near the floor, for the return trip to Dr Roylott's room. The snake would have fallen from the topmost hole, or used the rope as a guide of sorts; after biting the victim, the snake then used the floor-level hole to go back to its home.

JH: Ingenious! But still Watson failed to see the snake at any point. What if the snake were never properly in the room, but had merely popped its head through the (top) ventilator hole prior to entering, and it was at that point that Holmes saw it and lashed out, causing it to return before Holmes could strike a match?

HY: After threatening Holmes in London, what did Dr Roylott do in London? Also, why didn't Holmes and Watson think that Dr Roylott would hurry back home to bully his daughter – and, if necessary, to throw them into the river as he had thrown the local blacksmith?

JH: Another sneaky two-part question! As to what Roylott did in London: Helen said that 'he spoke of coming into town to-day upon some most important business,' but she did not say when he said this.

If it were said that morning, then it may be that Roylott had <u>not</u> previously intended to visit London, but made an excuse so that he might follow Helen. However, Helen herself says, 'I was too shaken to go to bed again, however [this after she had been frightened by the night's odd events], so I dressed, and as soon as it was daylight I slipped down, got a dog-card at the Crown Inn, which is opposite. . . [and thence to London and Baker Street.]' This reads as if Helen did not see her step-father that morning at all. Further, had Helen seen Roylott, and had he said that he – too – was going to London, there would be no reason why they should not travel together. (And, indeed, in that case Helen would most likely have been too nervous to visit Holmes!)

This all goes to suggest that Roylott had made the remark the previous day, and that in turn suggests that his visit was originally unconnected with Helen's own visit to Holmes, and that Roylott changed his plans slightly (even if only by getting out of bed earlier than he had intended) when he decided to follow Helen.

What, then, might he have wanted to do, other than follow his step-daughter? It seems to me that there are two possibilities, the financial, and what one might loosely term the social. We know that Roylott had killed once for monetary gain, and thus that money mattered to him; he might very well have been seeing his banker or stockbroker – or pawnbroker! - to rustle up a bit more cash. Again, he was a man of violent passions, and had no wife; he may well have wished to avoid a local scandal and have made some arrangement with one of the ladies of the town in London. (Depending on the exact nature of such a hypothetical arrangement, he may have needed extra cash first anyway!)

Either (both?) of these appointments might well have occupied him for the rest of the day. And he seems to have been pretty confident that he had scared Holmes with the poker-bending trick, and so he might not have thought that Holmes and Watson would visit Stoke Moran; Roylott may simply not have been any too concerned that there was any real danger. As to bullying Helen, Roylott most probably would have gone on to do just that – the perfect end to a perfect day – had the opportunity arisen.

9. "THE ENGINEER'S THUMB"

JH) The usual metal for forged half-crowns was pewter (lead/tin alloy). Watson himself says that 'Large masses of nickel and of tin were discovered,' on the premises. These metals would surely need a furnace for their transformation into fake coins, not a hydraulic press?

HY) As JH pointed out, the most effective and fast way to make fake coins is metal casting and plating. On December 3 2003, there was an Indonesian flight attendant arrested for using fake five hundred yen coins in Sakai-shi, Osaka. Nearly sixty such fake coins were found in that case in western Japan, and the flight attendant told police she exchanged her money in Bali into Japanese yen, and she did not know they were false. On December 5 of that year, there was a fire at an iron factory in Ipoh, Malaysia. From that burned-out site, police and fire department authorities found many fake five hundred yen coins and manufacturing machines, so that it was concluded that this was the origin of the fake Japanese coins. They first took impressions of the real coins, and cast them with brass. After, they plated them with nickel. That is the most common way to produce coins for cobblers.

But the German cobbler "Fritz" seems to be interested in a different method of forgery. I do not know why he did not like the ordinary way of forgery, but anyway he challenged himself to produce his own original method. I suspect that Fritz had the idea when he had been to a dentist, or Fritz himself was a dentist. Dental amalgam has been a popular filling material in dental treatment since 1826, and is consisted of silver, tin and mercury. Bliss Austin said "Nor could the material used to make the spurious coins have been an amalgam of nickel or tin, because ... and the latter does so to such a limited extent that it would have been of little use for this purpose" in "Thumbing His Way to Fame" (*BSJ* [OS] I, No.4 (October 1946), 424-32), but in that sense, his conclusion is not accurate. Dental amalgam cures without any pressure or heat, but the hydraulic press would be used for punching marks on both sides of coins. I am not sure such a huge press was needed for that purpose, but this system might not be made just for forgery.

Nickel would be used as a furring plate, which makes products harder and better glazed. Fritz would have them plated once more, perhaps in gold, silver, or brass.

Some scholars wonder why no mercury was found there, but the boiling point of mercury is only 357C. On the other hand, fire is from about 600 to 1100C. It is easy to evaporate mercury in "a house of fire". When the Big Buddha of Nara was made 1300 years ago, an amalgam of gold and mercury was painted on its surface, and then a big fire was set around the Buddha. It was a primitive way of gold plating in ancient Japan.

However, if Fritz chose a traditional casting system, it would have been much easier at less cost. He did not need such a huge hydraulic press, but just a small furnace and a casting machine which could be carried anywhere by just two people. In addition, the plating system would need only a small tank. Fritz had a new idea, but it was not effective or useful.

JH) Hatherley said, 'the face and manner of my patron had made an unpleasant impression upon me, and I could not think that his explanation... was sufficient to explain the necessity for my coming at midnight.' So why did he go?

HY) It is money, money money!

Hatherley said "Two years ago, having served my time, and having also come into a fair sum of money through my poor father's death, I determined to start in business for myself, and took professional chambers in Victoria Street.... During two years I have had three consultations and one small job, and that is absolutely all that my profession has brought me. My gross takings amount to twenty-seven pounds ten. Every day, from nine in the morning until four in the afternoon, I waited in my little den, until at last my heart began to sink, and I came to believe that I should never have any practice at all."

This resembles Conan Doyle's case. In his autobiography

I made 154 pounds the first year, and 250 pounds the second, rising slowly to 300 pounds, which in eight years I never passed, so far as the medical practice went. In the first year the Income Tax paper arrived and I filled it up to show that I was not liable. They returned the paper with "Most unsatisfactory" scrawled across it. I wrote "I entirely agree" under the words, and returned it once more.

However, Hatherley's income a year was only a little less than fourteen pounds, which was less than ten percent of Doyle's first year income. In addition, he had his office in Victoria Street, and had a clerk. It is said a specialist in London would earn a little less than five-hundred pounds a year at that time. Such a person would pay forty-two pounds to two servants. That servant received more payment than Hatherley.

Charles Booth estimated a household whose income was under twenty-two shillings a week as poor, in *Life and Labour of the People in London* (3rd ed, 1902-03). The lowest non-poor household yearly income was a little more than fifty-seven pounds. It is four times Hatherley's income. He was a member of the poor class, based on his earning. He could maintain his life and his office from the inheritance from his father, but if it was large enough to support his whole life with its interest, he would not have considered opening his office. It is easy to suppose he spent a large part of his inheritance, and had not too much left at that time. Colonel Stark offered him fifty guineas, which is fifty-two and a half pounds. He could thereby be free from poverty. This was the reason why he accepted such a doubtful offer.

JH) Holmes asked about the horse which drew Colonel Stark's carriage: 'Tired-looking or fresh?' and that gave him a clue as to how far it had travelled. But he also asked: 'Did you observe the colour?' What on earth did the horse's colour matter?

HY) This was one of Sherlock Holmes' favorite investigation techniques as when he adopted the disguise of a groom in SCAN. If the horse had any characteristic colour (not pink or violet, but white or a "silver blaze" type would be outstanding), he planned to search such horses kept by grooms in the area, or ask horse doctors in nearby towns. However, the horse was "chestnut", a very popular colour, and it would be impossible to trace it from that point.

These questions by HY, are also answered by myself.

HY) Why did the woman who cried 'Fritz' speak in English, and why did Colonel Stark answer in English?

HY) Hatherley said Colonel Stark had "a German accent", "several German books were scattered" on the table in his house. But I suspect Colonel Stark and Elise were not really German. In emergency situations, any persons would speak in their own tongue, not in a foreign language. They might have been disguised as Germans, though they were really English. Or they might be German-English, like Queen Victoria or the Prince of Wales. They were English, but their ancestors were German, and their father or mother was German. It is said the Queen and the Prince had a German accent, though they were born in England.

HY) Why did Colonel Stark abandon his intention of killing Hatherley?

HY) As there was a big fire in his house, Colonel Stark might have been injured by some explosion caused by the chemicals used for plating or other processes of forgery. If the Colonel was unconscious, Elise or Ferguson might have brought Hatherley near the station.

HY) Why did Colonel Stark make false coins in England, and not Germany, his homeland?

HY) Even if Colonel Stark was already suspected by the authorities, there were many nations in Germany at that time, and there were many coins issued by each small nation in Germany. It would be easier for him to move around Germany, and to make many designs. Even if he was not able to stay in Germany, he could go to other eastern European nations or Italy, which was also full of small

231

kingdoms. Britain was a united nation which had talented police, and it is not easy to escape from this country because of the sea.

I also wonder why the Colonel did not print false bank notes. It was easier and cost less.

The first chapter "A Scandal in Bohemia" is published in *The Ritual*, Autumn 2000, No.26 (The Northern Musgraves).

The second chapter "Case of Identity" and the third chapter "The Red Headed League" are published in *The Ritual*, Autumn 2001, No.28, and *The Shoso-in Bulletin* vol.11, 2001

"The Five Orange Pips" chapter is published in   *The Shoso-in Bulletin* vol.13, 2003.

JOHN HALL has written several works of Sherlockian pastiche, as well as many articles of the Canon, together with a Holmesian chronology, *I Remember the Date Very Well*, studies of Holmes – *Sidelights on Holmes* – and Dr Watson – *Unexplored Possibilities*.

HIRAYAMA YUICHI (The Japanese Vase) was the editor-in-chief of *The Shoso-in Bulletin*, and co-editor of *Japan and Sherlock Holmes* (Baker Street Irregulars). He also published some works on Japanese detective stories and translations of foreign mysteries.

Links

MX Publishing is closely involved in the Save Undershaw campaign
– the campaign to save and restore Sir Arthur Conan Doyle's former
home. Undershaw is where he brought Sherlock Holmes back to life,
and should be preserved for future generations of Holmes fans.

Save Undershaw   www.saveundershaw.com

Facebook   www.facebook.com/saveundershaw

You can read more about Sir Arthur Conan Doyle and Undershaw in
Alistair Duncan's book (share of royalties to the Undershaw
Preservation Trust) – An Entirely New Country and in the amazing
compilation Sherlock's Home – The Empty House (all royalties to the
Trust).

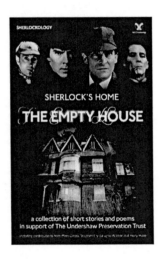

The uniqueness of this book is the essays and activities that include both serious and farcical writings about Arthur Conan Doyle's, Sherlock Holmes. A travelogue that compares Reichenbach Falls and Trummelbach Falls for Professor Moriarty's demise; and notes from a visit to Trinity College at Oxford to view Monsignor Knox's writings and entries in the Gryphon Club Book provide the reader with engaging insights into Sherlock Holmes' world of scholarship.

of the world's largest Sherlock Holmes publishers, dozens
 ıew novels and books from the top Holmes authors –

ıncıuuıng Alistair Duncan, winner of the 2011 Howlett Literary Award
(Sherlock Holmes book of the year) for
'The Norwood Author'

www.mxpublishing.com

New in 2012 [Novels unless stated]:
Sherlock Holmes and the Plague of Dracula
Sherlock Holmes and The Adventure of The Jacobite Rose [Play]
Sherlock Holmes and The Whitechapel Vampire
–– Holmes Sweet Holmes
The Detective and The Woman: A Novel of Sherlock Holmes
Sherlock Holmes Tales From The Stranger's Room
–– The Sherlock Holmes Who's Who [Reference]
Sherlock Holmes and The Dead Boer at Scotney Castle
The Secret Journal of Dr Watson
A Professor Reflects on Sherlock Holmes [Essay Collection]
Sherlock Holmes of The Lyme Regis Legacy
Sherlock Holmes and The Discarded Cigarette [Short Novel]
Sherlock Holmes On The Air [Radio Plays]
Sherlock Holmes and The Murder at Lodore Falls
Untold Adventure of Sherlock Holmes
Sherlock Holmes and The Terrible Secret
Sherlock Holmes and The Element of Surprise
Sherlock Holmes and The Edinburgh Haunting
The Hound of The Baskervilles [Play]
56 Sherlock Holmes Stories in 56 Days [Reviews]
The Many Watsons [Reviews]
The 1895 Murder

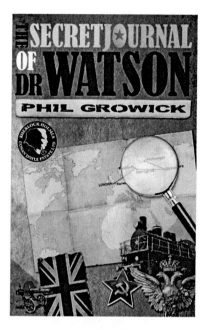

Also from MX Publishing

Sherlock Holmes Travel Guides

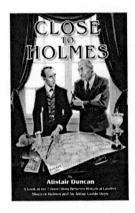

London   Devon

In e-book an interactive guide to London

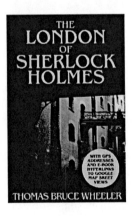

400 locations linked to Google Street View.

Also from MX Publishing

Cross over fiction featuring great villains from history

 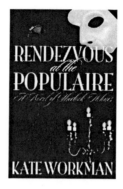 

Fantasy Sherlock Holmes

www.mxpublishing.com

CPSIA information can be obtained at www.ICGtesting.com
Printed in the USA
BVOW011857070713

325122BV00007B/60/P